BIAS

A K-POP ROMANCE

BY

 ★LUCY GOLD★

Published by Giliad Press.
Cover photos courtesy of RA, Paweł Czerwiński, and Micheile Henderson on Unsplash.
Paperback ISBN: 978-1-64032-277-6
Hardback ISBN: 978-1-64032-281-3
Ebook ISBN: 978-1-64032-278-3

A note on Korean language: Since this book is for English speakers, the dialogue is written in what it roughly means in English rather than a direct translation – for example, when answering the phone, Koreans say "Yeoboseyo" which literally translates to something like "Can you hear me?" But in this book, they say "Hello?" since it functions as essentially the same thing and won't jolt the reader.

It also might be nice to know that based on the Korean sound "eo", Wooyeong's name is pronounced "Woo-yong".

우영
WOOYEONG
ONE MONTH PREVIOUS

"I heard Hak Beomsoo was dating a fan."

We were taking a ten-minute break from filming our latest music video. Dyeong sat next to me in a metal folding chair, his hair midnight blue and wet from gel, fingers fiddling with the silver bracelet on his wrist as he spoke.

"Hak Beomsoo who's an idol?" I asked doubtfully.

Dyeong watched some staff adjusting the lights aimed on the set in front of us. *"Was* an idol. There's no way he would do that while he was in an active career. It'd be suicide."

"Dating a *fan*?" I scoffed. "Please. She only likes him because he's a K-pop star."

매디슨
MADISON

1

The guy was handsome.

He was stalling, like he didn't want to leave just yet. He kept glancing my way over his fancy sunglasses, brushing his thick, wavy hair from his smooth forehead as he leaned against the wall of the coffee shop. It was cold out, and his breath was streaming out in clouds from his parted lips.

I sipped my coffee and turned my gaze ahead, afraid he would see me looking at him. I looked around me instead, watching people drink from their portable cups and mugs on the outside patio of the coffee shop. It was January, and yet they still seemed to be enjoying themselves outside. Everyone, including myself, was bundled up like the sun was going to go out.

The guy shifted his position, and my gaze flicked back to him automatically. His sunglasses were so shiny they were like a mirror. He adjusted them on his face so I could no longer see his eyes, and then started striding toward me.

My heart did a double-take and started beating very fast. He got closer and closer... I glanced up at his face –

But he walked right past me and stopped at the table behind me, where he said flirtatiously to the beautiful girl with silky black hair sitting there, "Hello, what's your name?"

My face flushed red as I hastily turned my head back around, but not before I heard her little laugh and sly reply. She was probably used to handsome guys asking her for a date. Even guys as handsome as that one.

I stood up, gulping down the last of my coffee so I could leave. Even in Korea, I was invisible to the opposite gender.

I tossed my paper cup in the trash and walked quickly away, feeling like an idiot. It didn't happen in the USA and it wouldn't happen here.

I'd been in Korea for two weeks so far, just transferred for a job. Some small part of me had been hoping, I guess, that maybe things would be different for me here. I sighed, feeling irrational as I flagged down an orange taxi.

It stopped, and I got in the seat, the heated air smacking me in the face and spreading warmth to my toes. Letting out a breath of relief, I pulled out my wallet and looked at the address written in my looping handwriting, on a piece of paper jammed between some Korean won banknotes. I recited it aloud for the driver and he acknowledged it, the car starting to move.

The view outside the window was beautiful. Seoul, South Korea – a place that felt almost unreal now that I was finally here after so many years of studying the language. It had started with Ambition, my favorite K-pop band. After watching so many of their videos, and the interactions between Wooyeong, Tai, Dyeong, and Chin-hyuk, I had felt a strong desire to understand them. That's why I had learned Korean. I'd kept at it for five years, trying as many different ways I could to become proficient. It had been thrilling to realize that I understood what they were saying, and even more thrilling, later, to realize that I was starting to grasp the finer points of their humor and remarks. I still remembered the first time I had understood a full sentence – It was a surprise VLive and Dyeong and Wooyeong had been together in the car, teasing each other. Dyeong had stopped to answer a comment offhandedly, a grin still on his face – "Where's Tai? He's with Chin-hyuk in the studio."

I could hardly believe it – it was magical. Moments like that had fueled me to keep going in studying the language, no matter how hard it was.

Seoul was the next step. There wasn't anything for me back in my boring town in the US. This – this was an adventure. Something new.

The street we were driving through was narrow. Shops were jam-packed on either side, selling everything you could imagine. We'd already passed by three more coffee shops, a burger place, a few company headquarters, a cosmetics store, and a bunch of other buildings I couldn't recognize. Signs, mostly in Korean with the occasional Romanized lettering, were everywhere. There was an abundance of concrete and slick glass windows, and whatever trees and shrubs were planted here were leafless because of winter.

Everything still looked so new to me. Two weeks wasn't enough to get used to it. There was something so unique, so *exciting* about the city that I couldn't describe.

We passed an advertisement for tteokbokki – cylinder-shaped rice cakes in a thick, red spicy sauce that I'd seen the members of Ambition eat.

I'd never tried it. Or any Korean food, really. It just wasn't available in my city in the US.

The tteokbokki were glistening in their sauce, topped by vibrant green onions. It made me hungry just looking at it. I'd been in Korea two weeks and planned to stay here at least another year – it was about time I tried the cuisine.

"Sir," I said cautiously, trying out the Korean words in my head before I said them, "where is a place to get good food?"

"Are you looking for American or Korean?" he asked me, glancing in his rearview mirror at my obviously foreign face.

"Korean."

"Eumsigi Yogi Itta," he replied, nodding. "The food is so delicious, but is a cheaper option. They serve all the banchan."

I thanked him and pulled it up on my phone. The rest of the ride I spent in thoughtful silence, until we pulled up at my street. I paid him and got out, slamming the car door behind me.

I breathed in the refreshingly cold air, feeling pretty good. Tonight I'd go to that restaurant. It would be the start of my new life here – where I really acted like a native. I couldn't wait to taste the food I'd seen Ambition eat for so many years.

I took the stairs up to my apartment, unlocking the door and stepping inside. I shrugged off my winter jacket, flung it across the room, and collapsed onto the electric blue sofa that doubled as my bed at night. (Turns out they had IKEA here in Korea too). This apartment was so small it didn't really have a bedroom, and it would've been more expensive to buy a separate sofa and bed anyway. My new home looked like it'd been hit by a tornado, but at least I'd remembered to collapse my bed back into a sofa again this morning.

The table in front of the sofa was so cluttered, I couldn't even see the surface. A bunched-up red sweater, brochures for local Korean shops, notebooks, an empty coffee mug, a box of lightbulbs, and the trash-collection information for my apartment were just the beginning. Peeved, I shoved my feet into the mess so I could prop my legs up as I sat on the sofa, making a water bottle, a box of tissue, and some knotted-up earbuds topple to the floor.

"Living the dream," I muttered to myself as I slipped my phone from my pocket and clicked on Ambition's latest music video, *Wistful Paradox.*

Harmony started rolling out of my cheap phone speaker. I closed my eyes in bliss, listening to the bittersweet notes roll up and down, so familiar and beautiful. My eyes opened as Chin-hyuk started singing, in perfect, upbeat unison with the harmony in the background. He flashed the camera a killer grin as he started the choreography in front and center. Fitting for the leader.

His hair was baby-blue here, contrasted by his white costume. He had a petite face – small chin, small nose. His facial expressions were fierce, dynamic, and his hair whipped around as he danced.

Wooyeong joined in. His voice was low and husky, his lips curling into a devastating smirk as his intense gaze stayed on the camera.

Butterflies filled my stomach. It didn't matter how many times I'd seen the video – seeing Wooyeong still did that to me sometimes. Usually when I thought I'd finally gotten used to it, and I was least expecting it.

He'd been my bias ever since I knew about Ambition at their debut, when I'd called myself an Aim – the name of their fanbase – for the very first time. It wasn't just the fact that he was the most handsome person I'd ever seen. The other members of Ambition were definitely handsome too (even though I was never attracted to them like I was to Wooyeong). It was his little mannerisms, his personality, that I had also fallen head over heels for. Even when he was laughing and messing around, there was something so *solid* about him. A stability, a calmness. Just listening to him talk made the world feel like a safer place.

I had a huge crush on him. It had just been a reality of my life for the past six years.

Tai jumped into the screen next to Wooyeong, showing off his own dancing skills. The sight of his face made me smile, especially when he delivered that adorable grin of his. I'd seen him dissolve mild bickering between the other members, comfort scared fans, and make people happy for no reason at all. On the VLives he was even the most relaxed.

The music was quieter for a few seconds, the beat more prominent, as it was Dyeong's turn on the screen. It was easy to see why he'd been named the main visual as well as the rapper, because he was stunning. He rolled his neck at this part of the choreography, showing off the most beautifully-cut jaw I'd ever seen. His midnight-blue hair looked wet. His eyes were serious as he rapped, somehow harmonizing with Tai's, Wooyeong's, and Chin-hyuk's voices.

When the song ended I just sat there, not moving, letting the last notes echo in my head even though my apartment was silent and still. After their voices were gone it dawned on me just how alone I was.

I had just moved to Korea for a job two weeks ago. Other than people at my work – the fancy camera company, Gi – I knew nobody. There was no one to call on when I needed help. It was odd after coming from my home in the US, where I was the middle child surrounded by four siblings, and something was always going on. Right now there was no talking, no noises of people moving around, no incoming texts from friends, just...

The sound of my breath. But I wasn't lonely – not yet.

I pushed myself up off the sofa, unable to stand the silence any longer. It was tempting to play another Ambition song, but I had chores I needed to do. My apartment was a wreck and I needed to do laundry if I was keen on wearing a clean shirt tomorrow.

I bundled up in my parka and headed back out toward the laundromat with a laundry sack slung over my shoulder, shutting the door behind me, shivering in the cold. Why were Seoul winters so *freezing*? If it was snowing, I might be able to tell myself it was worth it. But the concrete just looked gray and bleak.

The air smelled like roasting coffee. I inhaled deeply, tempted to duck in one of the many shops for another hot cup. So much caffeine would probably make me a part-time insomniac though.

The neighborhood coin laundry was close. I opened the door, my eyes skimming the Korean lettering on the sign as a taxi whizzed by behind me on the road. I'd been learning the language for five years and could read it as instantly as I could English, even when the font got crazy.

The air was warm and smelled like fabric softener. There were only a few other customers inside. I did a double take as I recognized the girl switching her clothes into the dryer in front of me. She was the one that the guy at the coffee shop today had tried to flirt with.

It was no wonder she'd caught his eye. Her black hair was long and cut at a perfect angle, framing a symmetrical face that was as elegant as it was beautiful. Even in a winter coat and white sneakers she looked like a model, or maybe a character from a Korean drama.

We shared similarities, but not enough. Even though we were about the same height and both slender, she looked lithe and graceful while I felt clumsy. Where her hair was sleek and long and inky-black, mine was brown and wavy, chopped a little past my shoulders. Our eyes were both brown, but hers were bronze-honey and rimmed with thick black lashes, where mine were a flatter, dirty color with (way less noticeable) dark brown lashes.

She looked up at me through those beautiful eyes of hers, curious as she noticed me watching her. I tore my gaze away, turning to the washer in front of me.

While I inserted money into the machine, I glanced back again at the girl. She was leaving, walking with a sashay to her step as she hit the street.

Of course the handsome guy at the coffee shop had gone for her instead of me. I'd never been asked out on a date, why would it start now? Guys liked beautiful girls like her, not girls like me.

With my crush on Wooyeong, I'd always known that it wasn't going to happen. Not only was it virtually impossible, but I wasn't anywhere near good enough for him anyway.

Maybe that was why it had always been so easy for me to fall for him, when it usually felt like I shut my heart away. With him there was no chance of rejection because the most I would ever see of him – if I was *lucky* – was thirty seconds at a fansign.

There was a heaviness in my stomach. I didn't feel like going back to my messy apartment alone, so I decided to walk around instead. It was so cold my teeth hurt, so I kept my mouth shut and breathed through my nose. Maybe the icy air would numb reality along with my fingers.

The direction I was walking were streets I hadn't explored before. The road was narrow, one-way, and parked cars and motorcycles lined the edges. There were bright, trendy shops here as well as old and worn brick ones that had seen better days, with passersby going in and out. I rubbed my fingers together in my pockets, trying to warm them, breathing in the smell of garlic and funky smoke from a barbeque restaurant, hearing the chatter of people talking to each other and the roar of cars in the distance.

I didn't know why I was walking – just to walk, I suppose. I came to Seoul for adventure. For new things. I wanted to experience the Korea that the people here saw every day.

K-pop had been the one to introduce me to this new world. I felt lucky that I'd been able to be there for Ambition's debut six years ago, for more reasons than I could count. They'd been a bright glow in my life when times seemed dark, and a link to what was really out there.

The scenery was changing to be more city-like the farther I went, and it was a little less bright than before – the late-afternoon winter sky was turning darker gray. The buildings here were bigger, shinier, more upkept. There was a Homeplus Mart right across the street, taller than one would expect for a supermarket, with many floors and windows. It looked more like a business building than a place one would go shopping.

I had nothing else to do right now. I should at least go check it out, so I'd know what to do when my fridge ran out of rice, Spam, fresh fruit, and eggs. You'd be surprised how many days straight you could eat scrambled eggs with rice. Along with coffee from the endless number of shops that seem to multiply like bunny rabbits, it had been my breakfast every morning before work. Lunch was an instant ramyun cup and dinner was – you guessed it – more rice, this time with Spam and whatever fruit I had on hand.

I was just too exhausted trying to sort everything else out that I didn't have the energy for more, whether it was ordering at a restaurant or buying ingredients and trying to find how the heck to cook them. My parents always teased me about my love for food, but after so many new stimuli and things to figure out that once seemed intuitive – like even grabbing a shopping cart, which here required you to insert money – a bowl of rice and Spam at the end of the day worked.

But it'd been two weeks, and I should start integrating more like a local. Equipping my house with real Korean food – I could do that. I *wanted* to do that.

I crossed the crosswalk and entered the Homeplus Mart. It was busy here, with people going by with shopping carts, eating pizza from the food court, and talking to each other. I tried to stay out of the way, taking the escalator to the level that had the groceries.

I probably shouldn't bring anything home today. I wasn't ready for that, since carrying all of it would be a pain. But I could least check out what they had, and plan ahead of time.

Everything was clean and well organized, almost sterile, with white floors and attractively organized displays. The instant ramyun, cakes and sweets, packages of snacks, and jars were all in neat rows. The sheer variety was overwhelming.

The well-lit *slickness* of the atmosphere – with everything about it just screaming superstore – made it feel like there might as well been a sign in neon lights flashing Welcome to the Big City. It was like the efficiently organized IKEA of grocery stores – cool, and found only in major hubs. It made the grocery stores back home look small and drab.

I realized my mouth was open and I shut it. I was in the busy capital of Korea now, where this was normal. I arranged my face into a neutrally bland expression, because everyone else didn't need to see that I was not used to major cities.

I walked by the noodle section, past couples and families all bundled up in their winter jackets shopping. I was tempted to navigate toward the wall of Spam, but there was no way I was getting more of that for a long time. Some more variety of spicy ramyuns, perhaps, and some premade sandwiches, and some green onions. With vegetables and real meat. I wasn't that great at cooking, but how hard would it be to chop up some meat and put it in a pan with cabbage and bell peppers? Basics. I needed basics.

I made a mental list of things I passed by, like a bag of kimchi (starting with the small ones) and bulk dried rice. I took pictures of all the cheapest brands so next time I could just grab and go. By the time I had taken the elevator to the home supplies section to look at necessary (but really unexciting) things like sponges and silverware, it was already six-thirty.

My stomach growled. I jammed my phone into my pocket and made my way down to the main floor, the delicious, warm aromas of the food court wafting to my nose. I was so, so tempted to buy something, but I'd already decided where I was going today. I could eat at Homeplus the next time I went shopping.

Outside, it was alarmingly dark – night, mixed with all the city lights twinkling around me. The air was infused with energy, all the comings and goings of thousands of people all with their own lives, all heading somewhere. It was so beautiful and mysterious and romantic at night.

~{★ 9 ♥}~

It was even more freezing cold than before, but I didn't care this time. I felt warm down to the core. And even better, snow was starting to fall from the sky.

I looked up and smiled, feeling a thrill shoot through me like liquid euphoria. The streetlights illuminated the snowflakes that were now starting to pad the ground in a thin layer of white. I slipped my phone from my pocket again and pulled up the restaurant the taxi driver had recommended me earlier today. According to the map, it was just a few blocks away.

I hurried along the sidewalk, parka zipped up tight, my breath coming out in icy clouds. My hair was being coated in thick, fluffy snowflakes. Some of them tickled my nose; I didn't bother pulling my scarf further up my face. Somehow the day didn't seem so bad anymore. I couldn't help a slight smile as I scuffed my shoes across the layer of white that was starting to create a thin film on the ground, hearing a child squealing with laughter and delight in the distance as they too enjoyed the beautiful bounty.

It felt like hardly any time at all before I saw the restaurant sign glowing blue. I ducked into the door, being hit with a blast of warm air that smelled like beef and chiles and sesame oil. I was heading toward a seat when an older woman with a black apron and a frown intercepted me.

"Are you eating by yourself?" she said in Korean.

"Yes," I answered back.

"We don't serve single portions here. You want to stay, you will have to order double."

I didn't know what to say for a few moments. I'd heard of this before – sometimes the restaurants will lose money if they serve just one person because of the plethora of side dishes they must provide. But I didn't know this restaurant was like that. And I didn't want to pay double. Or walk another mile with no destination in mind, while it was dark and freezing outside.

"You too!" the woman added sharply to someone behind me. I turned around in surprise, thinking maybe if there was another lone diner, we could eat together. I saw a guy with smooth pale skin, spiked earrings in one ear and captivating dark eyes that made my gaze immediately fly to them. One-fourth of a second was enough to process, without even really seeing him, that he was out-of-this-world *hot*. Another fourth of a second and –

Oh my gosh. It was *Wooyeong*. Lee Wooyeong.

매디슨
MADISON
2

My mouth fell open. But it was all happening so quickly that I was barely comprehending the reality of what I was seeing. I closed my mouth just as fast, right when his dark eyes locked on mine and he said "It's okay. I'm with her."

My stomach exploded into butterflies. He seemed to take my wide eyes as agreement and moved a little past me to talk to the woman, seeming not to notice me staring after him in shock. It *was* Wooyeong. It was like my brain had caught up with reality now. He was wearing all black, from his jeans to the beanie on his head.

He was much taller than me – taller than I expected. I'd seen him on a screen so many times in so many ways, and now....

I stared at his all-too-familiar profile. His pale face was almost glowing, while his eyes were smoky. My stomach was filled with a strange, sick feeling and I took short breaths, trying to quell it as goosebumps erupted down my arms. I couldn't think. I was short-circuiting.

"Is that so? You're together?" the woman was saying to Wooyeong, looking at me dubiously.

She wasn't talking to me because she assumed I spoke mostly English, which was not a stretch. But just as Wooyeong opened his mouth to reply, I interrupted in clear Korean, "Yes, we are. I just thought he wasn't coming. He's always late."

I sucked in a sharp breath, probably looking just as shocked as the woman – and Wooyeong, whose surprise looked like it was mixed with amusement. My face flamed as our eyes met for the briefest second.

"Hmph," the woman said. She turned away, and Wooyeong started toward a wide table in the corner with two seats across from each other. I followed, numbly. Another girl looked up as we passed and her eyes widened at the sight of Wooyeong, even though she didn't seem to know who he was. He was just remarkably hot, with a striking face that would turn heads in a crowd. He looked like a K-pop star – because he *was* a K-pop star.

I was pretty sure I was burning a hole in his back with my gaze. I forced myself to look away, staring at my feet as we walked.

Wooyeong slid into the seat and folded his arms across the wooden table, opening the menu as the woman kept staring at us suspiciously from near the door while trying not to look as if she was. I sat across from him. It was a relief to sit down – my legs felt weak. I let out a shaky breath.

As soon as the woman was gone, Wooyeong set down his menu and looked right at me. My heart was beating very fast.

"Your Korean is excellent," he said, sounding fascinated. "How much do you speak?"

His *voice.* The same voice I'd heard for six years through my phone. I shivered, so nervous that I could look anywhere but his face.

"A lot. Enough to be comfortable around Seoul." I could barely speak. I was gripping my legs under the table. My face was crimson.

"That's impressive," he replied, but I didn't see his expression because I still couldn't look at his face.

I nodded, unable to do anything, cheeks still burning. I unbuttoned my parka just to have something to do, hoping he didn't notice the way my fingers trembled. I felt both sick and giddy. Should I tell him I knew who he was?

I'd dreamed about meeting Lee Wooyeong for years while knowing for a fact it would never happen. And now that he was right in front of me, *across the table*, I was completely immobilized.

This was never meant to be a real-life crush. I didn't know what to do. I bit my lip and picked up the menu just as a distraction, hoping it hid my bright red face. Knowing he was right across the table – close enough to touch, in all his solid realness – was making all my thoughts scatter in my head so that the only thing left was my hyperawareness of him.

I scanned the options without really seeing or understanding them. Plus – this was the first time I'd ever eaten real Korean food, besides an ice cream I got from a street vendor. I had no idea what to order. But I couldn't focus. I couldn't even decide whether I wanted to talk to him or whether I was so overwhelmed I just wanted to run from his presence.

I took a few shaky, deep breaths. I repeated the line to myself four times before I said it aloud. "Um, do you know what's good here?"

The 'um' was not planned, and totally American English. I cursed myself.

Wooyeong looked up at me. He seemed surprised and casual, like he was just another person in a restaurant. "I don't know. This is my first time eating here. A friend recommended it to me."

"Oh." I felt my face burn as I looked down at the menu again. There was a small pause and then I said, "This is my first time eating real Korean food, so... is there... anything you might suggest? I don't know what to get."

There was visible interest sparked in his eyes now. "You've never tried Korean food?"

I nodded. It was difficult just *looking* at his stunning face. He was the very picture of a stormy bad boy, with his spiked earrings glinting silver in the warm restaurant light.

Wooyeong's mouth quirked up in a smile, nearly melting me all over again. He looked down at the menu, then up at me. "You eat spicy food?"

"I eat *everything*," I said seriously, leaning forward a little.

"Okay," he said, sounding almost slightly amused as he glanced me up and down, then back at the menu, then back at me, like he was trying to evaluate how much I could *really* take... or maybe what I would like best.

My heart was in my throat as I waited.

"How about the daeji kalbi?"

His eyes were distracting. They were dark, but large, and with a calmness to them. An openness. Like he was too involved in what he was doing to guard against the world. They were very casual, very relaxed. Disarmingly so. I'd never seen that when watching Ambition's videos.

I felt surprised, but I didn't know why. "Okay. And the side dishes?"

"Ah, the usual banchan." Wooyeong looked down at the menu again, and then gave a shout to summon the waiter. I knew this was the way they did it in Korea, but I'd never seen it for real, and I was fascinated.

The waiter was a young man not much older than Wooyeong. Then again, sometimes it was hard to tell. He smiled at us and prepared to take our order, but also gave Wooyeong and me an odd look. It was clear by his makeup that Wooyeong was a celebrity, and I was a white foreigner. We couldn't be a stranger pair, I'm sure.

Wooyeong ordered confidently, only glancing once at me when it came to the drinks. "I don't drink alcohol," I said, so he turned back to the waiter. "...three Yakults, please."

"What did you get?" I asked once the waiter left.

"You'll find out," Wooyeong said. And smirked with that irresistible, unintentional smirk that made his thousands of fans swoon. *Other* girls would've blushed. I...

Blushed.

I tried to hide it by turning away and looking across the restaurant, anywhere besides his masculine face and dark eyes, feeling my face burning pink. There was no way a smirk like that should be legal.

"So what's your name? Where are you from? The US?"

I turned back to him, taken aback that he was asking me. "Um, Madison. I came here just two weeks ago – from the US, yeah. Haven't eaten anything but food I brought from home and instant ramyun. But I love food so I'm excited to try it."

Being near him was making my whole body electrified. I looked down at my entwined fingers in my lap, which were still trembling – from anxiety or adrenaline I couldn't tell.

"I love food too," Wooyeong said, sitting up straight, interested. "I like sharing Korean food with people. It's so good. I think it could become really popular internationally."

I tried not to look too astonished. I never knew that about him. "You like to cook?"

Wooyeong nodded. "I haven't cooked all my favorite foods yet though."

"I would love to learn how to cook Korean food," I said, and then felt my cheeks prickle. *That* sounded desperate. And obvious. And not what I was trying to hint at. "So far I'm really happy just tasting it first though."

He laughed. It was the first time I had ever heard him laugh in real life, and it was both familiar and unexpected. It made a chill run up my spine.

"Oh, well we'll see," Wooyeong said, and his expression was unreadable – except for a happy sparkle in his eyes that was a dead giveaway.

I couldn't help a smile, looked down and then back up. "You're Lee Wooyeong," I said, more of a statement.

The expression on his face instantly shifted. "Yes." He sounded cautious.

"You're a great dancer," I said, trying to ignore the way I could feel that I was blushing. He probably just thought I looked this way all the time – pink. "One of the best I've ever seen. And I've watched a lot of K-pop performance videos. The way you move…" I trailed off, trying to find the right words, though I'd bragged to so many people I knew about him using the same description. "It looks impossible for a human."

"Thank you," Wooyeong replied, laughing a little. Politely.

"Actually, Ambition is my favorite band," I said. Things were slipping out of my mouth faster than I could control them, and I felt a vague sense of panic. "All of you are very talented. I've been stanning since your debut."

Shut up, shut up! my mind was screaming at me. I looked down at my lap.

"Thank you," he said again, warmer this time. But there was still something slightly reserved about his manner now.

And I couldn't blame him. This was no longer a normal interaction, however much we tried to act like it was. I rubbed my thumb across the edge of my sleeve repeatedly, regret stinging in my chest.

That was when the waiter came back with a huge platter, loading the table up with side dishes, or *banchan*. Kimchi, fresh lettuce, lots of things I didn't recognize, rice, and the daeji kalbi, which looked like the star of the meal.

"Daeji kalbi and bap," said Wooyeong coolly, nodding at them, then at the banchan. "Mu ssam, sigeumchi muchim, dubu jorim, gyeran jjim, kimchi jeon, japchae, kimchi, and dongchimi."

I couldn't help feeling a little overwhelmed. I swallowed the lump in my throat. "Woah."

Wooyeong pushed forward the gyeran jjim – bubbling egg – for me to try. It was in a large, heavy dish and steaming hot, almost still boiling. The custardy egg inside was pale yellow and slightly frothy, topped with scallions.

I was sitting at a table with one of my favorite idols, which was surreal. If the food hadn't been here I didn't know what I would do. It was a welcome distraction to involve myself in, especially after this awkward exchange where I'd confessed to being a fan. My insides were a mess of emotions – sad, regretful, nervous, giddy, excited…

I dipped in a spoonful of gyeran jjim, blew on it, and then put it in my mouth, trying to ignore the way he was watching me and hoping he couldn't see the way my hand was shaking. The gyeran jjim was soft and velvety, with a mild but addictive taste.

"This is delicious," I said, eyes wide. Wooyeong smiled at the expression on my face as he loaded up his own plate with food. "Now try the kalbi."

I took a piece of the daeji kalbi with my chopsticks. Spicy pork spare ribs, if my Korean didn't fail me. They were orange-red, slightly charred, and glistening. Even just looking at them was like beholding a piece of heaven.

My mouth watered before I took a bite of the moist, juicy pork, flavors exploding on my tongue. Spice, garlic, char, sweetness, depth, umami. I was pretty sure my eyes might've actually rolled back in my head.

For a second I forgot I was actually talking to Lee Wooyeong, and about our awkward little exchange before. "Holy cow! I *never* ate food like this before!" My mouth was starting to feel like it was on fire. "This is *amazing!*"

"You think so?" He was leaning forward earnestly with a faint smile. Seeing me panting, he cracked open a small bottle with a red foil top and handed it to me. It was cold and read *Yakult* across the label, which was what I'd heard him order earlier.

I took a sip, the coldness smooth in my mouth. It was not like I expected it to taste – instead being very tangy and sweet with a strong taste of citrus. It calmed down the spice a lot. The bottle was tiny, which was probably why he'd ordered three.

"Thanks," I said a little sheepishly, but took some more daeji kalbi anyway. Along with my steaming rice I piled up the various banchan, like water radish kimchi, sesame spinach, and explosively spicy kimchi pancake. I'd never tasted anything like this before. The flavors were bright, punchy, almost bombastic.

Wooyeong was surveying me curiously as he ate. "How did you end up here in Seoul? How old are you?"

His gaze on me made me painfully self-conscious, unable to focus, with thrills running down my arms. It was almost impossible to talk while looking at him.

"Twenty-two," I said, cheeks flushed from the spicy food, the warmth of the restaurant, and him. "American age. I grew up in a small town in the US, wanting adventure. I was already learning Korean, so when I graduated, I chose a degree that allowed me to focus on international business. Coming to Seoul was my dream. I was so happy when a company here accepted my job application." I stopped, snuck a glance up at him. He was watching me with interest, waiting for the rest of my answer. My cheeks prickled again at our eye contact, and I looked quickly back down again. "That was recently. I just moved here two weeks ago. How old are you?"

I already knew, but I wanted to hear him say it. "Twenty-three American age," Wooyeong said seriously, "and twenty-four Korean age."

"How did you end up in this restaurant?" I asked. It seemed funny, like a mirror question of the one he'd asked me. But I was actually curious – and deep down, confused. How did Lee Wooyeong, a beautiful, masculine, smoldering-hot K-pop star whose band was rising to match EXO and maybe even BTS, end up *here?* Across the table from *me?*

"Too much instant ramyun and too tired to cook," he said. "I enjoy trying out restaurants anyway. So I came here, remembering my friend's recommendation. He loves this place."

I made a "mm" of acknowledgement as I ate, glancing up at him as I listened. He looked formal, sober.

"So is Seoul everything you hoped it would be?"

"Well, it's very cold," I admitted.

"You don't like that?"

I gave a sheepish laugh, picking up some sesame spinach with my chopsticks. "Not really."

Wooyeong mixed some sauce from the kalbi in with his rice. Even though he wasn't smiling, he seemed pleasant and friendly – maybe I'd already gotten used to his serious personality after such a long time. "Just wait for the summer. If you're staying that long."

"That's definitely the plan."

We were too busy stuffing our faces to talk much further. The food was delicious, each individual component well-done and flavorful, and even better together. The chewy sticky rice, funky, tender kimchi, spicy pork, velvety egg, snappy vegetables, and soft sesame spinach were so good it was like an orchestra in my mouth. I loved food – *loved* it – but this was *beyond* my expectations. It was like I was floating into heaven. I couldn't help letting out passionate "MMMMs" every once in a while, but trust me, words couldn't express.

Wooyeong was quiet as he ate. We finished at about the same time, and I leaned back, sipping more Yakult yogurt drink to calm the fire that made my cheeks red and my mouth hurt.

Wooyeong called for the bill, also something normal here but not in America. The waiter came back and dropped off the check and I looked at the total price, pulling my battered wallet out of my pocket and thumbing through my Korean banknotes. I put exactly half of the price on the table, glancing up to see Wooyeong looking at me, and the money, intensely.

I must have looked as startled as I felt at his expression, because he snapped out of it. "I'm sorry – you're paying for half?"

"Yes," I said, eyes still widened. It wasn't a date – it's not like he should pay for both of us. We were random strangers who just agreed to sit together so we could get into the restaurant.

Well, /was a random stranger; Wooyeong was definitely not, not to me. And then I realized –

"Oh!" I said. "Korean manners, the oldest person pays. I forgot about that. In America, both people paying equal is common, even if they already know each other..." Which we didn't. "It's sometimes rude in America to assume that someone else is going to pay for your meal, so I was paying half so you don't feel obligated to pay for me..." I was saying too much. I shut my mouth.

He looked surprised, but like he understood now. "Oh, no, it's alright. That's fine." He reached into the back pocket of his black jeans and pulled out his wallet, deftly flipping it open and counting banknotes.

How did he manage to look so *hot* doing just the basic things? Even when he was casual, he looked like someone should be filming him. The fluid way he moved, his nimble fingers, the way his pale skin glowed in contrast to his neat black clothes. The masculine, graceful shape of his nose, his lips, his sharp jaw. And his eyes. Beautiful. Large. Dark. I don't think I would ever get over how dark they were.

Wooyeong glanced up to meet my eyes, surprised, like he could feel my gaze on him. I fought the urge to look away, embarrassed, but my eyes still wandered to the dishes down on the table.

"I could eat this every day for the rest of my life," I said as a change of subject. "You eat this *all the time?*"

"Well, not all the time," Wooyeong said, a slight smile starting to tug at the corners of his mouth. "There's so much else out there. What else have you tried?"

"I ate a vanilla ice cream from a street vendor," I admitted. "But that's it."

"I love sharing Korean food with people," he said eagerly. "You should try tteokbokki, for sure – and rabokki. Those are delicious street foods. Mandu, buns, fried octopus – well, I suppose I could go on all day."

Watching him was making me feel giddy. I swallowed. "Wait, wait –" I pulled out my phone, laying it flat on the table, where he could see I was making a note. "Rabokki, tteokbokki, buns?"

"And mandu and fried octopus," he reminded, leaning forward as he watched me type. "Ooh, I can tell you the best places to get them too – Bukchon Son Mandu makes good mandu, with shrimp being my favorite, but there's also a street vendor who's practically magic –"

I accidentally tapped the wrong characters in my haste and had to backspace, trying to catch up at mad speed. I didn't want to miss anything he said, not only because I was lost and had no idea what I was doing (though that was most of it). Lee Wooyeong was giving me food suggestions – that didn't happen every day. And never would again, so I was enjoying it now.

"Ah!" he gasped. "And Mashi Joayo. You *have* to go there, it's delicious! It's fine food while not being too fancy and expensive. A meal sets you back about 25,000 to 35,000 won but it's worth it. The flavors – they're very clean. And their kimchi is some of the best I've ever tasted."

"Mashi Joayo? That sounds familiar." Maybe I passed by it before.

"Actually, it's less accessible to foreigners," he said, thoughtful. "The staff aren't very trustworthy to anyone who looks like they're not Korean, more than usual – tourists hardly ever go there. It's easy to get confused, and then of course there's the very complicated menu."

"Mmm," I said, biting my lip. I could speak Korean, but definitely not advanced Korean.

"Why don't I take you there?" Wooyeong offered.

I stared at him, thinking I'd misheard. "What?"

"You *have* to eat there. It's delicious! I'll take you, so you can avoid the confusion."

I was stunned. It must've shown on my face.

"It's one of my goals to share Korean cuisine," he added, but his expression was turning hesitant as he watched me.

"Oh, yeah," I agreed. "Of course. I would love to go to Mashi Joayo. I was just surprised."

There was a beat of silence. Then I slid out of my seat, ignoring the butterflies in my stomach and standing up, grabbing my parka and shrugging it on. "Thank you," I said. "For all that. Should we exchange...?"

~{★ 19 ♥}~

I was too afraid to continue. *Numbers?* Yeah, like Wooyeong was going to give me his *number?* Yeah right. I was delusional.

He slipped a paper into my hand. I looked up at him, surprised. He was standing up now, much taller than me, and my skin burned with warmth even though he hadn't touched me while giving me the paper. My fingers closed involuntarily on the precious slip.

"My email," he said. "I'm free on next Saturday, for lunch. Does that work for you?"

"Yes," I said, hardly able to tear my gaze away from his striking face. "I should give you mine, too. In case you want to cancel."

He said nothing as I scribbled it on a small scrap of paper and handed it to him.

"See you at Mashi Joayo," he said, and then walked out of the restaurant, leaving me to look after him, stunned.

우영
WOOYEONG
3

The taxi pulled up to the sidewalk.

SMK Entertainment's lights were bright, as usual. They glowed white, the windows on all twenty-two stories brilliantly lit up because of all the people still working inside.

The clerk at the front desk, Eun Ae, looked up when the automatic door opened and smiled at me in recognition. She was about ten years older than I was, with shiny black hair pulled back to reveal smooth skin and a wide face.

"Hey Wooyeong," she said. "How are you doing?"

"Good," I said. "Just got back from dinner."

"The boys didn't want to join you today?"

"I told them I refused to have any more instant ramyun."

She laughed as I made my way to the elevator, ignoring the security guard and punching in the floor number. I didn't have to think about it, after six years.

The hallways were clean and bright, with shiny white walls and a floor slightly scuffed from all the traffic that passed through on a daily basis. I passed the glass doors of some dance performing rooms, hearing a lonely thump-thump of shuffling feet as someone practiced their choreography. But since it was late in the evening, there was no one else around. I made my way through the empty halls and to the solid gray dorm doors, finally arriving at ours, near the end, Number 10. It was already unlocked, as usual.

"Hey!" I called, my abrupt shout echoing through the dorm. It was clean and modern and a little bit bigger than an apartment. I unlaced my leather boots and sat down on the sofa in the living room, tired.

Dyeong walked in, his eyes glued to his phone as he scrolled. He looked up at me. "You're back," he said unnecessarily.

"Yeah."

"Chin-hyuk's out," he said. "Went to grab some chips before our VLive."

"Oh, so we are doing it tonight?" I traced my finger in slow circles across the glass surface of the coffee table. "You don't have any makeup on."

"The staff are setting it up downstairs right now. It's only going to be about half an hour long. I'll just put on a mask or a hat." Dyeong threw himself onto the couch beside me, his wiry form languid as he clicked through his phone. A shiny, brand new iPhone of the latest model – paid for by SMK so he could use it in VLives when reading people's comments, and for taking selfies for Instagram. I'd declined their offer to get me one too. I didn't really care.

It fully hit me then that I'd just handed out my personal email to a fan.

I couldn't help it. Lately I'd been feeling so cynical, so jaded... but in that moment it'd been different. As if cold water had been dumped over my head. I'd forgotten I was a K-pop idol then, even though I'd still been in full show makeup and come straight from SMK.

Something about her had made me feel at ease. Like we'd known each other already, almost, though that wasn't quite it. At the core, I really didn't know her at all. She made me curious to know all the things she hadn't told me. I mean, an American who'd learned fluent Korean and come to Seoul? That wasn't common. Korean was one of the hardest languages for an English-speaker to learn and vice-versa. If she'd known even a little of it I'd have been impressed – but she'd known a *lot*.

None of us Ambition members had ever learned a full language. Sure, we'd memorized a smattering of English, Chinese, Japanese, and Spanish, and "hello" and "I love you" in the language of every country we'd ever toured in. But for her, an American, to learn Korean? And to be able to hold a conversation with native speakers?

That took considerable intelligence. And self-discipline.

I wondered what other things about her she hid behind her shyness.

Maybe that was why I had invited to meet again on a whim. She was quietly smart without flaunting it, interesting, and was excited and adventurous about trying new Korean food. I'd never found someone that I'd been able to share that passion for food with before.

Even now I felt that lightness, that enthusiasm in me that I was trying to hide from Dyeong. Would she love sundae? Eomuk tang? Had she ever tried kimchi friend rice before? I couldn't wait for Mashi Joayo. I was already thinking about what I would order. She said she'd eat *everything* – a smile played on my lips as I remembered her seriousness – but I still wondered if there might be one or two foods she avoided. Like octopus, maybe. Everyone had their preferences.

Dyeong didn't like clams, Tai wouldn't eat vegetables, and Chin-hyuk hated most banana-flavored things (and bananas themselves). Madison surely had something she didn't like, even if she didn't know it yet.

I wouldn't think that there would be a lot of Korean food available in the small US town she described. Du Yohan, my close friend who went by the stage name ONEDAN, had visited on a long tour and said it was hard to find food from home outside of bigger cities. And if she didn't cook – did she cook? I should ask her – that limited her options even more, since she wouldn't even be able to use the from-scratch ingredients.

I felt *excited* as I thought of all the things I could share with her. I hadn't felt excited in a long time.

It almost alarmed me. That cold-bucket-of-water-over-my-head feeling wouldn't go away. *Snap out of it, Wooyeong.*

I was very conscious of Dyeong next to me as he scrolled through his phone, having no idea what was running through my head.

I wasn't going to tell him. About tonight, about meeting Madison, and definitely not about inviting her to Mashi Joayo with me.

Deep down I knew it was unwise. Meet a fan, have a nice conversation, sure. One meeting never hurt anyone. But offer to meet again? That went against one of the golden rules of K-pop – don't be seen with people of the opposite gender, especially if it's only you and them. It looked too much like dating, even if it wasn't.

Yesterday, if one of the members had come home and told me that they'd arranged to meet someone again next week, and that someone was not only a *fan* but a *girl*, I might've blown my top. That was unquestionably stupid.

But this felt... this just felt different. Maybe it was a bad idea, but I couldn't be *Lee Wooyeong of Ambition* all the time. Sometimes I had to be just Lee Wooyeong. Who was allowed to relax and make new friends.

That's all she would be – a friend. That was the only way she interested me.

~{★ 23 ♥}~

It's not because she wasn't pretty; she was beautiful. But c'mon, this was the K-pop industry. I personally knew lots of beautiful girls – like *extremely* beautiful girls. Take-your-breath away beautiful. But just because we joked around and held a conversation sometimes when we met at parties or all kinds of awards didn't mean I had any romantic feelings for any of them.

In K-pop, you get used to having unearthly good-looking friends. It's like the Hall of Hotness.

This girl wasn't any different. I'd proved that I could successfully stay just friends with exceptionally beautiful people, without any struggle or conscious effort on my part. So I knew if I told Dyeong that I was meeting her at Mashi Joayo, he wouldn't be worried about *that*.

That wasn't the issue. It was the rumors that were the problem. All of us in Ambition knew how valuable our reputations were. They could make or break you. And if someone glimpsed me and Madison together and took a picture, that would be very bad.

People like me weren't allowed to date. When you're the crush of thousands and half of fans' devotion is to you personally and not just your music, dating could make them stop supporting you. Because they'd be watching their unrequited crush fall in love with someone else. That's hurtful.

So even if I wasn't dating a girl, just people *assuming* we were could be very bad.

Tonight had been a rare night. I'd gone out in full show makeup, not covering my face or hiding who I was. The last time I'd done that was months ago.

I hadn't washed off my makeup because of the VLive I knew we were supposed to be doing tonight, and bringing a mask would be pointless because I'd be eating.

I guess I'd been ready to deal with the possible consequences this time – and I'd gotten lucky, though I'd spotted a group of people staring at me and whispering, pulling out their phones, right before I ducked into the taxi.

If I was going to meet Madison again, no one could see us together and recognize me for who I was. There wouldn't be another time like tonight.

I wondered if someone else in the restaurant already *had* recognized me and snapped a photo. There was always that risk.

Which meant seeing her again was a doubly bad idea.

Dyeong was… just as experienced as I was, just as jaded sometimes, and definitely just as level-headed or more so. Especially right now, when I *knew* with my head that what I'd done was a mistake.

Strictly speaking, it never even should've happened.

So of course he wouldn't approve. He would tell me to cancel. Just like my intellect was telling me I should.

My fingers crunched the paper she'd given me in my pocket in case I wanted to cancel. Funny how she'd insisted on giving me an out. I hadn't even thought of it at the time.

But I didn't *want* to. Because I felt exactly the same way as when I'd offered to take her.

And something about her just seemed… trustworthy. That's what my instincts were telling me. I was a decent judge of friends.

Dyeong shifted in his position. I glanced at him instinctively.

"So how'd it go?" he said lazily. "Yohan's been kicking you to go to that place for a while, right?"

I felt apprehension rise up, another shocking feeling I hadn't experienced in almost as long as I could remember. I opened my mouth, pausing, unsure of what I was going to say…

And then the door swung open. We both looked up as Chin-hyuk walked in, his arms rustling with plastic shopping bags.

Chin-hyuk was our leader – a few inches shorter than me, with a smaller frame in general, somehow. He wore his designer clothes casually, not afraid to crease his white button-up or wear out his black jeans. Even his straight lavender hair looked easygoing, hanging in a way that, after many years of experience, I could tell was due to him moving around rather than half a can of hairspray and an hour's worth of work by the stylist. Looking at him, you would never guess that he was a fierce high-note hitter or a leader – until you worked with him.

"I thought you were just getting chips," I said incredulously, staring at the many bags on his arm, but I could still feel my relief from not having to answer Dyeong.

"I did!" he answered cheerfully, running a hand through his silky, shiny lavender hair. Loose strands glided from between his fingers. The hairstylist hated it when he did that – it messed up all the careful work she'd done. Me and Tai had laughed at him once when we'd overheard him being chewed out during a photo shoot.

~{★ 25 ❤}~

"You should do that onstage sometime," I said. "The fans would go wild. It's hot."

"I did it on accident," Chin-hyuk laughed as he walked to the kitchen. He stopped short, just noticing the mass of dishes in the sink. "What's this?" he asked, aghast.

Dyeong glanced at me with wide eyes, trying to tell me not to give him away. Chin-hyuk was a very clean person who kept law and order when it came to our mess. Dyeong could wash them later when he wasn't looking.

"Don't ask me," I said, strolling casually past Chin-hyuk, lifting one of his shopping bags from his hand on the way by. "I ate out."

Chin-hyuk grumbled something to himself as I unpacked the bag, setting his own on the counter. Pringles, kkokkalcorn, crab chips, and a whole bunch of water bottles.

"The chips are for the VLive," Chin-hyuk explained. "The water bottles are extra. I didn't pay for them. Manager Pak wanted me to pick some up just in case." He looked up at us. "Where's Tai? It's about to start."

Dyeong went to go fetch him from the bedroom. I watched Chin-hyuk as he arranged the water bottles on the counter, throwing the plastic bags away. Neither of us said anything.

"How are you doing tonight?" Chin-hyuk said. "You're quiet."

"No more than usual. I'm fine."

He leaned on the counter, fiddling with the label of one of the bottles. "I worry about you sometimes," he said quietly. "You get more cynical every year. More guarded."

I didn't say anything.

Chin-hyuk sighed. "I'm just concerned for you, is all."

"Like you always are," I said, a small smile tugging at the corner of my mouth. "You're a good leader."

"There's a smile," Chin-hyuk said. "I was beginning to miss them." He lapsed back into pensive silence.

Dyeong came back into the kitchen wearing a black mask, with Tai following close behind.

Tai, at six feet, was the tallest of us, with Dyeong earning second place at 5'10" and me third at 5'9". He absolutely towered over Chin-hyuk, the shortest, at 5'6". His warm eyes, the color of hot chocolate, had melted many fans' hearts. It was harder to be melted when those hot-chocolates had looked at me appealingly after eating my ramyun without permission.

"Are we ready?" he yawned, reaching up to rub his eyes – and then stopping, probably as he realized he still had the same performance makeup on as me and Chin-hyuk.

"Let's go," said Chin-hyuk, giving me one last long, thoughtful glance before heading to the door holding the bags of chips.

The VLive had gone well. There had been a lot of people watching, and they loved us, as usual. The comment section had been moving so fast I could barely read it. I had tried responding to a few questions I could understand, throwing in a couple English "I love yous" and Spanish "Te amos". I had even given the camera a wicked playboy wink, probably something that was going to be all over social media tomorrow. But it was the good kind of attention. The kind that fueled Ambition's popularity and renewed our fan's devotion.

I had been a little distracted during the filming. It had been hard not to think about Madison. She'd known me – and was a fan. Had she been watching? I wondered what that must be like for her. Must be strange to see me in person and then in a VLive broadcast just hours later. Suddenly I felt stupid for winking, though I couldn't pinpoint exactly why.

I stared up at my ceiling in the dark as I remembered, hearing Tai's breathing from the bunk below me, and hearing Chin-hyuk shift his position in the bed behind mine. Dyeong was probably out like a rock. He was an extremely deep sleeper – we'd have to check whether he was still alive in the morning, as usual.

I let out a heavy sigh, still looking up at the ceiling, my hand on my stomach as I thought of one of the comments I'd seen, *Wooyeong is the ideal boyfriend*.

It wasn't like I was unhappy with being adored by thousands of people around the world. That could be fun. I enjoyed it. You had to, if you were in this career. Fans posted pictures of my face, raved that I was the hottest man alive, or the cutest, depending on the pose. They said my personality was amazing, I was perfect hugging height, and they would give anything for the chance to touch me. That was fine.

It was just that no one had cared until I debuted with Ambition.

매디슨
MADISON
4

I was running late for work.

I scrambled around, grabbing my work bag and parka and slipping on my shoes. I made it out the door of my apartment into the blasting-cold, dewy early morning air, where it was still dim outside and a taxi was waiting. That was when I realized I had left my phone inside.

"One- one minute!" I stammered to the driver, gasping, running back into the building and taking the stairs to my place, where I busted in, snatched my phone from where I left it on the table, and ran back.

By the time I arrived at the taxi again and shut the door behind me, I was severely out of breath. I smoothed down my hair as we pulled away, still feeling panic and dread in my stomach.

Ever since Wooyeong gave me that piece of paper I'd been a scatterbrained wreck. Distracted, daydreaming, nervous. I muttered an English cuss word as I opened my work bag, rifling through to make sure everything was there.

Get it together, Madison. I was a competent, working adult. At least that's what I kept telling myself.

And I was probably going to be late. I sighed, leaning back on the seat and covering my eyes with my wrist.

It was so, so easy to think about him. He had been taking over my mind. How was I going to survive the remaining three days until I met him again?

I still couldn't believe it had actually happened. I'd spent practically every waking minute trying to rationalize it, trying to think it through, worrying and speculating and looking at that piece of paper with his handwriting on it to prove to myself it wasn't just a dream I'd made up.

But it hadn't done anything. I felt just as unprepared and stunned as the first moment.

Hearing the innocent little sound of the VLive notification a few days ago had given me shivers. I'd stared at the phone, then flipped it over to see the text of the banner, out-of-breath. I'd wanted so badly to press it, and at any other time, I would've – but the thought also made me so nervous I was almost queasy.

I'd heaved several deep breaths, trying to calm down, but it didn't work. I ended up not watching it, somehow unable to bring myself to face him again, even anonymously. Even now I hadn't watched the replay, almost afraid to.

It was different now that he was real.

I still couldn't rationalize it. Your world-famous bias doesn't just *pop up* in front of you, even if you do live in Seoul. There's no way. Yet it had happened, and even more shocking, he wanted to meet *again*.

My head was full to the bursting with wild possibilities and ideas of where this was going, but I shouldn't think about them. In fact, I'd already thought of all this *enough*. I was stuck on repeat.

I nearly yelped as I realized the taxi had just pulled up to my work. I'd done it again – gotten lost in the tangled mess that was my thoughts.

I darted out, my hand firmly clutching the handle of my work bag, running up the steps to Gi's white building and its glass blue-framed door. Inside I nearly ran into a woman, who moved aside, just missing me. "Oh my gosh!" she said, wide-eyed.

It was Jeongsook – my coworker, whose desk was next to mine. She'd been very gushy and happy to me, and seemed like she was doing her best to be nice. I appreciated that. She was very pretty – large eyes with perfect makeup, smooth dark brown hair that she always left down to fall in waves in front of her face, rosebud lips. She was always impeccably dressed, too; today she had on a cream pencil skirt and jacket with high heels taller than any I would've dared to wear. "What's wrong, Madison Hart?"

"Nothing," I said, trying to smooth down my hair as casually as I could. "I thought I was running late."

Jeongsook laughed, a bubbly sound, as she checked her wristwatch. "You have twenty seconds to spare."

"I have to set up things at my desk," I said, giving an apologetic bow. "Bye, Jeongsook!"

~{★ 29 ♥}~

The day passed very slowly. By the time it was done, I had nothing to do but just head home, so I decided to take that shopping trip at Homeplus I'd planned right before I'd met Wooyeong. It took me an hour, and some more time after I got home to organize everything; it seemed that I had more utensils, bowls, plates, pots, and pans than actual food. My cupboards and fridge still looked sad.

I clumsily cooked myself a real dinner, cleaned up, and then gave a frustrated sigh as I stared out the window, realizing I had nothing else to occupy my time.

This was the longest week of my life.

I obsessively kept checking my email for something saying he'd canceled. It *had* to come. There was no way this was actually going to happen.

But on Friday night I still spent two hours picking out exactly what I was going to wear if it did. Nothing seemed right.

Just keep it simple, Madison, just keep it simple. Not because of some fluffy ideology, but because if I didn't, I was likely to end up ruining everything.

I rummaged around in my tiny closet, pulling plain shirts and jeans out of the box I had yet to unpack. Should I go more classy, more casual (ha – as in *faked*, because it would take me an hour to look 'casual'), or more girly? I'd left behind most of my clothes in the move, not that they were much different from what I wore everyday here.

A long coat – yes. It'd be cold. And the coat would mostly cover anything I wore anyway.

In the end, I ended up picking out the fanciest thing I owned- a pretty cream blouse I'd bought for work and my average soft blue jeans. It was either that or a t-shirt.

I hardly ever wore makeup, but this was a special occasion. I couldn't remember any time that I wanted to look pretty this desperately. I spread my small stash out on the floor, biting my lip as I picked through them.

If I showed up looking too different or too dolled-up it would be suspicious. And he wasn't a clueless "normal" guy – he would notice. He and the other members already had to spend time in the makeup chair every time they did a performance or concert.

I ended up setting aside a single tube of mascara and a bit of lip color for tomorrow, too scared to do anything else. It would have to do. Not that making a good impression mattered anyway – this would probably be the last time I would see him.

~{★ 30 ♥}~

I carefully laid out the clothes and makeup next to each other and then stood back and looked at them, letting out the breath I had been holding in a rush. This meeting seemed to be inspiring more panic in me than anything else.

매디슨
MADISON
5

Before I knew it, it was Saturday. This was it. The day where I'd either see him again at Mashi Joayo or figure out that he'd canceled without saying anything.

I opened the door of the taxi, ducking out, my heart skyrocketing to my throat as my shoes hit the concrete of the sidewalk.

I glanced around at the busy scene, slamming the car door. It pulled away, going slowly around all the pedestrians in the road, its tires making gravelly noises on the asphalt.

This part of Seoul was new to me. Maybe I'd been here before, but I didn't remember. It was smack in the middle of the city, with buildings packed on all sides, an odd mix of old and new, stunning skyscrapers and brick apartments, and buildings that I didn't even know what they were for. A highway ran past, which was the road my taxi had taken for a short stretch to get here. The sound of car engines whizzing by filled the cold air.

The area I was standing was purely pedestrian. A man on a bicycle flew by on the other side of the road, and businesspersons in suits, perhaps on lunch break, traveled in packs. There were even men and women with large shopping bags, coming from some complex around the corner. There was every unsortable manner of people here, all with their own missions.

I heaved a breath, standing there in the middle of the sidewalk while people went past me on both sides. I looked through all the crowds, my eyes scanning for one familiar form that was nowhere to be found. There were so many people here I could easily miss him – he could be anywhere.

I took another deep breath to calm the nervousness in my stomach, my hands smoothing over the front of my gray woolen coat to make sure it was straight. My breath streamed out in a cloud in front of me. I looked down at my black boots then back up at all the moving people. Still no Wooyeong.

I swallowed, stuffing my hands in my pockets and starting to stroll forward toward Mashi Joayo, shoes clicking dully on the sidewalk.

It was unbelievable that I was looking for Lee Wooyeong here. It felt unreal, like something that was happening to someone else instead of me.

But he wasn't here yet, so my head was still clear. I hoped with all my might that I didn't melt into an awkward, nervous wreck as soon as I saw him.

Maybe he wasn't coming. This felt preposterous. Why would he want to meet me? He probably realized his mistake.

No... he would've told me. I'd given him my email. He was coming. He just wasn't here yet.

I shivered. It was cold, the wind blowing my hair back from my face. I wondered if I'd chosen wrong in leaving it down. It suddenly felt plain and frumpy, not to mention the breeze that was messing it up. Should I have put it up instead? I swept it away from my face, and started to braid it behind my head, feeling panicked. Why couldn't I be one of those girls who always had a beautiful hairclip with them or something? Even that would be welcome right now.

Someone tapped me on the shoulder.

I whirled around, gasping slightly, feeling panicked. *Oh no. Not right now!*

A guy with slick, reflective black sunglasses towered over me, a hoodie pulled over his dark blue turtleneck and black baseball cap. I took a step back reflexively, my hands falling from my hair, staring at him with wide eyes.

"Don't be scared," he said, his voice sounding actually concerned. "Don't you recognize me?"

My gaze fell upon his lips. I knew them all too well. My cheeks colored and my heartbeat started going very fast.

"Yes," I admitted, my voice coming out breathier than I expected as I looked up into those impenetrable sunglasses. It was difficult to keep my concentration when I was very aware of his lips quirking in a smile.

Don't look, don't look, I cursed myself. He was going to think I was a total weirdo. I looked away instead, at the shiny building across the highway. It was a relief.

A beat of silence passed where we just stood there.

~{★ 33 ♥}~

I felt my cheeks flush red again as I realized that my hair was one-third braided. I reached up and feverishly released it, my fingers clumsily shaking it out and raking through to the bottom. I did it fast I could, not looking at him, feeling him watching me.

He didn't comment, even though he'd seen me trying to fix my hair in the first place since he'd walked up behind me.

"Where'd you come from anyway?" I muttered, so embarrassed I didn't know what else to say, strands of my hair now blowing in front of my face.

Wooyeong half-turned his body and pointed down the sidewalk, where it continued for a time and then bent to run down another road, hidden from view. "Sorry – I'm always late, remember? I was strolling around the blocks behind that building."

My blush deepened at his teasing and I froze, mortified that he remembered what I'd first said to him.

"It's cold out here," he said, when I stayed silent. "Would you like to go inside?"

I nodded mutely. We headed down the sidewalk to Mashi Joayo, side-by-side. It was both odd and wonderful to be conscious of his figure next to mine. I snuck a glance at him. He was looking forward – as much as I could tell under his sunglasses. Though he had a broad, masculine chest and shoulders, there was something almost graceful about him. Perhaps it was the way he carried himself, which it seemed he was unconscious of. There was a litheness about it that seemed to speak of his experience and power as a dancer.

He'd slayed every choreography I'd ever seen him do, making it look effortless every time. It made me jealous of the smoothness of his motions, even while he was moving faster than what seemed humanly possible. I couldn't describe the mesmerized awe I'd felt when watching their first dance practice so many years ago. People like him couldn't be real.

But he was, and he was next to me. He reached the door first and held it open, snapping me out of my reverie.

"Thanks," I said, going inside, walking a little faster so he wouldn't have to wait. I became painfully self-conscious again, and aware of the formal politeness between us.

The first room in Mashi Joayo was large and airy, with a lofty ceiling and fawn-colored walls. It was bright and modern, and I could see the diners at their tables beyond a half-glass wall. The air was filled with the chatter of people talking and the smell of clean carpet and food.

A server in a white uniform greeted us, smiling. Because I was clearly a foreigner, she might've thought Wooyeong was too – until he started talking in rapid and crisp Korean. "Table for two, please," he said. "Preferably somewhere near the corner of the room."

She nodded and escorted us all the way across the dining space and to a corner, just as Wooyeong requested. She laid out two menus, napkins and silverware.

I pulled out a chair and sat down, smoothing down my coat. Wooyeong had already picked up the menu, his lips moving ever so slightly as he read silently. I looked down at the table, which was already adorned with silverware. The spoon was metal, and so were the chopsticks, in the Korean way. I couldn't remember where I had first learned this, or whether it struck me as odd after seeing so many wooden Chinese and Japanese ones.

When the waitress arrived, Wooyeong didn't hesitate to order. "We'd like the house kimchi, the radish gimbap, and gamjatang with water, please."

I was glad he was in charge, because the menu looked insanely complicated. I smoothed my coat again, my fingers brushing over the wool. I unbuttoned the first few buttons to release some heat now that we were indoors, and looked up to see Wooyeong watching me.

"What is it?" I said, startled.

"Mm? Oh, I was looking to the side even though I was facing you. Sorry. You can't see, through my sunglasses…"

"Oh." I tried to act calm, fingering the chain around my neck just for something to do. My fingers felt hot and clumsy. Why was this so uncomfortable?

"So how have you been?"

I stared at him, somewhat taken aback. His voice seemed warm and genuinely curious. Weren't we just here for the food? Was he asking for more than a 'fine' answer or was I just mistaken?

I didn't know what to say. Right now, all I could think about was him. Even though we'd just started this second meeting, I was already aware that it was our last.

I wished… I wished that I could see his eyes, even if they would distract me.

"Could you take off your sunglasses?" I asked softly. "Or are you afraid someone's going to recognize you?"

Wooyeong stilled. Then he slowly, slowly reached up and slid his sunglasses far down his nose so that they were almost falling off, until I could just see his intensely dark eyes. They were made darker by the shadow underneath his cap.

It nearly knocked the breath from my lungs, seeing their familiar, beautiful shape.

His voice was neutral. "Is this okay?"

I nodded.

"There's no one here that's going to see my face except you and the waiter, since I'm facing the wall," he said, voice low. "Did you take the chair facing the room on purpose, or by accident?"

I looked down at it in surprise. "Um, by accident. I'm glad it worked out that way though. It's strange talking to someone when you can't see their eyes."

"I'm sorry about that," he said. "I have to do this sometimes." He gazed at me. "But it's okay for now."

I nodded again, not knowing what to say. I picked up the menu, seeing a complex mass of small text.

"You never answered how you were," he said.

I put down the menu, slightly embarrassed. "Sorry... um..." I couldn't think of anything to say. "What do you want to hear?"

"Whatever you want to tell me."

I looked at him for a few moments. Wooyeong's dark, unwavering eyes never left mine.

They were so beautiful I had a hard time looking away. I pushed down the emotions filling up inside of me, glancing down at the table with effort. Today my hands were shaking less in his presence. At least that was an improvement.

"Well, I did try out one of the places you mentioned. The mandu shop. It was amazing."

I'd gone there not only because I was in desperate need of good food, but also because I wanted to follow his advice before I faced him again, the very least so we'd have something to talk about. Funny how I'd forgotten before, the very minute I saw him. His presence made every thought I'd had mysteriously fly out of my head.

Wooyeong nodded, but I got the strange feeling he wasn't satisfied with my answer. I would've thought he would've wanted to talk about it. When I didn't say anything else – I didn't know what to say – he pressed on. "What else have you been up to?"

"I went to work," I said, struggling to come up with something to say. "My life's really not that exciting. I don't have any secret, interesting hobbies lurking about, if that's what you're wondering."

He let out a breath that sounded like amusement. "No secret, interesting hobbies? None at all? What a disappointment."

My face burned. Wooyeong looked surprised to see it, adding "I'm teasing you. I'm not serious."

"I know," I said, but he'd hit the vein of truth. He was a brilliantly talented and interesting person, and I... was boring. It reminded me why my crush on him should go away, since we were horribly matched. He could do so, *so* much better than me, and he would. I'd be out of the picture. "What about you?"

"I'm not letting you change the subject just yet. What do you do at home then, when you're not working or eating mandu?"

"I listen to music, watch dance practices, read, sleep... sometimes I watch shows too." I was trying hard to keep the insecurity off my face. "As you can see, nothing unique or exciting."

"That's what I do when I'm at home," Wooyeong said. "Most people can't be exciting and unique *all* the time. Besides, aren't you passionately interested in food?"

"Well, that's somewhat of an overstatement. I just... like to eat."

His expression was calm, but somehow I got the oddest sense that he was smiling. "Is that why you learned Korean?"

I shook my head. *I learned Korean because of Ambition, but mostly because of... you.* There was no way I could ever muster the nerve to tell him that. Even if I did, would I just end up looking pathetic?

"You said that's what you do when you're at home, but you also said you liked to walk," I said, hoping he didn't think me evasive.

He hesitated but then said, "Yes. I do. It makes me feel good. Peaceful."

"Even in the Seoul winter?" I said in disbelief. "Does walking around through crowds and across the concrete when it's freezing still make you feel peaceful?"

"It does," he admitted. "Not as much as when I'm somewhere beautiful, obviously. But I can't wait until they schedule a break from –"

He stopped. "Work," he finished generically, "so that I can go for a real hike."

~{★ 37 ❤}~

"Is there any place you have in mind?"

I didn't miss the way he'd avoided mentioning what he really did. He didn't want to talk about being a K-pop idol, or about being famous, so I wouldn't talk about it either. Not that I was keen about it before – it had felt awkward. A fan and an idol. By mutual consent it seemed like we were going to act like that had never happened, and we were two normal people.

Wooyeong's voice was enthusiastic – as enthusiastic as he could be while still sounding calm and serious. "The Inca Trail, the Appalachian Trail, Dragon's Back Trail... too many to count. I love the wild ones. I spend so much time in big cities that I miss the adventure of being out in the middle of nowhere."

It was odd to hear things from him I'd never known before. I'd thought that with all the talking and interviews and videos Ambition had done, they'd revealed themselves – who they were, what they liked, their dreams. But I had to admit that as much as I knew about Wooyeong, there were huge parts of him that were still a mystery. By actually being in his presence I had the strangest impression that I knew who he was even less than before.

"Adventure," I said. "You had me at adventure, and I know nothing about those trails, or hiking."

The waitress arrived back with the food, cutting off Wooyeong's response. She set first a bubbling black pot of stew, with chunks of meat and potatoes and vegetables in a red broth, topped with fresh leafy greens I couldn't recognize along with slices of chiles. The smell was tempting. Next was a neat white bowl of kimchi, a small platter of what looked like sushi rolls, and our two waters.

"Ah," Wooyeong said. "I can't wait. So those seaweed-wrapped rice are called gimbap; it's kind of like Korean sushi. I heard that's very popular in America."

I nodded.

"I ordered the radish kind. Next is their house kimchi – it's very fresh and fragrant and crunchy. I think it's refreshing. Mashi Joayo's kimchi is one of my favorites. And lastly, the stew. It's gamjatang – pork bone stew. It's rich and spicy. Just a bowl of that feels like miracle elixir for your health."

The flavors exploded in my mouth just like before. The kimchi tasted just like he'd said, but was a bit too strong for me. The gimbap was phenomenally fresh, the radish juicy and peppery, and the stew was full umami. It was salty and rich and meaty with a strong chili flavor.

It truly was amazing food, though I liked the banchan place we'd been to as well. I would eat at either of these.

I guess Wooyeong wouldn't be with me if there was a next time. I snuck glances of him as I ate, glad that he was asking me questions of what I thought of it. It gave me an excuse to look at him.

The conversation wasn't nearly as personal as it had been before the food arrived, but we talked anyway. Anything K-pop related wasn't brought up, but we discussed the weather, Seoul, the US, movies, and other random things that always revealed a little more about him to me. Some of the information was new to me, some of it wasn't – like I learned he only liked black coffee, no sugar, nothing creamy. He didn't like too-sweet drinks. I thought it fit his serious personality rather well.

But soon it was time to pay, since the waitress arrived and dropped off a check. I tried not to reveal my disappointment.

Wooyeong shifted his position, leaning forward slightly so he could reach into the back pocket of his jeans for his wallet, which made his sunglasses slide the last quarter-inch off his nose and onto the table. He uttered a little surprised half-laugh, making me stunned by the full force of his uncovered face and his smile. My heart skipped a few beats.

But the expression of surprise on his face was enough to jolt me out of it. He didn't pull out his wallet. Because it appeared it wasn't there.

"Uh-oh," he said, pushing his chair back and standing up. He patted all of his pockets and even his hoodie, finding only his phone. "I think... I've lost my wallet."

"While you were walking?" I asked. "You're *sure* you brought it?"

He nodded, never looking away. "It might be in the front of the restaurant. Let me go look for it." He picked up his sunglasses again and hurriedly shoved them onto his face.

I sat in my chair and watched him walk away, feeling helpless. Then I pulled out my own wallet – much less languid and hot than I'd seen him do it our first meeting – and hurriedly counted out the banknotes, slapping them on the table as I stood up and followed him out.

The wind hit me hard as soon as I stepped out of the door, blowing my unbuttoned coat lapels back to expose the skin near my collarbone. I flinched against its icy force, but didn't bother to do anything, turning around and seeing Wooyeong hunting down the path we'd walked. Through the several pedestrians, I could see the sidewalk was clear.

I ran to join him, falling into step beside his powerful stride with some effort.

Wooyeong turned around in surprise, abruptly stopping so that my shoulder almost collided with his chest. I took a step back, my vision of his eyes blocked again by the sunglasses so I could only see his parted lips.

"You're here? You already paid?"

"Of course I did, I'm not going to sit there and let you look all over for it by yourself."

He made a noise in the back of his throat I couldn't interpret, taking a deep breath and looking sideways down the sidewalk. "Thanks," he said. "It appears... it's not here. So it's probably on the path I walked."

"Someone could've found it," I said. "We took a long time to eat since we were talking."

He glanced down at his feet, pulling out his sleek black phone. "My number is in there. If someone found it, they haven't called, which means it's probably stolen."

I didn't miss the edge of worry to his tone. Besides all of the things in his wallet gone, I could just imagine someone recognizing him as Lee Wooyeong of Ambition and posting it all over the internet.

"Well, we have to find it," I said. "How far did you walk?"

"I did circles," he said. "Around certain blocks. There's no straight path."

"How about we split up to look for it?" I suggested.

Wooyeong turned to me. He must've seen the struggle on my face from not being able to see his eyes, because he said "Sorry," and lowered his sunglasses. Then he heaved a breath. "Yeah, let's do that. If that's okay with you."

"That's perfectly okay with me," I said quickly. "I just don't want it to be stolen."

"Here, give me your phone."

I stared at him.

"If we're going to split up, we should be able to call each other and say if we found it. I'm going to enter myself as a contact."

"Oh! Of course," I said, feeling stupid, but also shocked at the suddenness of it. I handed him my phone and he handed me his. The solid black glass was still warm from where he'd touched it. I entered my number, putting my name as *Madison Hart*, my fingers clumsy and trembling from the adrenaline of being around him.

"I entered myself as Wooyeong," he said, handing mine back to me. "No Lee."

I nodded, slipping it back in my pocket and trying not to think about the fact that his fingerprints were now on my phone, giving back his. "Okay... so you went that way?" I pointed to the right, to the corner where he'd come up behind me.

"Yes," Wooyeong said. "I stuck to the sidewalk until it wrapped around near a fashion complex, and then I went left towards the 7-Eleven." He paused. "And... a lot of other places that I don't even know how to explain right now. I'll cover those while you take that path. If you need more directions call me, okay?"

"Okay," I said, hurrying, starting on the path that he'd walked.

I took a few deep breaths of the cold air once I was far enough away that he couldn't hear me. Adrenaline was rushing through my veins, but I also felt stunned. We'd exchanged numbers. Just like that.

"You're on a mission," I muttered to myself as I hurried down the pavement. Wooyeong needed his wallet. That was important.

I rubbed my forehead. It didn't matter how stunned I was. I had to pay attention.

I walked past people around the corner, searching at the edges of the sidewalk, where people might've missed it. If it hadn't been stolen already, it would be in a place not obvious, or else many people would've already seen it by now, picked it up, and called the number on the inside. The wind rushed past my exposed collarbone again and I shivered, reaching up to button my coat, not taking my eyes off the sidewalk.

There were sometimes railings outside the stores, or little wire bins full of goods to sell, like shoes and fake flowers. I checked around and behind them, seeing nothing but the bare concrete.

I hoped so badly that no one had stolen it. That could create a lot of trouble for him.

The fashion complex was reached fairly quickly. "Left until the 7-Eleven," I murmured to myself, trying to remember what he'd said. I walked, scanning the sidewalk and nearly bumping right into a woman standing in front of a store. Luckily I saw her at the last second and dodged around, and she didn't even notice me because she was listening to someone in her cell phone. There were lots of people around here and it was hard to notice a wallet through all the feet.

Wooyeong hadn't bothered to describe it – I guess he'd forgotten, or just assumed I'd known because I'd seen it once. At the time I'd been more distracted by his hotness, but I'd remembered it being black, just like the rest of his clothes. Black leather.

There was nothing made of black leather to be found here, nor anything dropped on the ground. I reached the 7-Eleven and stopped short.

"Did he go beyond here?" I murmured to myself, rotating on the spot. My fingers brushed my phone in my pocket. I could call him...

No. He hadn't walked the direction I'd walked. Maybe his wallet had fallen in a place only visible when heading one direction.

So I turned around and did the same path again, even up to the exact spot where he'd surprised me from behind. There was nothing I could see.

I pulled my phone out of my pocket and stared at it, taking a few deep breaths of the cold air. After I could stall no longer, I clicked it on, found *Wooyeong,* and hit the call button.

He answered it first ring, which was fortunate so that I didn't have time to hang up in a nervous panic. "Hello," he said.

"Hi – um, I didn't find it," I said, regretting that it was true. "I'm sorry. I did the path twice, from both directions. I'm in front of Mashi Joayo now."

He was silent for a beat. "Me neither," he said. "I haven't walked the full way yet though."

Wooyeong's voice coming from my phone was giving me chills. I rubbed my arms, glad he couldn't see me.

"We'll find it," I said, although I'm not sure I actually believed it. "Where else can I walk?"

He was silent again for another beat. "You can go home if you want to. Anywhere you go will be a place I already walked, but you can double my path and check I didn't miss it... if you like."

I could feel something – remorse? Panic? – gripping me. This was too sudden. I wasn't ready yet. I didn't even get to see him one last time. And besides, his wallet was still lost. I really wanted him to find it.

The way he said 'if you like' at the end gave me butterflies. "Yeah," I managed to squeeze out. "I'll do that."

There was a short pause, but I noticed he didn't try to talk me out of it. "Straight ahead towards the skyscraper with the blue logo, then turn left. Baegjo-gil is the street you should be on. I'm on it right now, you'll find me if you walk far and fast enough. I'll call you when I turn onto a different street, that way you won't get lost."

"Sounds good," I said, mouth dry, already walking quickly in the direction he'd specified. He said goodbye and hung up. I kept my phone in my hand instead of putting it back in my pocket.

I got on Baegjo-gil and went slower than before, trying to look in every nook and cranny. My adrenaline leapt up when I spotted a dark rectangle next to a store door, but it turned out to be just a smashed, folded piece of paper that might've once been on a portable coffee cup.

Just like before, there was nothing here either. We'd been looking for almost an hour already.

My phone rang again from Wooyeong. I quickly pressed *Answer* and brought it to my ear, heart beating fast. "Hello?"

"I found it!" he said, sounding bright and breathless. "It was leaned up neatly against the curb almost like someone had put it there. I almost didn't see it. Nothing's missing either."

"Thank goodness!" I gasped.

"Where are you?"

"Baegjo-gil right by..." I looked around. "A coffee shop with a red exterior."

"Oh, okay, I'll be right there!"

"I'll meet you," I said, starting to hurry forward.

That was the exact moment I spotted him running down the road. Our eyes locked across the crowd, his phone still pressed to his ear. He smiled.

"There you are," he said, his low voice in my ear startling me. In that moment I'd forgotten we were still on call.

He drew closer, slowing down until we came to a stop in front of each other. For a second we just looked at the other person, a slight smile still on his face.

"I guess we should hang up now, huh?" I said awkwardly, lowering my phone.

He didn't answer, but silently lowered his phone too. "Thank you," he said, both of us moving to the side near a shop wall to be out of the way of the flow of people. He was holding the wallet out so I could see, pushing his sunglasses back all the way up covering his eyes.

"It was nothing," I said. "I'm just glad you found it."

~{★ 43 ♥}~

Wooyeong smiled and opened his mouth, then stopped as if suddenly remembering something panicky. "Oh –" He pulled out his phone and checked the time. "I was supposed to be back an hour ago, I really need to leave –"

"Well, hurry!" I said, waving him on urgently. "Don't bother with me, just go!"

Wooyeong flashed me a smile, but I could tell he was stressed-out. "Thank you!" he said. "For everything. I'm so sorry."

"Go!" I told him, and he uttered a rare laugh, already running away in the direction he'd come from, his head turning left and right at the intersection as he clearly looked for a taxi.

I watched him go until his black hoodie disappeared from sight, my heart swelled with bittersweet happiness.

I'd thought that, by living in Seoul, I'd been in the process of my one and only real dream. Finally achieving it, and living out the results. End of story.

But now I was forced to realize that wasn't the case at all. Whether I liked it or not – whether I was ready for it or it was even rational – I had another dream.

우영
WOOYEONG
6

I jumped out of the taxi and jogged to the automatic doors of SMK, my pulse racing, yanking off my hat and sunglasses. I held my hand up in greeting as I went by the startled-looking desk clerk, who was Ilsung Kim today. His eyes were round underneath his glasses.

When I was in the elevator I swept my hair back into place with my fingers, arranging it on my forehead by instinct as I panted. This was not good. Not good at all. I'd told them I'd be back a long time ago, and now I might have to face their questions.

Please, please let no one be in, I wished fervently. Losing my wallet had been unexpected, and had caused a huge delay.

And then afterward...

I'd lied to Madison.

I really had lost my wallet, but then I'd found it leaning against the curb.

That's when she'd called me. I had the opportunity to say "Hello, I found it, we can both go home now."

But I hadn't. I'd just said "Hello," heartbeat going unusually fast as I stared down at the wallet safely in my hand. And then she'd said she hadn't found it – of course.

"Me neither," I'd said, trying to control my tone.

After we'd hung up I let out a little breathless gasp of incredulity. Why had I done that? I'd lied, purposely, just so I could stall. That's what I'd been doing. Stalling. I hadn't *wanted* both of us to go home, resume our lives separately. I was searching for something, some reason to drag it out a little longer, to see her again.

I'd paced up and down the sidewalk, thinking furiously, wallet tucked snugly in my back pocket. I'd gotten her phone number. I could call her. She's paid for the meal. I could offer to repay her. Yes.

I'd felt too guilty to stall much longer. Madison had absolutely no idea that I'd just lied to her, and she was out in the cold when she said she'd hated the cold, as I remembered from our first meeting. I couldn't make her do this. I couldn't even fathom why I'd done it in the first place. The other members would never believe it – Wooyeong didn't *lie* and *plot* just so he could see someone longer.

I wanted to be there to say goodbye in person. I'd headed back down the path I had come until I spotted Madison in front of a coffee shop, her hair blowing all around her face in the harsh winter breeze. That's when I'd called her again and told her I'd found it – trying to play it off like a happy coincidence that I had been close enough to see her one more time.

I really had been glad that I'd found my wallet, but underneath it was the rush of adrenaline and *satisfaction* that what I'd done had worked. I was still aghast at myself, hardly understanding it.

And in all that was going on, I'd forgotten about being late.

This was not going to be good.

But if no one was in the dorm, they'd never know. That was the way I wanted it. This day had *not* gone as planned....

I straightened my hoodie, taking a deep breath just as the elevator's doors slid open again with a little chime. I stepped out into the empty hallway and started running toward our dorm, dodging a surprised crewman who was coming out of one of the studios with a clipboard.

"Sorry!" I called to him as I made it to our dorm, wrestling the door open.

The sight that met my eyes was singularly formidable, more than I'd feared: Dyeong, Tai, and Chin-hyuk all sitting in the living room watching me. Waiting for me.

My heart sank. All the carelessness I'd felt today with Madison vanished in an instant, leaving me heavy as a stone.

"Hello," I said resignedly.

"Where did you go?" Chin-hyuk demanded. "I called you, twice. You didn't answer. We were expecting you back at least an hour ago."

"I should've called," I admitted. I *had* received his calls, but I'd only answered Madison's. Which now seemed like a very stupid thing to do.

Facing Chin-hyuk was the worst. His tone was never angry – and it wasn't today either. Just calm disappointment in me, infused with kindness, like he was just glad I was okay.

It nearly killed me. I couldn't remember the last time I'd made him respond like this.

"Where were you?" asked Tai, who looked more curious than anything else.

Dyeong glanced at me from his chair, his legs casually crossed but his face totally unsmiling. All the fans thought that expression was hot. It was different when you were the cause of the annoyance, and knew it wasn't just a pose. His gaze made me want to shrink inward – but I didn't.

I swallowed, needlessly adjusting my black hoodie with a tug on both sides. I glanced down, then back at them, not sure what to say. *I lost my wallet*? That would be true, but it wasn't the whole story, which they would definitely ask for.

I inhaled slowly, trying to calm the defensiveness I could feel rising.

"I was at Mashi Joayo," I said. "I invited someone I met last week at another restaurant. And then I lost my wallet, and we both had to look for it." I dug in my pockets, holding it up so they could see, lamely. "I'm sorry I didn't take your calls. I should've at least sent you a text so you knew I was okay."

There was a long, tense pause.

Then Dyeong tilted his head lazily, his eyes piercing through me. "But you didn't, because you didn't want to explain something we wouldn't want to hear," he said softly. "Tell me, who is this mystery person?"

His tone was dangerous. Tai's wide eyes flicked worriedly to Chin-hyuk, waiting for him to intervene. He didn't. He was watching me, his cautious gaze going from Dyeong to me, expecting an answer.

I heaved a breath, suspecting that Dyeong already knew some of the truth. That's why he was asking me. Daring me to say it aloud – that I'd risked being out in public with a girl.

"Her name is Madison," I said, not moving from my tall stance, "and she's an expat from the U.S.A. who learned fluent Korean. She was excited about trying Korean food, so I offered to take her to Mashi Joayo."

The air was frozen. No one said anything for a long moment.

"Wait, you met this person before? Was it last week when you went to that restaurant?" Chin-hyuk said.

"She's *American?*" Tai gasped.

"And you met her *again* today?" said Chin-hyuk.

"And you didn't tell us?" Tai asked incredulously.

~{★ 47 ❤}~

I nodded.

"It should be fine if this was the only time," Dyeong said, his face struggling with his surprise. "And this was the only time – right?"

Chin-hyuk was nodding slowly. Tai was just looking around at us all, his gaze fast, watching our reactions.

I could tell by their faces that Dyeong, at least, wanted me to answer *"Yes. It was the only time. I'm done now, and have no plans of meeting up again."* Even Chin-hyuk, who would never push me into anything I didn't want to unless it was one more dance practice, was biting his lip apprehensively.

I took another deep breath. This had all moved so fast, I'd barely had time to honestly ask myself what I wanted, let alone tell them. But I knew enough.

"I would like to meet her again."

Dyeong slammed his fist into the arm of his chair, making Tai jump and Chin-hyuk look over warily. "*Dang* it, Wooyeong! You think you want to put us through this?"

I didn't have the words to answer.

"Just because the dating ban ended a year ago doesn't mean you can just freely hang out with girls! If rumors started spreading, Ambition's popularity could plummet! You could ruin it for us, not just yourself!"

I swallowed. Tai was looking worried for the first time, a crease between his straight brows.

"You – you're being careful, right?" he asked.

"Of course I'm being careful," I said. "I know it's risky. But..."

"Idols still have to make friends," Chin-hyuk said quietly. "We still have to have some small part of our lives that belongs to us and not to the fans."

"Yes," I said, jumping on his defense. "That's what it's like. She's my friend. I don't think of her as anything more than that. If I were to cut off contact even though I enjoyed her company, just because I was afraid dating rumors would start spreading..." I looked at Dyeong, hoping he would see the sincerity in my face. "I would hate that. I hate it when I feel restrained by our success."

Chin-hyuk was nodding, his eyes glazed over as he stared at the coffee table. Just yesterday he'd commented how cynical and guarded I was, and – I had been. But the feeling I got from being around Madison broke through that. I felt alive.

Dyeong leaned back. "I know what you mean, and I feel bad for you, but sometimes it just can't be helped. Do you remember what happened to 4XA?"

I did. All too clearly. It was the most recent drama in the world of K-pop, still an ongoing controversy.

"The youngest member got caught up in a dating scandal. They were doing so well, but the group collapsed. The official disbandment news was released just a few weeks ago." Dyeong's eyes blazed. "Cherry of ChocolatePop. A photo was released on Instagram of her holding hands with a guy. They lost half their fans and are still suffering from the blow. Jaejoon of Dragonn. A photo was released of him with a girl, with him smiling at her like they were dating even though he kept repeating he wasn't, just like *all* of us do. Fans at the next concert started a chant of 'Liar' –"

"I get it," I interrupted. "I know it's a risk. But I'm being careful. It's not going to hap –"

"It was just two times, no harm was done," Tai said. "Right?"

"Besides," Chin-hyuk said. "It's not like she knows who you are."

I tried to find something to say. There was an awkward pause. Then I said, repeating Tai, "There's no harm d –"

Dyeong wouldn't let me get away with it, cutting me off. "Does she know who you are?"

I glanced down. It was all they needed for an answer, Dyeong looking like he wanted to murder me and drape my dead body across the back of the sofa. But before he could open his mouth Tai burst out "She knows who you *are?* What about all those stories about obsessed fans who destroy you if they can't have you? All it takes is one social media post and you're done for!"

Chin-hyuk sucked in a breath, covering his eyes with his hand.

"I know that!" I said. "It's fine, she's not... not like that."

Tai just looked at me silently, unbelief on his face.

"That's enough," Chin-hyuk said uneasily. "I'm sure you're more than aware of how careful you have to be and what will happen to you as well as *us* if you're seen together." He gave me a pointed look. "Even if you're just friends and intend to stay that way. It doesn't matter what's true. It matters what people *think.*"

"Yes," I said shortly.

"Ambition has gotten so far, we have so much to lose." Dyeong waved his hand intensely, not listening to Chin-hyuk's command. "Why do you think Chin-hyuk broke up with his girlfriend before he debuted? Why do you think me and Tai pass up so many nice, cute girls that we'd love to take out on a date but can't? Do you think *you* don't have to do the same?"

I didn't answer.

"You know we all have our pick! We meet all sorts of people at the fansigns and concerts! And you know what? Sometimes I still regret not reaching out to some of them! I still wonder where they are and what they're up to, what they're like! We could take someone out on a date, or hang out with girls who are just friends. But we *don't!*" Dyeong leaned forward, then hissed *"This* is why we're successful."

"I get that," I said, struggling not to respond defensively. "But I also stand by what I said before. I *need* this. She's my friend. I'm going to be careful."

I walked forward, still in the living room but on my way to the door of the bedroom. "I'm going to see her again."

Chin-hyuk nodded slowly. "If you think it's wise."

I inhaled, dipped my head in a slight bow of regard, and then turned, going into the bedroom and shutting the door behind me.

I heaved a huge breath once I was on the other side. I ripped off my hoodie, throwing it onto the floor and heaving myself over the edge of the bunk bed I shared with Tai, where I lay down on my side.

I hadn't been this upset in a while. I felt like a mass of emotions but couldn't sort through them.

Pulling out my phone would just be avoiding the root problem. So I didn't distract myself. I just lay there, thinking.

I had been so happy earlier. The happiest I'd been in... I didn't know how long. I'd felt carefree. Light. Madison had made me laugh. I enjoyed being around her.

Now it was creating a rift in Ambition.

I'd already made up my mind. There wasn't going to be a change.

It suddenly, fully sank in that instead of just having her email now, we'd swapped phone numbers.

I slipped my cell out of my pocket and turned it on, making the home screen light up with a picture of a tiger and a text notification from my friend Du Yohan, early this morning – he always got up before me. I still had to respond to that one. I navigated to my contacts, seeing her name pop out like it was the biggest one there.

I stared at it for a long time. *Madison Hart.*

매디슨
MADISON
7

I pulled out my sofa-bed, throwing off the midnight blue seating cushions and extending the mattress. I put on the sheets and tossed over the comforter, which was a pale pink with flowers – uncharacteristic of me, but I'd fallen in love with it while shopping in Shinsegae Department Store. It had just seemed so Korean, somehow, at the time. Maybe that was stupid. But I really wanted to feel like Seoul was my home.

I climbed into bed, wedging into the soft pillows and pulling the comforter up to my neck as I looked out the window. It was dark outside, now that it was ten o'clock, except for the glitter of distant city lights.

I pulled out my phone – smudged with fingerprints, mostly mine but maybe even some of Wooyeong's. The thought gave me a strange, light feeling in my stomach. I clicked the power button and the screen lit up.

It was still on the recent calls tab. There was his name. *Wooyeong.*

"Just Wooyeong, no Lee," I whispered to myself with a smile, remembering. It feels unreal.

I navigated to his contact. If someone ever saw my phone, they would see this. If they knew Ambition it might make them ask questions, even jokingly, thinking that I knew someone with the same name as a celebrity.

One thing was already clear – he was super careful about his privacy. He didn't want to be recognized, didn't even want to talk about being an idol. Around me, anyway. So this – entering his real name when someone might see – it was strange. A breach of character. Almost like, when his wallet had been lost, his guard had been completely lowered too.

I backspaced his name, cringing on the inside, hesitating. I didn't want to delete the words Lee Wooyeong himself had put in my phone. But I did and typed *L.W.*

instead, because it was probably what he would want, even though it felt like I was destroying something sacred. I didn't have to worry about someone looking over my shoulder when calling now.

I guess I was instinctively trying to protect him too. That's what good friends did... if we were friends. I didn't know. I didn't even know if we would see each other again at all.

Probably not. These two encounters would probably be something I'd remember for the rest of my life as I watched him from afar.

I smashed my face into the pillow, letting out a sigh. But what if Wooyeong *did* want to see me again? Everything felt so uncertain – and like a dream I'd wake up from. It was already too good to be real. What were the odds of running into your bias, and even more crazily, him inviting you to meet again? It was impossible. If you asked anyone, they would tell you: Things like this didn't happen.

우영
WOOYEONG
8

I had waited until I was alone to call Madison. It had been one full day, and it was finally afternoon, in the middle of a photoshoot. It was Dyeong's turn. He stood in front of the white sheet and posed, rolling his head back languidly, parting his lips, and basically just doing whatever the photographer guides told him to do. He was in a mesh shirt that showed off plenty of skin and the muscles of his wiry arms. Chin-hyuk was nowhere to be found and Tai was waiting nearby in a fold-up chair, watching the shoot with interest while a hairstylist did last-minute adjustments to his shiny black hair, like moving the loose strands one centimeter to the left or right on his forehead.

One centimeter didn't seem to matter, but I knew the stylists knew what they were doing.

"Is it okay if I step out for a few minutes?" I asked Manager Pak, who was standing there with crossed arms, watching the photoshoot while occasionally jumping in to change or suggest something.

"Go ahead," he responded. "You've got ten minutes since Tai is the next one up."

I nodded, catching a glimpse of myself in one of the mirrors before I made my way out of the bright room. They had made the skin around my eyes smoky again and enhanced my sharp jawline, perfected my brows and made my skin look flawless. Both my ears were also loaded up with macho-looking earrings, which is why they felt heavier. My black muscle tank with carefully ripped edges and threads stood out against the skin of my shoulders, and two silver chain necklaces hung from my neck.

Okay, so I was definitely not stepping anywhere outside. I'd stand out like someone had spray-painted K-POP IDOL around me in a circle with neon yellow.

Our dorm was quiet. I went up there, jogging so I would get there and back again in time. As soon as I was on the other side of the door, I pulled out my phone and the contact page *Madison Hart*, staring at the screen.

Odd that I hesitated before pressing the call button. *So, I thought you'd have to try street food as a new person in Korea, why don't I take you there? No... Hey, are you free in a few days? I have a debt to repay, since I lost my wallet last time –*

I pressed *call*, annoyed with myself. I never rehearsed what I was going to say before a phone call. Never. I always just knew exactly what I wanted. This should be no different. So why was I coming up with sentences in my head? It was even odder than me hesitating.

It rang. And rang. And rang. And... went to an automated voicemail.

"Darn," I muttered, looking down at the screen. I sucked in a deep breath, my hand going up to run through my hair and then stopping right before I touched it. I lowered my hand, remembering that I couldn't do that right now since the stylist had just spent an hour making it look *perfect*. I would be in so much trouble if I'd made even one strand of hair move out of its fake-casual place.

I sucked in another breath and then hit *Call* again. Was it just me or did the ringing seem abnormally long?

It almost went to automated voicemail again before it cut off, and then her familiar voice said "Hi. I guess you accidentally called me?"

I held the phone away from me so she wouldn't hear me laugh. "No, I did it on purpose. I felt bad last time since you had to pay for Mashi Joayo and I want to pay you back – I only have a few minutes right now, but I was wondering if you wanted to go to the street-food hotspot and get some tteokbokki."

I wondered if that was better or worse than the sentences I'd rehearsed in my head. There was a pause on the other end that seemed painfully long.

"In a few days, maybe," I added. "If you're free."

"Oh," she said. "Oh. Sure, I'd love that. Isn't that the rice cakes in the spicy sauce?"

"You got it. Have you tried them?"

"No, not yet. That sounds great," Madison said. "Um – I'll let you go now since you're busy."

"Okay," I said. "I'll call you later to suggest a time, if that's alright."

"Yeah," she said, her voice softer than usual. "Sure."

We said goodbye and hung up. I lingered for a few seconds, feeling unreasonably victorious for a task as small as inviting someone to eat tteokbokki. I stuffed the phone in my designer-pants pocket and opened the door to the dorm, jogging downstairs.

There were still a few minutes left of Tai modeling to go. When I arrived, Manager Pak was adjusting his body position – shoulders back, head tilted slightly forwards, camera focus on the eyes. Slight smile, as Tai always had – it was my job to be the sizzling-hot bad boy and for Tai to be the adorable but manly puppy, just because the respective looks came naturally for us. The photographer snapped a few more photos and then it was my turn.

I set my phone on the metal folding table and the stylist checked that everything was okay before I started posing at the staff's directions. It was over fairly quickly, but even so it was hard not to get distracted at the thought of being around Madison again.

I departed to meet Madison in the street market at twelve-thirty on Saturday, checking my appearance in the mirror and tightening the scarf hiding my face before heading out. Dyeong was sprawled in a chair in the living room, glowering at me.

"I'll watch social media for news," he said ominously.

I didn't reply, going out of the dorm and closing the door behind me with a soft click.

When I spotted her at the street market, the afternoon sky white with clouds and the air crisply cold, I was still trying unsuccessfully to push what Dyeong had said to the farthest back of my mind.

"Hi," she said. She had on a black turtleneck underneath a light gray parka zipped up tight. A single chain necklace hung around her neck but the charm has disappeared beneath her parka. A pair of gloves stuck out of one pocket. Her hair, a light, gentle brown, fell softly past her shoulders.

"Ready to get tteokbokki?" I asked. My voice was slightly muffled through the scarf, and I was hiding my idol-giveaway hair under a hood.

"Absolutely!" she said, her face lighting up. She put her hands in her pockets and we started walking together side by side down the road, like it was the most natural thing in the world, past the vendors hawking dumplings, ramyun, grilled octopus, spicy pork, and battered-and-fried vegetables.

~{★ 55 ♥}~

It was too easy to be comfortable around her now. We'd gone beyond acquaintances – we really were friends.

I wondered if she'd thought that word to herself the way I said it aloud to Chin-hyuk, Dyeong and Tai.

I was conscious of that memory now as I watched her. Their faces – their caution, their questioning. Madison had no idea that she was the subject of an entire conversation, an important argument, even, among us.

I spotted a sign with Tteokbokki spelled on it and my eyes widened. "Look! There it is!" I quickened my pace and strode forward, Madison falling behind me so we wouldn't take up too much room in the crowd. I looked over my shoulder to make sure she was still with me as we made our way to the vendor.

"Do you smell that?" I asked her over the din of voices and footsteps and food sizzling. "Sticky sweetness? Rich, smoky, spicy gochujang?"

Madison sniffed the air, but shook her head and made an odd expression. "I smell octopus," she admitted.

I made a mock-frustrated noise in the back of my throat. By this time we had reached the vendor, with enough room for her to stand next to me, peering with interest at the tteokbokki pot.

There was something so... different about having her here next to me. I did enjoy the company, just like I'd enjoy it if Tai or Chin-hyuk or Dyeong or Yohan went with me. But something about seeing her soft brown hair and her shorter frame next to mine just felt *right*.

"Two bowls of tteokbokki please," I said to the server, a surprisingly young girl with a bun and very light skin. She had to be just within a few years of Madison, definitely younger than me.

She giggled. "Sure," she said flirtatiously, eyeing me from under her lashes as she spooned two servings from the bubbling pot.

I took a deep breath, glancing sideways, my gaze accidentally falling on Madison who was looking at me slightly incredulously with one eyebrow raised.

I looked away uncomfortably. Sure, girls flirted with me all the time, but it wasn't like I flirted back, except if I was at concerts or fansigns, but that was when it was my *job*. With Madison next to me it just felt different – uneasy. I wanted to get out of here as soon as possible.

"Thanks," I said awkwardly as Madison took the bowls and I paid.

"You don't have to pay for everything, you know," she said as we walked away, her still holding the steaming tteokbokki bowls in each hand, graciously not commenting on what just happened. "I feel like a freeloader."

"Well, you payed for Mashi Joayo," I said. "Not like you had much of a choice. It's fair, don't worry about it."

Madison brought the tteokkbokki closer to her face. "This smells heavenly."

"Can I have mine?" I asked, holding my hand out. "We'll eat it while we walk."

So we did. Strolling slowly, observing all the signs and products and food out for sale. I was weakened at the sight of some egg-bread, but was stopped from buying some because there would be no place to put it, since one hand was holding my bowl and the other a pair of chopsticks.

"This is so good," Madison groaned, panting because of the spicy chili sauce. I made a satisfied noise of agreement while I took another chewy rice cake.

"This is one of my favorite foods," I said. "Whenever I'm traveling and homesick, this is what I crave."

She nodded, seeming to think about it. "When I go back to visit my family, I can definitely imagine wanting some of this badly."

"What are they like? Your family?"

Madison glanced down and smiled as we strolled. "Well, they're very affectionate. Both my parents are, probably the most I've ever seen. I used to be embarrassed by it because it made me feel like a little kid. And I have four siblings. Our house was always busy."

I chewed the tteokbokki. "Four siblings! That's a lot. I have the opposite – only one brother, and he's older than me. He's so formal. My parents are more grave as well."

"Like you?"

I smiled. "Sure. But we both are very similar in temperament, you and I. More reserved and serious. So be careful how you describe me."

Madison bit the side of her lip in an attempt to stop herself from smiling. "Alright. We even dress in the same dark colors. So, is your family... affectionate even though they're serious?"

I remembered my parents being formal a lot of the time, and my brother was very solemn and studious. But there were moments that stuck out in my memory. "Not most of the time, but it showed. Every time I called my mom when I started training in high school, she cried."

"Your poor mom! Well, mine didn't want me to come here. She tried to stop me."

I looked at her, trying to read her expression. "What? Why?"

"She was just so worried. Since I was a female by myself, and all the way across the world – and she'd miss me. I had to call her every single day for the first week I was here, convincing her that I was doing fine." But then her mouth fell open and she stopped, drifting over to another stall.

"Hey, where are you going?" I asked, following close behind.

"What's that?" she asked, pointing to the stall where an old woman was frying circles of dough in a vat of oil, giving off a sweet scent that mingled with the rest of the smoke, perfume, savory food, and new-plastic smells on the street.

"Hotteok," I said. "Molten brown sugar fried in bread. Would you like some?"

She nodded. "Once we're done eating this, maybe we can go back."

"Deal."

We kept walking. I watched her. I liked the focused way she ate, like it really was something to be experienced rather than just a boring job to be done. She looked like she really liked it. I couldn't help a smile.

"Hey," I said, pointing to a stall that caught my eye, with a sign reading *Handmade Leather Wallets and Bags*. "Those wallets look like mine." I stopped. "Hey, I think they *are* the same as mine." I picked one up from the display, my thumb brushing over its slick black leather surface, a smile on my face. "This must be where they bought it."

"Who bought it?"

"My family. At my first concert, my parents, my brother, and my best friend Du Yohan showed up in the front row and surprised me." I let out a soft breath, remembering how much I'd cried after the show, how happy I had been. "It was the best moment of my life. And then they gave me this wallet afterward as a congratulations gift." I smiled wistfully, still holding it. "I forgot how it feels when it's new. I wonder if I should buy another one."

Madison nodded, not saying anything, though I could tell she was listening intently. That was one of the things I liked about her – she *listened*, as friends were supposed to. It was a rarer and rarer quality nowadays.

"What about you?" I asked, putting it down and turning to face her.

She looked surprised. "What about what?"

"What was the best moment of your life?"

Her lips parted like she was going to say something, and then she closed her mouth and looked away after one long moment. "I don't know," she said. "Arriving in Seoul."

Something about her tone told me she wasn't telling the whole truth, but I knew how important Korea was to her nonetheless, even if it wasn't the most precious moment of her life. I guess we'd only met three times, and I was odd for expecting a real answer. I still felt a pang of curiosity and disappointment.

We were quiet for the next few minutes as we finished up the spicy tteokbokki. It was a silence that I wished wasn't there – because it forced me to face my own thoughts. I watched her eat, her soft hair lifting in the breeze, her mellow brown eyes glancing down as she accidentally spilled a drip of sauce on the ground, the way she unconsciously shoved her gloves deeper in her pocket to make sure they wouldn't fall out. She was more than just exceptionally beautiful – as I'd first seen her. She was *lovely.*

This was a problem. *We're just friends,* I thought sternly. *That's the way it's going to stay. That's what you told Dyeong and you weren't lying.*

It was unexpected, surprising, that I should even have to remind myself of that fact. She was a *fan.* There was no way of getting around that.

It was all that mattered, even though we were friends, maybe even becoming good friends.

That was enough, and that was the way it was going to stay.

매디슨
MADISON
9

We headed back to the stall with the sweet frying breads, waiting for a minute as the person in front of us got their serving and left. I looked around, drinking in the sights of the bustling market. Ordering at the chicken ginseng soup stall next to us are a few middle-age men, one of them with a backpack, all wearing leather jackets and hats. And all holding big, professional cameras with wide lenses. One of them glanced around in the crowd shiftily, like they were looking for someone.

I opened my mouth in a silent gasp. *Paparazzi.*

I bent my head low so my hair covered my face and ducked around to Wooyeong's other side, tugging on his sleeve. He was facing away from them when he looked down at me in surprise.

"What is it?" he asked. His gaze was on my eyes, then my hand, which was still clutching his sleeve. The trepidation on my face as I opened my mouth must've been evident because he started to turn around to look for the threat.

Before I could stop myself I reached up and put my hand on his cheek, pulling him firmly back to face me. His dark eyes were fixed on mine with shock, his skin burning hot under my fingers.

"Paparazzi," I said quietly and urgently, panic mixing with butterflies in my stomach. "Don't turn around."

He didn't move, still gazing intensely into my eyes. I felt my cheeks prickle as my hand slid off his face and I looked down, now fully processing what I'd just done.

Wooyeong's lips parted. His gaze flicked above my head at the crowd ahead of us as he fingered a few banknotes in his wallet, pulling them out and handing them to the stall owner as he received the small pile of hotteok, bringing it close to his chest. Then he glanced down at me again, slipping his wallet nimbly back into his pocket.

"Let's go fast," he whispered, looking slightly more fearful than I would expect him to be.

I didn't even bother responding. We were already, by unspoken agreement, moving quickly away from the stall and the paparazzi, in the opposite direction, gaining speed when we were far enough away so that they couldn't see us. Then we started running, our footsteps slapping the road, dodging around the crowd, sometimes side-by-side, sometimes me moving behind him to fit through the masses of people, his broad shoulders clearing the way in front. We ducked around a group of tourists with backpacks, then a family holding shopping bags.

Then for no reason Wooyeong started *laughing*. Bright, robust, full-on laugher. He was slowing down because of it. People were looking over.

"Wha –" I couldn't even manage the words because all my breath was focused on running, but a smile spread across my face involuntarily.

He was still laughing and for some reason I started laughing too, and then we were both just two maniacs cracking up as we sprinted down the street with people and stalls on either side. Our footsteps were faltering. Wooyeong was laughing so hard that he started coughing in the cold air and we both started doubling over. He moved to the side of the road, toward a narrow alcove between stalls that was draped with a plastic sheet.

The space inside was hollow. He lifted the sheet for me and I went inside, him following after, letting it fall to cover us.

Everything was bright white in here because of the light shining through the plastic. It was just a little bigger than a telephone booth, and we stood facing each other, panting and smiling.

Wooyeong's cupped hands on his chest unfolded to reveal the paper cup stuffed with hot fried hotteok pancakes.

"Just made it," he said, his voice still breathy from his panting. He let out another short laugh and made a move like he wanted to slide down the wall and sit down, but he couldn't; there was just not enough room.

We waited a few minutes without speaking, catching our breath. Then I reached out and took a hotteok. It was still warm, the bread slightly browned and crispy on the outside but soft in my fingers. I tore it in half, revealing the sweet, gooey dark brown insides.

I handed one half to Wooyeong, steam rising up between us. He took it and smiled, and we both bit into ours at the same time.

It was hot, spreading warmth through my mouth. The bread was chewy and slightly sweet, almost milky, balancing the filling – which was nutty and caramellike, with the taste of brown sugar and cinnamon. I closed my eyes, letting out a little moan.

"Oh. That is *so* good," I sighed.

Wooyeong nodded. "Yes, it is," he said, finishing his quickly. There were two left – one for me and one for him. He took his, but kept holding the paper cup until I was done eating my first half, waiting for me. Then he held it out.

I took it and we both enjoyed the dessert in silence – a comfortable, happy silence. It felt warmer in here now, maybe the result of the plastic trapping in our body heat. Or maybe it was that we were not standing very far apart. I wouldn't even really have to step forward to hug him.

Wooyeong took the last bite of his hotteok, crushing and folding the grease-stained paper cup. Then he sighed in contentment.

"I'm so glad we managed to escape," he said, laughing a little again.

"Why are you so giddy?" I asked. "You made me laugh too! I could barely run!"

"I don't know," he admitted as we grinned at each other, his cheeks slightly flushed from the exercise and the warmth of the hotteok. "It was just so funny. Both of us sprinting away like thieves being chased through the market! I felt like I'd stolen the hotteok!"

"It was totally legit. You paid, I watched you."

The smile faded from Wooyeong's face.

I watched him with a crease between my eyebrows, startled and not understanding, wondering if I'd done something wrong.

Were we too close? I pressed as close to the wall as I could, trying to fight the hurt I felt. He was probably just worried about being discovered. It wasn't personal, right? That's what everyone always said. Most of the time when something seemed personal, people were just concerned with their own thoughts.

"What is it?" I asked, trying not to sound too worried.

"Oh – nothing." He gave a quick smile, one intended on reassuring me, that vanished just as quickly.

I was still hurt and confused. Wooyeong drew his tongue across his bottom lip as he looked outside, drawing the white plastic sheet away a crack so we could see.

Many people were going by, but none of them were the leather-jacketed men I saw before.

"They could be anywhere by now," he said seriously. "Even making their way up here, this way. We did take a while catching our breath and eating the hotteok."

"Don't you have anything to cover your face more?" I asked.

Wooyeong rewrapped his scarf so that it went to the bridge of his nose. "Better?" he said, voice muffled.

I nodded, trying to get back to normal just as it seemed he was. "Yes. So where should we go now?"

"Hmm." He scuffed his shoes on the ground and then looked back outside through the gap he'd made with the sheet. I noticed he was wearing sports sneakers just like I was, except his were black-and-white and mine were brown and smaller.

"Seoul Plaza," Wooyeong breathed as if he'd suddenly realized, turning to me with his eyes widened. With most of his face covered, they stood out, distractingly stunning against his smooth pale skin. Would the sight of his impossibly familiar features ever cease to give me chills?

"Seoul Plaza?" I repeated.

He nodded. "It's not far from here. Let's go."

We ducked out of the space, lifting aside the flap and being fixed with an accusing look by a nearby vendor. But he didn't have time to call to us since we were already on the move, hurrying out of the district and onto a side road that was empty.

I snuck glances of him as he looked straight ahead, excited for what he had planned. When we got to a main street, there were many people in coats – families, young and old with their friends, couples. None of them glanced twice at us as we headed down the concrete sidewalk under the bright, light gray sky.

Only when we got close to Seoul Plaza did I see the sign and realize where he was taking me. "Ice skating?" I gasped.

Wooyeong just glanced at me and smiled. I was glad to see him smile again. He seemed to be back to normal, as if nothing had ever happened.

I tried to let the nagging worry at the back of my mind fade away. Maybe we were both hiding the whole truth from each other – fine.

And that's when we rounded the corner.

Sprawling in front of us was an open-air gigantic ice-skating rink, bigger than any I'd seen before, oddly placed in the middle of the city surrounded by buildings.

I stifled a disbelieving gasp with my hand. "Oh my gosh! Is this where we're going?"

Wooyeong nodded and smiled, gesturing to the pretty formal-looking building at the end of the expanse. "That's City Hall right there. They ice over this place every winter."

I walked over to the wall in front of the rink and stared at the beautiful sight in amazement while Wooyeong went to buy tickets. I couldn't believe it. The ice itself was crowded by a lot of people, even though it still remained a crisp white. Rising up around the edges were buildings and skyscrapers in warm brown tones, while two ad-screens mounted high on the wall of a skyscraper flickered in bright colors, reminding me just how much in the city we were. An open-air ice-skating rink! Smack dab in the middle of Seoul in front of City Hall!

I let out a short giddy breath. The rink was rimmed by a short wall, with spectators like me leaning on it while they watched the action. So when a kid slid to a stop, grabbing the edge right next to me, I jumped back a little.

The kid stared at me from under his helmet. "Hi," he said in English.

"Hi!" I said back, giving a little wave.

His face broke out in a wide smile and he skated away.

"Madison!" Wooyeong called. I turned around to see him standing at a counter twenty feet behind, at a little building that was lending ice skates.

I hurried to join him at the counter, where an attendant had set a Wooyeong-sized pair of chunky ice skates on the surface.

"What's your shoe size?" he asked me when I was next to him.

I opened my mouth and then suddenly realized I didn't know the answer. I'd been about to blurt out my US shoe size – not my Korean one.

"Um, I don't know my Korean shoe size," I admitted sheepishly.

"Hold out your foot," the attendant said. I did, to show him. He scrutinized it for a moment, and then came back with a pair.

Wooyeong and I sat down on a bench to secure our ice skates. Mine fit perfectly, much to my amazement, besides being a little tight in the toes.

"Oh! We have to get helmets," he said. "I forgot."

He picked up a red one, securing it under his chin, and handed me a yellow one. I tried it on. "Too small," I said. "I think this is kids'-size."

He looked around for another one, this one also yellow, and gave it to me. I tightened the strap under my chin, hoping my hair didn't look unflattering.

"You ready?" Wooyeong asked, standing up.

I stood up too, feeling weird to be walking on skates outside the rink. "The last time I skated was ages ago," I said anxiously. "And I wasn't very good then either."

"You'll get the hang of it! C'mon, let's go!"

We clomped to the rink opening and then stepped out onto the ice. I nearly slipped right then, but managed to grab hold of the wall.

"Woah," Wooyeong said, reaching out to grab me by the arm but stopping when he'd seen I'd caught myself. But we couldn't dither here – there were people waiting behind us. This rink was jamming with ice skaters.

I tried moving forwards. The ice was incredibly slippery even in skates. I threw out my arms to balance myself, pinwheeling them.

Wooyeong grabbed hold of my arm and pulled me gently out of the way, sliding me forwards with him. My breath caught in my throat as I stared down at the ice, thinking I was going to fall.

"My parents took me here every winter!" Wooyeong yelled over the sounds of many other people skating and talking. There was a steady stream going past us, in a continual loop, around and around the huge rink. "It's really fun! I'll try to catch you if you fall, okay?"

I nodded, unable to say anything as I focused on not slipping. People – kids, even – were skating by us quickly, showing their experience.

Wooyeong tugged me forward a little. I let out a short squeal, leaning forwards and then back again, almost falling over.

He laughed and took hold of my other arm. "I got you! You're okay!" he said.

We were facing each other now. I gripped his forearms. "Don't let go!" I yelled.

"How about we try to go slowly?" he asked, his eyes twinkling.

"You're enjoying this!" I accused him, but then he pushed forwards with one skate-stroke, making me go backwards since I was in front of him. I gasped, clutching his forearms tighter, my legs wobbly.

"If we're going to skate together you're going to have to move your deathgrip to my hand instead," Wooyeong said, laughing a little. "Here." He gently pried me off his arms and then took my hand in his, squeezing it tight, our gloves thick between us. "Ready?"

"Yes," I said even though I wasn't. All I could think about was the fact that he was holding my hand. His strong grip was reassuring and safe.

What's the best moment of your life?

I'd lied. The best moment of my life was not when I'd set foot in Seoul. I might've said that, once, but not anymore.

The best moment of my life was meeting him.

I studied his face as he looked around for the best place to start skating, feeling an unexpected lump in my throat. Six years of longing, and I still wasn't any closer to having my unrequited crush become something more.

Because he was Lee Wooyeong – a K-pop star. And as happy as this day was, and this friendship seemed to be, they both had to end sometime.

Our paths of life were completely separate. And the more I thought of it, he seemed to know that too – judging by the fact he never talked about Ambition or his idol life with me.

It made a sharp piece of sorrow jab at my mind. I took a breath of the frosty air, promising myself I'd just enjoy this while it lasted.

Wooyeong skated forward a little with long strokes and I copied him, still pinwheeling my free arm, but his hand supported me and made it so I didn't lose my balance as much. We joined the stream of skaters, close to the wall as possible since we were slow. Wooyeong had a big grin on his face and I couldn't help smiling back, a thrill sparking in my heart as the wind rushed past us.

After we'd made one full circle, then two, I was starting to get the hang of it, and also forget about holding his hand. I mean, I didn't *forget* – but instead of being distracting, it now just felt like the most natural thing in the world.

In fact, even when we started going faster and surer, and I wasn't losing my balance anymore, neither of us let go.

"Can we join the fast stream?" I asked him as we skated leisurely on the outskirts, with people gliding past us.

Wooyeong looked at me, cheeks flushed with cold; he pushed his scarf up from where it'd been falling down, pulling the ends to make it snugger on his face. "Are you sure? Are you ready?"

I nodded quickly. "Just don't let go, okay?"

"Alright," he said, and I could tell by the crinkles in the corners of his eyes that he was smiling.

We skated forward, building up speed, me still tightly holding onto his hand and him to mine, until we integrated with all the other skaters. A couple of kids half our height flew past, seeming to make fun of everyone else there with their easy competence.

I felt exhilarated as we skated quickly, with long stokes, keeping pace with the general crowd. The wind made my hair flutter but it felt good, since I was so toasty warm.

We were almost at two full circles when I started losing my balance again. I must've hit a patch wrong or bent my skate the wrong way or something, because suddenly I was slipping backwards, going to fall on my butt. I gave a shout and felt Wooyeong's strong hand pulling me back up but it wasn't enough; we just kept gliding forwards with me sinking lower and lower to the ground as I tried to use his hand to leverage me back up. Before I knew it we were stopping with Wooyeong pressed close behind me, his arm linked under mine and his hand still holding my own in an awkward, but effective, support to stop me from bashing my knees or rear end on the ice. So close, I could feel the warmth radiating from him, and smell the tantalizing scent of his cologne that made me want to close my eyes and take a deep breath.

Wooyeong was laughing as he switched his position so that he was holding me under the arms, trying to lift me back to my feet again. I felt my back against his chest as I staggered, my feet unsteady as a newborn fawn's. I was laughing too, almost taking it as a given that he'd stopped me from hurting myself just from pure trust. I looked up at him as I slipped again, seeing his happy face and the scarf that had come off completely, dangling limply and crookedly on his shoulders.

"Come on!" he said, beaming. "You can do it! Let's go!"

I grabbed his shoulders he tried to raise me up again and he wobbled a little, drifting on the ice, but at least we were both standing up now.

"Thanks!" I said, brushing my wild hair out of my eyes as I let go of his shoulders and took his hand again, noticing how his grip was extra-firm this time.

We skated around many more times, Wooyeong's scarf fluttering behind him in the wind, his smile exposed for all the world to see as we glided, fast and freely, on the ice with the buildings of Seoul rising up around us under the bright sky.

I'd had a crush on him for six years, as far away as I was, even though we'd never met.

But I realized that now, it wasn't just a crush. Against all my intuition, even though it would just end in heartbreak, I was in love with him.

우영
WOOYEONG
10

A couple weeks passed. It was just the start of February, and Ambition was so busy preparing for our next comeback in the middle of March that I didn't even have time to see Madison. We emailed back and forth a few times, and then started calling. When I would get a break for fifteen minutes I would duck somewhere quiet and we'd talk, even briefly. It had become a habit of mine. I'd never called anyone so much in my life.

Tai, Chin-hyuk, and Dyeong noticed my change in behavior – different, they said, and suspiciously cheerful – but they'd only caught me on the phone a few times. I didn't want to draw attention to it, especially with Dyeong, who still seemed uneasy – and edgy, sometimes – about me having a girl for a friend.

Maybe it was talking to her so much that did it, but I realized... I wanted her to be more than a friend. Even though she had no idea. Even though I was an idol and she was a fan. Even though I'd told myself multiple times that it would never – *could never* – happen and furthermore, it was just a bad idea, plain and simple. I'd struggled with the same thing that day when we'd been eating hotteok.

But I couldn't help it. And no matter what I told myself, my heart still jumped whenever I heard her voice.

"Do you like her?" Dyeong sprung on me one day, right after I'd finished a phone call with her and hung up. He'd come around the corner, and I hadn't seen him.

I'd been surprised, struggling with the delay of the truth – which was that yes, I unquestionably did like her – and what I was going to tell him.

I kept my face blank. "No. She's just a friend."

He looked at me a long moment. "Good."

That was probably the first time I'd ever lied to Dyeong.

But I couldn't tell him the truth. And it wasn't a *real* lie – it was a harmless one. I had no intention of dating Madison or even letting her know how I felt. It was never going to happen. That's what I repeated to myself over and over, what I knew I *should* do. What I was currently doing.

She was still a fan. Even though she was my friend. Even though I was crushing on her hard... maybe more than a crush.

This was why it was a bad idea. How would I ever know that she loved me for *me?* Lee Wooyeong, and not just Main Singer/Dancer/Visual Lee Wooyeong of Ambition?

I had it under control, though. Everything was under control. So I wasn't really lying to Dyeong, not in a harmful way. Just because I had strong feelings for her didn't mean that I would actually go through with them. I could still choose what to do. And I knew with my head that dating her would be complicated, no matter how strong my feelings were for her. Besides, she had no idea. She didn't like me back at all. Not once had she ever flirted or let the conversation lead anywhere but what was strictly platonic.

Since she didn't like me, didn't want me, our relationship couldn't go any further anyway.

That worked out fine, even if it ached a little. Yes, everything was under control.

매디슨
MADISON
11

Wooyeong had his first real day-long break for weeks. I learned when he called me at my desk at work. I kept my voice down so the other employees wouldn't hear me, listening to him explain, sounding happy and excited.

"Tomorrow," he said. "What time do you get off?"

"Five."

"I was thinking we could go to the Dongdaemun Design Plaza. They have this really neat thing called the Rose Garden. It's a bunch of LEDs, it looks amazing at night."

"Glowing roses?"

"Basically. If you leave right after work we could make it before sunset and see them all turn on."

"Okay, I can do that," I said, already excited at the thought of seeing him again. Other times over our calls, I'd been extremely careful with my emotions, part of me knowing just how impossible my desire for him was. But I hadn't seen him in so long that I couldn't help but feel anything but elation.

There were voices in the background.

"I have to go," Wooyeong said. "See you tomorrow?"

"Yes! Bye!" *I love you.*

I put the phone down lightly with a sigh of heartache. I was trying to get back to working, pushing aside a pile of paperwork, when Jeongsook leaned over from her desk next to mine. "What was that about?"

"Oh," I said. "Um. I'm meeting a friend."

"That's nice," Jeongsook sighed. "I haven't met up with my friends in a couple days."

I haven't met up with mine in almost a month, I thought but didn't say it. Wooyeong was not a regular friend.

"Would you like to go shopping with us?" Jeongsook asked. "There's three of us. They're already excited to meet you anyway since I told them you're an American who speaks Korean! We're going to head to Myeongdong. They have the *best* skincare selection, and makeup too. You could use some moisturizers."

"Ah... hehe... we'll see. I might have an appointment I already need to fulfill." I was aware of the fact that I didn't have that shiny, moisturized 'glass skin' look that a lot of the other women did at this Gi office. I didn't blame Jeongsook for mentioning it, but the thought of going shopping for skincare and makeup made me nervous. I'd probably be totally lost.

"Well, you're welcome to come," Jeongsook said, blinking her nice lashes. Her eyeliner was perfectly symmetrical and swept up at the corners. "It's so fun!"

"Thanks," I said. We both got back to typing up our reports.

The next day, the work seemed to stretch on forever. I would've sworn I was working on a single Excel sheet for four hours, interrupted only by one of the Overseas Marketing Managers dropping by to run an English ad by me. *Gi – the superior camera.*

"Looks good," I said mildly, handing the paper back to him. "No grammatical errors."

I suspected they just ran English ads by me after a sister company had released an ad with embarrassing syntax, somehow passing by the translator without a second check. I glanced up at the clock, thinking it must be at least four-thirty already.

It was only three in the afternoon. I swallowed a sigh of frustration.

When five finally arrived, I said goodbye to Jeongsook right on time and bundled out the door, still in my work clothes – a long-sleeve good-quality V-neck in cream and some nice brown pants. I hoped I didn't look boring and stiff, but there just wasn't enough time to go to my apartment to change. Besides, it's not like I would probably take off my long parka or anything.

"Dongdaemun Design Plaza," I told the taxi driver, shivering as I straightened out my parka collar. It was rumpled and sliding around, since I'd been in such a rush. I tugged at the sleeves and smoothed down my flyaway hair, trying to get into a presentable condition.

We pulled out onto the main road full of speeding cars. My stomach was full of butterflies. I couldn't wait to see him again. It'd felt like so long...

But then my phone rang with his caller ID. I picked it up, nervous.

"Hello?"

"Where are you?" he asked.

"I'm taking a taxi to the Dongdaemun Design Plaza," I said, half confused as I stared out at the scenery zooming by. "Why?"

"Well, it was going to be us, but… I hope it's okay that someone else comes. I didn't really have time to tell you. He just all of a sudden declared he was going."

"Who is it?" I asked.

"Tai."

My mouth opened. I was speechless from shock.

"Is that okay?" he said, sounding concerned. His voice didn't sound particularly cheerful.

"Of course. I mean, yes," I said. "Yeah, that's okay."

Tai. I was going to see Paek Tai. I nearly let out a gasp of incredulity and happiness. Why would it not be okay to see Tai? I'd dreamed of meeting all the Ambition members ever since I started getting interested in them at their debut.

"I mentioned to him that the Rose Garden was featured in one of his favorite dramas and then he wanted to come," Wooyeong said. "He just kind of sprung it on me… I didn't know what to say…"

"That's completely fine," I said. "I don't mind. It'll be great, actually."

"Alright," Wooyeong said. "See you in fifteen minutes."

"I'll meet you on the corner right after the subway before DDP so we can walk together. Goodbye!"

"Okay, goodbye."

He hung up. I let my phone drop into my lap, feeling stunned again. No way – I was going to meet Tai. That was going to be so cool.

It's not like I ever had a crush on Tai. Yeah, he was amazingly good-looking in his own way, but all the Ambition members were. My one and only real bias had always been Wooyeong. It was just that I thought all of the members were so cool and unique and talented.

I was so excited. Meeting Wooyeong had been disarming (probably due to his out-of-this-world hotness and my gigantic crush on him) but this would be different, hopefully. More relaxed on my part.

I wondered how Wooyeong felt about it. After all, he never discussed anything related to his stardom, not even his soul brothers Tai, Chin-hyuk, and Dyeong.

Maybe it would make it easier for me to be around Wooyeong if someone else was there. My crush on him – the longest crush I'd ever had, starting six years ago – had worked because there was no possibility of rejection, no possibility that it would ever be real.

But now that I was actually talking to him, that I *knew* him, and furthermore, that I *loved* him – my heart just hurt more. So having Tai... having him there would probably be better.

우영
WOOYEONG
12

"So I get to meet the infamous Madison at last," Tai said as we walked, our footsteps steady on the concrete.

I didn't respond. How would she react to meeting Tai, another member of her beloved group? Would it become clear that she would take any Ambition member for a friend and I wasn't special?

I didn't want her to be too happy. She had me. Meeting Tai shouldn't make her outrageously excited. She should be used to the idea of Ambition as people she could see in real life now. It should be casual.

I still didn't know who her bias was. What if it was Tai? What if she started flirting with him?

This is a mistake. I never should've allowed him to come.

Or maybe it was just me being selfish. So what if Madison liked another member more? Maybe I just didn't want to find out.

And the others had no idea I desired her as anything more than a friend. They thought it wasn't a big deal.

So I wasn't sure why Tai kept going on and on.

"I mean, if she can make you go against the no-girls-in-public rule, she must be pretty unique," Tai continued. "If you didn't want to lose her that bad. I mean, gosh, when you were facing us that one day – well, Dyeong cared the most, I didn't really mind what you did – I'll tell you that you looked all stoic and manly, standing tall and stiff with that tic in your jaw." He considered. "Actually, it was pretty impressive. You looked cool."

"Thanks," I said neutrally, trying to figure out whether he was insinuating anything or not.

"I mean, you've never acted like that before. You were one of the most hands-off members of our group, especially when it came to *fans!* I mean, it's me and Chin-hyuk who have always been the friendliest. The manager has to tell us to tone it down all the time."

I didn't say anything. It was true, so I couldn't really argue.

"And then all of the sudden you're hanging out with someone – number one oddity – and then they're also a fan? Number two oddity! I still don't know what to make of it. And then as I mentioned, you getting all stoic. You've *never* done that with Dyeong before." He glanced at me, then his left eyebrow jumped slightly. Judging by his reaction I was going into 'reserved mode' again. But he looked back at the road, kept talking.

"Must be worth it," Tai continued. "She must be exceptionally smart, or exceptionally fun, or exceptionally kind, or exceptionally pretty..."

The people in front of us parted to reveal a figure with light brown hair and a parka standing on the street corner, facing away from us, her arms wrapped around herself. My heart jumped into my throat.

She turned slightly, black boots repositioning. Tai was going on and on, but I wasn't hearing what he was saying as we drew closer, but still far away enough that I could frame the whole thing like a picture – a distant, beautiful girl on a distant street corner, in striking contrast to everyone around her.

Then she turned around.

Tai seized my arm in a sudden grip. "My gosh, that's her."

He didn't need an answer from me. He already knew. It felt like something was caught in my throat, leaving me breathless, unable to say anything as I stared at her familiar form.

Madison had now seen us. Her face brightened in recognition and she started striding toward us.

"Wooyeong, you weren't messing around," Tai said in a low voice, sounding stunned.

We were now within hearing distance, and Tai shut up as she cleared the rest of the space between us, stopping short and staring at Tai with wide, thrilled eyes.

"Nice to meet you," he said in English as he stepped forward, eyes sparkling. The accented English that was utterly adorable and made fans melt, and he knew it. He reached out his hand for her to shake. "I'm Tai."

Madison's cheeks were turning bright pink. She covered her mouth with her hand, timidly reaching out to shake his with her other. "I'm – I'm Madison," she said in stammering Korean, then let out a tiny laugh of disbelief.

Tai had on his full, genuine, dimpled gigawatt smile that made even the most stoic girls swoon at its cuteness. Madison, it seemed, was not immune to his charm. She let out another embarrassed, happy laugh as she pulled her hand away.

I bit the inside of my cheek and looked sideways, feeling a quiet possessiveness fill my heart. A jealousy. Was she like this when she met me? No, she was far more guarded. Today she seemed like just another fan – but she wasn't. Not to me. Not to Tai.

I should probably take command of the situation.

"You know Tai, of course," I said with a half-laugh that wasn't very happy. "The introduction was rather unnecessary."

Madison nodded in agreement, her smile still wide and her cheeks still pink. Tai was looking at her warmly, a smile on his own face.

Unless it was onstage, Tai didn't flirt with people just for the sake of it. I knew that. He only flirted with people he was attracted to.

I cleared my throat, feeling a low, fluttering rumble in my chest – anger. It shocked me. I knew I had been falling for Madison, but I thought I'd had it under control. I hadn't thought that I would get like this – that I would feel so possessive over her. "We should get walking."

"We have a lot of time," Tai said, his crinkled-up eyes still sparkling. For the first time in my entire life, I felt like slapping that expression off his face.

I bit down on the inside of my cheek even harder and looked away restlessly, trying to keep myself in check, waiting for Madison to decide. But she said nothing.

I looked back at her. She was gazing at me with her eyes slightly scrunched-up in thought. She sensed something was off but didn't know what it was, trying to read me.

Of course she didn't know. She had no idea how I felt about her. She thought of me as just a friend.

I flashed her a smile to show I was fine, noticing her still-pink cheeks. But even just seeing that, I *wasn't* fine. I was starting to realize just how badly I was falling for her. Now it seemed obvious. It didn't matter how much I repeated to myself that we were just friends, or that I shouldn't date a fan.

~{★ 77 ♥}~

I wanted her and couldn't have her, because she didn't want me back.

"Let's go this way," Tai offered since no one was saying anything. We started walking, Tai chattering all the way, commenting about this or that. He occasionally stopped to show Madison certain sights, talking about music and life. She was eating it up, an eager expression on her face.

We stopped and stalled for a few moments, standing here like tourists. They were carrying on a happy conversation without me, and I could feel my shoulder muscles tighten.

"Don't get territorial," I could practically hear Dyeong muttering in my ear. *"She's just your friend, isn't she? Back it off."*

My jaw was clenched. I stood there and didn't move.

Tai had playfully caught a strand of her hair that was flying in the wind and it glided between his fingers. He laughed, and Madison was smiling, her cheeks flushed pink. It took all my willpower not to take a few steps forward and physically separate them by shoving myself between.

But Madison wasn't mine. My jaw was clenched so hard that my molars were feeling the strain. Half of me wanted to stride up and passionately kiss her on the lips right now, declare it.

Instead I turned and looked out at the city skyline, not really focusing enough to see it. I could still hear them laughing behind me. *Self-control,* I thought, taking in a sharp breath. Self-control, like I always had. Calmness. Somehow I couldn't muster up those things now. For the first time I could feel a savageness in my chest threatening to do exactly what I felt. It was angry and very, very jealous.

I'd never felt this before in her presence. Then again, I also had her all to myself, all the time.

Not now.

"Come on," I called, my voice coming out rougher and harsher than I expected. "I want to get there before dark."

"The whole point of going to the rose garden is that it *is* dark," Tai called back, his voice neutral. Maybe I was misreading it and he was cheery as usual, or maybe he just didn't like my tone.

I started striding ahead, black shoes clicking on the pavement.

"Hey, wait!" Tai said, and then in a moment he and Madison fell into step next to me, Madison first on my left and Tai on my right.

"I want to get there before dark because I want to see them turn on after sunset," I said, feeling considerably calmer now that she was here. "That'll be nice, don't you think?"

Madison smiled and nodded when my glance fell on her. "Definitely. I can't wait. How much farther?"

"Just a few streets," I said. "I looked at the map."

Half-melted snow from the afternoon sun had now turned rock-solid as the temperature dropped with evening. It was in little piles in the corners of the sidewalks and streets, sometimes paired with slick patches of ice.

I pulled out my phone and checked the time. "Sunset is about at six so we have a good fifteen minutes," I said.

Tai rubbed his hands together. "Ah, good," he said. "And maybe dinner can be some dosirak at that 7-Eleven." He nodded his head at the green-and-orange striped sign across the street.

I didn't nod or say anything in acknowledgement. I didn't want to eat dinner together. I just wanted Madison as far away from Tai as possible.

I knew it was selfish. Madison could and would choose for herself who she wanted to hang around. It's not even like I was being protective of her. No, Tai was kind and his intentions, even if they were romantic, were completely innocent. He would probably be a fantastic boyfriend. I already knew that about him.

It was better anyway that she didn't like me back, wasn't it? That's what I'd told myself over and over. It wasn't as complicated this way. I couldn't get into as much trouble. Dyeong and Chin-hyuk would approve more.

I knew that, so why did it feel so bad?

But I was wrenched from my thoughts when in one split second, something went wrong.

매디슨
MADISON
13

It happened so fast that I didn't realize I'd stepped on a patch of ice. My foot seemed to buckle, twisting painfully, and then all of the sudden I was on the ground, my head luckily kept upward so it hadn't bashed into the pavement. I lay there dazed for a split second, feeling the hard impact on my body and the burning that was on fire in my ankle.

"Madison!" Wooyeong and Tai were yelling. Wooyeong was right there crouched beside me, but I was hardly aware of him through the pain.

"My gosh!" some nearby person was exclaiming. "Is she all right?"

"Ow, ow," I said, squeezing my eyes shut. My left ankle was in agony. I clutched my knee to my chest with my foot held limply in front of me, rocking back and forth. "My ankle."

"Are you okay?" they both asked. Both of them were crouching next to me now, their eyes worried – Tai's milk-chocolate ones, Wooyeong's dark and stormy ones.

"Do you need help?"

A man and a woman, a middle-aged couple with their arms linked, were leaning over me and Wooyeong and Tai all on the ground. It was the man that spoke in his rough, deep voice.

Tai shook his head. "No thank you. We're fine."

I nodded in agreement. I didn't need a whole pack of people trying to help – it wasn't like I was alone. I was grateful for their offer but too embarrassed to ever accept. "I'm fine," I managed with my best convincing smile.

"Did you sprain it?" Wooyeong asked as the couple moved on, my smile vanishing as soon as they did so. "Can you put weight on it?"

"Maybe," I gasped. I tried to rest it flat on the ground but it just hurt more. I shook my head, wincing. "It twisted the wrong way when I stepped on that patch of ice."

"She sprained it," Wooyeong said, deciding now, his voice low and deep and grim.

"Let me see," said Tai. His eyes looked into mine, begging me to trust him. "We should probably get your shoe off before it swells, Madison." He reached his fingers gingerly toward my laces.

I nodded, pressing my lips hard into my knee, not able to muster the control to say anything.

"Are you hurt besides your ankle?" Wooyeong asked, his hand going to my head, the touch of his palm reassuring but strong, almost like he was supporting it. He seemed to realize what he was doing, his hand instantly falling away from my hair as he looked down. "You took a pretty hard fall."

"I don't think so," I whispered, feeling like a little kid as Tai untied my shoelaces.

"We need to get her somewhere else," Wooyeong told him. "She needs to get this treated. She can't just walk back."

Tai wasn't looking at him; he was now gingerly, gently, slipping off my shoe. Though whenever my foot moved it made my ankle hurt worse, I didn't complain. "Where?"

Wooyeong made a noise in the back of his throat. He stood up abruptly, turning this way and that as people passed us by. "The hospital? Her apartment? SMK," he said.

"SMK's closest," Tai said, still not looking at him as he set my shoe on the ground and slipped off my sock. The cold air hit my foot, shockingly frigid. Tai's fingers trailed down the bare skin of my ankle to the top of my foot, making chills follow the light touch of his fingertips.

I shivered. Tai noticed the movement, looking up at me. "This hurts?"

"No," I said.

"Are you cold?"

My bare foot was burning hot, and the rest of me now felt chilly. "A little."

"We should go before it swells up," Tai said.

"Calling a taxi might take too long," Wooyeong said. He was busy scanning the street for one, but evidently wasn't finding it. "We're going to have to walk."

"How long will that take?" Tai asked, a little doubtful, though he couldn't seem to think of any other option.

I was already in the process of struggling to my feet, putting as little weight as I could on my ankle. "I'm fine! I can walk," I said, standing there. "You go on, I'll catch up to you."

Wooyeong ignored me, bending down and scooping me up without warning, one arm around my shoulders and another underneath my knees in a princess carry. I gave a little gasp of shock as I was lifted into the air.

"Am I hurting you?" Wooyeong asked, his voice gentle. I could feel the vibration in his chest.

This was the closest we'd ever been. *Ever.* My cheeks prickled with the nearness of him, the shock of what he'd just done. The uncrossable line between us that I'd felt for so long, the distance of *just friends and nothing more,* was scarily close to being shattered.

He was pressing me against him, holding me tight. The butterflies in my stomach were making me almost sick.

"No," I said quietly, leaning my head against his sweater. I could feel his solidness, hear his heartbeat racing.

I was too terrified to wrap my arms around his neck to relieve him of some of my weight. What if he took it as a romantic gesture? I didn't want to betray myself, like my flushed face wasn't doing that already. There was no way he could know. I would just be another girl rejected who'd fallen in love with the untouchable Wooyeong.

Wooyeong's dark eyes were fixed on my face intensely, on my features and vulnerable eyes. He slowly tore his gaze away, unreadable, asking Tai, "You have her shoe?"

"Yes." He strode toward us, stopping inches from me against Wooyeong's chest. He towered over Wooyeong. I'd always thought him lanky, but it was illusion of his height, which was over six feet; he was actually broader than Wooyeong. "It's a few blocks. Are you sure you can make it that far? Give her to me, and we can run. We'll get there faster."

Wooyeong was silent, his jaw hard and set.

"Come on, Wooyeong, let me carry her," Tai pressed. "She can piggyback. That position will hold her ankle steady so it won't hurt."

"I can do it," Wooyeong said, stone-faced.

"You're going to be slower. You can't run with her like I can. I'm stronger than you are."

Wooyeong looked down at me. "Are you okay with that?"

No, I wasn't. I wished he could hold me forever. "Yes," I breathed.

"I'm going to let you down," he said. "Stand on your good leg. I won't let go."

He slowly, gently lowered my legs to the ground. I clutched his arms, and he was still holding onto me tightly, just like he said.

Tai bent down low to the ground, his tawny coat brushing the concrete, his arms held out. I leaned over his back, putting all my weight on it and wrapping my arms snugly around his neck. He held my legs and stood up, giving a little bounce to make sure I was far up and snug on his back.

"Okay, let's go," he murmured, striding forward briskly. Wooyeong kept pace next to us, his posture rigid. Tai started to jog smoothly, picking up speed.

We rushed past people and crowds, my hair fluttering behind me, the wind harsh on my ears. My bare toes were already starting to feel icy at the same time my ankle was burning hot.

Every time he stepped I nearly winced, but my foot was barely moving – he was doing an excellent job. I closed my eyes, shutting out the people who were giving us curious stares, feeling Tai move fluidly and steadily beneath me like a well-oiled machine.

He was definitely strong, and fast. I was grateful for that. Even if I wished it was Wooyeong who was carrying me now.

I was suddenly very tired and very cold. I tucked my chin into the space between Tai's neck and shoulder, his silky black hair brushing my cheek. His coat was soft and smelled faintly of fresh, floral soap.

I could hear the breaths whooshing from his lips like a rhythm. We must be so close by now; it wasn't that far, was it? My arms circled closer, snugger, around Tai's neck to try to relieve him of some of my weight. There seemed to be a shift in his breath, and his strong arms tightened their support on my legs in response. I was grateful for how solid it felt.

I could hear Wooyeong's steady footsteps behind us, quick and pounding. But we were slowing down – a stoplight. Tai swiveled around so that we were facing Wooyeong, and the breath caught in my throat.

He was running up to us, shortening his strides so that he would stop too. He was pressing his sharp teeth into the side of his lip, his eyes so dark they were almost black, his expression hard but unreadable.

Tai was turning back around again as Wooyeong fell into step beside us, walking the rest of the way to the group of pedestrians waiting to cross. We stopped behind them, the traffic roaring by in a huge stream of shiny cars.

"Do you want to put me down?" I asked anxiously. Tai's breathing was heavier and clumsier.

He shook his head. Wooyeong wasn't looking at us. A stream of fog escaped from his lips, clear in the cold air. I couldn't take my eyes off his manly profile. That look on his face just a few seconds before... dangerously hot, and impossible for me to read. The butterflies in my stomach wouldn't go away.

I took a few deep breaths of my own to try to calm them. "You should really put me down, Tai. You're going to get tired just by holding me when we're standing."

"Put her down," Wooyeong said, still without looking at us.

Tai listened to the unsmiling command in his tone, bending down slightly and letting me slide off his back. I stood on my good leg, resting one hand on top of his shoulder so I'd keep my balance.

"Well, this is unexpected," said Tai. "Does this happen to you often, Madison?"

I laughed. "No... this is new. I've never slipped on ice before. I definitely hate winter now."

"It's not so bad when you get to go ice skating in Seoul Plaza," Wooyeong said quietly, his gaze flicking to me. His eyes were unexpectedly soft.

I swallowed, trying to quell my racing heart. "Yes," I agreed, looking away. "That wasn't so bad."

I didn't know why I said it – it made it sound like it hadn't been one of the most treasured memories of my life. But I was nervous, just repeating what he said.

"Did you guys go ice skating together in Seoul Plaza?" Tai said incredulously, turning around to face me, his shoulder shifting under my hand.

"Yeah," I said. "We were nearby."

Tai made a noise I couldn't decipher, but then the light changed up ahead and people started going across the crosswalk.

"Ah," he said, bending over again. "Hop on."

The cheerful way he said it made me smile, unable to help myself. I hoisted myself on his back again, arms around his neck.

"I feel like I'm giving you a horse ride," Tai laughed. "Except you're not a little kid."

"Far from!" I said indignantly, giving him a little slap on the shoulder. He let out a laugh, and I could feel the vibration of it as we quickly walked along with everyone else, Wooyeong keeping brisk pace beside us.

In truth, my ankle was hurting worse now, even if I wasn't showing it. But I allowed myself a wince as we hit the sidewalk on the other side of the road and started running again, pressing my face into Tai's soft coat occasionally to keep myself from crying out.

Tai was back up to his previous speed, his breaths heavier and clumsier, though his pace showed no sign of slowing. It was several minutes until he slowed to a jog, and looking up made me realize why.

We were in front of a huge, clean silver-white building spanned with endless windows, though the reflective glass made it so that I couldn't see inside right now. Next to the sliding glass automatic doors was a small sign:

SMK Entertainment.

I felt chills run up my body, almost making me shiver. I was going *inside* SMK Entertainment. I was stunned as we jogged up to the door, almost too fast for me to process, and inside.

There was a dark carpet on the floor leading to a stainless-steel elevator door directly in front of us across the room, and white lights on the ceiling lit the whole thing up brightly. A clerk at a desk, a pretty woman with wide cheekbones and hair pulled up and away from her face, gazed at us – well, at *me*, on Tai's back – open-mouthed.

"Hey Eun Ae!" Tai shouted, giving a wave. "Can you call the medics? We got someone with a sprained ankle here."

Eun Ae covered her mouth with her hand. "Of course," she said, picking up the phone.

Tai had stopped in front of the elevator. "Where do we take her now?" he asked, turning to face Wooyeong, who was right behind us.

"The dance practice room," he said, stepping in front to punch the elevator button. The doors slid open to reveal a clean interior. Tai followed him while I stared around with wide eyes, a strange feeling in the pit of my stomach.

~{★ 85 ♥}~

"We're going to the dance practice room," Wooyeong called to Eun Ae, his voice sounding huskier than usual. She gave a nod to show she heard, still on the phone.

Wooyeong pressed a number on the control panel and we started moving upward. I closed my eyes, that feeling in the pit of my stomach moving lower. I was in the *heart* of SMK Entertainment, moving farther and farther into it. I would never had thought this day would ever come. For some reason, I felt excited but also almost... apprehensive. Maybe it was the newness of it, or how suddenly it'd been decided, or the fact that my ankle was sprained and they were going to call medics as soon as we arrived in the dance practice room.

The elevator slid to a stop with a cheerful noise. Wooyeong didn't move, letting Tai step out with me first.

The hallway was also lit by white lights, giving it a very cold, corporate feeling. There were doors on either side, made of frosted glass with the SMK Entertainment logo. I swallowed. Were we heading to... *the* dance practice room?

I should be used to this by now. I knew the off-screen Wooyeong and even Tai now. I realized they were just humans like me. But being in here felt surreal. I wasn't... giddy, like I would've been before I met Wooyeong. But the same room I'd seen so many times in videos, to see it, to *be* there in person... right now this moment felt so present, so solid, while my brain was telling me it was unreal.

I held my breath as we arrived at a certain door that looked like all the others, but Wooyeong and Tai recognized clearly. By mutual consent they went toward it, Wooyeong swinging open the door and clicking on the light so we could go inside.

It did look like the same exact room in the dance practice videos – except the mirrors were uncovered. I could feel myself holding my breath.

The door swung softly, slowly shut as Wooyeong let it go, striding over to us as Tai let me down gently in the middle of the room.

The floor was hard but warm. I hastily yanked off my other shoe and sock, holding my feet side by side as I sat on the floor with my legs out in front of me. The sprained one was *definitely* swollen, and badly.

I let out a stream of air from between my lips. Well, at least that explained why it hurt so much.

"Oh, Madison," Wooyeong said, his voice coming out frustrated and sad.

"It's fine, I'm fine," I said immediately. "Let's just wait until someone comes to look at it."

Tai grimaced, watching me. "I didn't think about how uncomfortable the floor would be. I'll go grab something so you'll be comfier and some pillows so you can elevate your foot. That's the first thing we need to do." He hurried out, the door swinging slowly shut behind him as his figure vanished to the left.

Wooyeong and I were left in thick, audible silence that hung over us like a blanket. I hadn't been prepared to be left alone with him so suddenly.

"You need to elevate your ankle," he said, crouching down near my feet and unexpectedly reaching for my hurt one before I could react.

Wooyeong's fingers gently caressed my hurt foot as he slid his hands around it, keeping my ankle straight. I shivered involuntarily at his touch, my skin burning hot where his butterfly-light touch contacted my foot.

He lifted my foot so it was in the air, held perfectly straight and painless in his hands.

"Don't – don't you think this is a bit much?" I asked, my cheeks flaming red, unable to look at him.

"It's swelled enough already from Tai carrying you. I still think I should've. Even if we'd gotten there slower, I wouldn't have had you on my back. You'd be in my arms so your foot would have been elevated already."

It seemed like an unreasonable complaint against Tai, but Wooyeong had been acting weird – edgy, almost – the whole time. I didn't understand him, didn't understand why.

His skin against mine was like an electric charge running up my leg, distracting me, making it impossible to think. "Let go," I said softly, still unable to look at him, hardly able to muster up the focus to say those words. "Please."

Wooyeong slowly lowered my foot back to the floor, his hands leaving.

An agonizing beat or two of silence passed, neither of us talking or looking at each other, and then Wooyeong sighed and scooted up so that he was next to me. His position, crouched on the ground, was still formally a foot away. The distance between us felt like a chasm, yet uncomfortably close all at once.

I remembered suddenly that I had been the first one to actually touch him, to cross that line accidentally, at the market. My hand on his cheek, his shocked eyes. For people who had never even brushed hands while passing an object, it had been startling. For both of us.

The silence in the room was suffocating. I didn't know what to say, if there was anything to say in the first place. When did being around him become so hard?

"You know why you fell?" Wooyeong said, his voice low and husky. He wasn't looking at me, but was staring intensely up ahead, his hands crossed as he crouched on the ground, his long coat brushing the smooth floor. His profile was severe, set. "It's because you weren't holding my hand."

He turned his head and looked straight at me. Butterflies exploded in my stomach at the passionate intensity of his dark gaze. I was speechless.

"You told me 'don't let go'," he continued quietly. "But I did."

No words came to my lips. I wanted to tell him *That was when we were ice skating!*

"You can't have hold of me all the time," I muttered, my eyes staying on a fixed point on his chest below his collarbone. I just couldn't meet his intensity without looking away. My cheeks felt feverish and warm. "I have to live without being babysat. It was my fault I fell. I was stupid."

"You're not stupid," he said quietly.

"And yet hundreds of people passed through there, and did you see anyone on the ground or injured? No." I was staring straight ahead, my arms crossed tightly. I felt unexpectedly vulnerable, and I didn't like it.

"Anyway," I continued in a mutter, "so much for the rose garden."

"It's open year-round," he said. "We can always go another time. It doesn't matter."

The door swung open again and Tai burst in, almost hidden by a huge mound of blankets he was carrying – some pillows and what looked like two comforters.

"Oh good," he said. "I'm not late." He dropped the mound beside me and Wooyeong, grabbing two pillows and scooting them close to my hurt foot. "Can you lift your leg?"

I lifted it and Tai slid the pillows underneath. He also awkwardly doubled-up the comforters and managed to scoot them underneath me with my help.

I sighed. "That feels much more comfortable." Even my ankle felt better with the pillows.

Tai took off his coat and threw it in a rumpled pile across the room, dropping to a casual sitting position beside me, across from Wooyeong. He also took off his shoes and set them beside mine.

"Your poor coat," I said.

"Are you kidding? Almost all our clothes are sponsored. They're cheap around here. I have another one just like it." Tai ran a hand through his black hair. He made an odd figure in his plain cream hoodie and light blue socks. It was much more casual than I was used to seeing him, and he was in sharp contrast to Wooyeong, who was still completely dressed in his coat, turtleneck sweater, and black shoes. "Hey, by the way, Eun Ae called. The medic's on his way but he was looking at someone else a few floors down. Someone bashed their knee while practicing, I guess."

"It's okay. I just need to get ice on it or something to take the swelling down and elevate it for a while. I don't really need him to come. It's not like he can do anything."

"Yes, but he should just take a look to see how bad it is," Wooyeong said. "That's what he does for us."

"Yeah, last time we saw him was when Dyeong pulled a muscle in his neck," Tai said. "He was doing his rap part in *Crushed Flower* where he has to bend down and kind of jerk his head to the side." Tai imitated it to show me, his movements shockingly fast and smooth like only a professional dancer's could be. "For some reason that day it didn't go so well, even though he stretched."

The mention of Dyeong was like a little electrical jolt to my brain. I suddenly fully recalled that I was *in SMK Entertainment,* which meant that Dyeong – and Chin-hyuk – were probably just down the hall.

"I'll go get some ice for your ankle," Wooyeong said, rising. "Who knows how long he'll be."

"The first ice machine is out," Tai called as he left. "You'll have to use the one farther away."

Wooyeong made a short noise of acknowledgement as the door shut.

"It's getting dark outside," Tai said, looking at me. "You might not make it home soon."

There were no windows in the dance studio, so he must've passed some when he went to fetch the pillows. I inhaled a short breath. What was I going to do? I was an adult now in Seoul all by myself, with no one to call.

"You could always stay here," Tai continued. "Just for one night."

My mouth felt dry. "What time is it?"

Tai pulled out his phone. Though it was a sleek, shiny new edition, the screen was cracked like it'd been dropped multiple times. "Six thirty-five."

I nodded, feeling calmer. "I've got plenty of time then."

"Dinner, though," Tai said, running his hand through his hair again. "That's the next thing. I'm already hungry. You can eat here with us, I'll find something to cook up. The manager will probably allow us to break from our diets since you're here."

That was the first time I'd heard anyone address it so directly. Wooyeong didn't talk about this, didn't talk about any part of his idol life. "What are they like?" I asked quietly. "Your diets."

Tai looked sideways at me and laughed, presumably at the expression on my face. "Don't look so worried, Madison. We're not being starved to death. Our manager is actually pretty lenient. Mostly it's just... boring food and less of it. But we eat instant ramyun a lot too." He patted his cheeks. "It's all about making sure the jawline stays sharp."

I couldn't help smiling. I guess Tai had that effect on most people.

"Dyeong even cut back on calories *willingly*," Tai said. "Self-discipline. But as long as we stay looking fit and lean, Manager Pak is happy. He tries to make it our responsibility so we don't go binging on boxes of Pepero sticks and 'Oh Yes' choco pies behind his back."

"That sounds really good right now," I moaned. I hadn't even realized that I was starting to get hungry before.

"Sorry, we don't keep choco pies or Pepero in here. Too tempting. You'll have to smuggle it out of Manager Pak's desk. He's a sweet fiend. His office is *loaded.*"

Wooyeong came back in with a plastic bag full of ice, laying it gently on my ankle. I sighed blissfully at its cooling effect.

"Thank you," I said. Wooyeong gave me a nod in response but nothing more, sitting next to me in silence again.

Tai chattered happily for the next five minutes until the medic arrived, a very short man with kind eyes. He inspected my ankle, looking at the swelling compared to the other one. "This looks like a mild sprain," he said in calm English. "But it'll heal, in a few days. Just give it time and take it easy. As far as I can tell it doesn't look so bad that you need further attention."

This was a *mild* sprain? It hurt like *heck*!

"Okay, thank you," Wooyeong said as he left again. The medic gave a wave before the door closed.

"It doesn't *feel* mild," I muttered in an exaggeratedly resentful way, and they both laughed.

There was a silence.

"So... now what?" I asked. "I can't stay here forever, as comfortable as it is." I patted the comforter underneath me.

"You shouldn't go home already," Wooyeong said. "It's too soon. Stay here awhile."

"I was going to make some food," Tai said, standing up. "She can eat with us in the dorm. That way she can sit on the sofa."

"But – aren't Dyeong and Chin-hyuk in there?" I asked, trying not to sound too nervous. "I don't want to bother them."

"Nah, it's fine," Tai said, waving his hand and standing up. "They won't mind. I'll go make the ramyun."

"Instant ramyun," Wooyeong laughed quietly after he left. "That's about as much as he knows how to cook."

"Sounds delicious," I said. "I don't care what I eat. I'm just hungry."

"Me too," he said amiably.

We didn't say anything for a few minutes. I sighed. "I feel guilty for making everyone scramble around just for me," I said, resting my head on my arm. "You've already helped so much even just by getting me off the street. I don't know what I would've done if I'd been by myself."

"You could've called a taxi. Or me."

I glanced at him with a wry smile. "I guess."

Sitting and talking with Wooyeong in the dance practice room was one of the strangest things that had ever happened to me, but I didn't want it to end.

우영
WOOYEONG
14

Madison leaned on me as she hopped down the hallway on one foot, her hand on my shoulder.

"So... this is where you always go?" she asked.

"Yes," I said. "For the past six years, this is home. Down this hallway and then into Number Ten."

This was the first time she was going into our dorm. The first time she'd even been in SMK Entertainment and a dance practice room.

This was the first time that my friendship with Madison had intersected with my Ambition life.

I'd forgotten she was a fan. I was painfully aware of it now, like there was something sharp wedged in my chest. She was a fan in SMK Entertainment, about to meet the rest of her favorite idols.

Everything I felt – and everything I was telling myself to feel – was threatening to overflow. Even if it all magically fixed itself so that we could ever be together, how would I know that she appreciated me for me only? I'd managed to forget it for a while, let my feelings for her and our friendship be entirely separate from my idol life. Being here forced me to recognize that they never could be truly separate, and they weren't. Had I just been playing a pretending game the whole time I'd known her?

I swallowed the lump in my throat as we walked down the hall, not looking at her, feeling the steady pressure of her arm on mine.

My emotions were so tangled I couldn't sort them out, but I knew one thing – I was nervous. This was the first time Madison was going to meet Chin-hyuk and Dyeong.

We reached the door to Number Ten just as Chin-hyuk yanked it open from inside, looking at us in surprise, his gaze falling down on Madison – as close as it was, since he was barely taller.

"Hi," he said, eyes wide.

"Hello, Chin-hyuk," I said shortly, glancing down at Madison, who was looking at Chin-hyuk in as much flustered shock as he was looking at her.

He reached up and tousled his lavender bangs, talking so fast he was almost stammering. "I heard what happened, we moved the coffee table aside, Tai says you're staying for dinner –"

"Right," I said. "Thank you, Chin-hyuk." It was hardly ever we got visitors to the dorm, and even rarer that it was night. And of course, it was never, ever a girl.

He bustled out of the way, letting me help Madison to the sofa. They really had moved the coffee table aside. It was pushed off the rug, giving a big open floor space. Besides the two cushy chairs that were always there, they'd also pulled up a stool. It looked like a makeshift party.

"I'll... go get the pillows for the sofa," Chin-hyuk said, and rushed off in the direction of the dance practice room we'd just come from.

Madison lay down on the sofa, elevating her leg, her face flushed. "Are you sure this is okay?" she asked anxiously. "I don't want to bother you..."

"It's fine," I said, standing next to her. "We don't get visitors often, you're a novelty."

Tai was cooking ramyun in the kitchen; there was our largest pot on the stove filled with bubbling water. "Wooyeong, I need you to set the table! We're eating in the living room!"

"Coming!" I yelled, going to the warm, busy kitchen. Tai was moving quickly this way and that, gathering things he needed as warm steam rose into the air.

I grabbed five pairs of chopsticks and five bowls, one of them mismatched since we only had sets of four.

"Is there anything I can do for you?" I asked him. "You look frantic."

"Are you kidding me? I'm a *master* of making perfect shin ramyun, you should know that."

I suspected having Madison here was distracting him, but I didn't say it. "Where's Dyeong?"

Tai glanced meaningfully across the room, where Dyeong had pulled up a chair next to the sofa, conversing quietly with Madison.

I felt panic spike. I strode over to the living room and set the bowls down on the coffee table loudly. Dyeong looked over, but his expression was perfectly unruffled. "Hello, Wooyeong."

He'd better not have been telling Madison to stay away from me, or anything else furthering his own agenda. I was barely gone for sixty seconds.

This was the first time he had ever seen her, and I couldn't help wondering what he was thinking. But I couldn't read his calm expression as he stood up and turned on the lamps in the living room, giving everything a surprisingly cozy yellow glow.

Chin-hyuk came back with his arms bursting – unlike Tai, he needed two trips to carry it all – and dumped some pillows on the rug.

"Ramyun's ready!" Tai shouted.

"I'll be right back!" Chin-hyuk said, and rushed out again.

Tai carried the pot to the table, then came back for the seasoning packets as I grabbed two pillows from the floor and offered them to Madison. She leaned forward so I could put them behind her back.

"Thanks," she said, and I couldn't help noticing that her cheeks looked pink. She unzipped her parka, then struggled out of it, draping it on the arm of the sofa behind her.

She caught Dyeong's eye; he looked over her brown slacks and loose cream V-neck shirt. "Did you just come from work?"

"Yes," she said sheepishly. "I didn't have time to go home and change."

He made a small sniffing noise I couldn't decipher, almost smirking to himself as he bent down, stirring the ramyun.

Chin-hyuk came back and all of us settled in on the rug. Dyeong served up a bowl of ramyun, handing it to Madison along with a seasoning packet. "Careful," he warned. "It's very spicy for a foreigner."

She nodded and took the warm bowl, holding it in her lap. Dyeong passed the next one to me and I picked up a curly noodle with my chopsticks, tasting it. It was still chewy and springy – cooked to perfection, just like Tai said it would be.

All of us ate, talking, though Madison and I stayed mostly quiet. Dyeong, Chin-hyuk and Tai were carrying on an animated conversation, occasionally throwing in questions for Madison, laughing at something or the other. They were bantering about cooking skills, mostly targeting Dyeong since he couldn't even boil water.

It felt so homey, just like things were supposed to be – the warm, heavy bowl of ramyun in my hands; Chin-hyuk's faint, usual scent of lemons, lavender and mint that tended to infect the whole dorm; the metallic clatter of chopsticks and slurping as the five of us ate together; the warm yellow light casting its glow over everything; Dyeong's laughter; the soft rug beneath me as I sat cross-legged. And Madison, in the midst of it all, looking so natural and fitting as one of us. I wondered if that was just my perception. Did she feel the same way? Comfortable, here?

I loved her.

I didn't just like her, or think she was pretty. I loved her. I knew that now. Maybe the thought should've surprised me, taken me aback, but it didn't. I'd been falling more and more in love with her over all those days we talked on the phone, every day we were friends. The thought of losing her filled me with fear. I sucked in a breath as I realized there was no turning back.

She kept adding more of the spice packet to her ramyun, and her cheeks kept getting redder and redder. I tried to fight the smile that kept quirking my lips.

I couldn't imagine life without her in it anymore. I swallowed the lump in my throat, glad that Dyeong was distracted asking her questions.

All of them were so interested in her. They could barely rip their gazes away, so fascinated with the person who'd managed to break the cynical, jaded Wooyeong. They were talking about anything and everything – music, places to go in Seoul, travel, complaining about exercise, siblings, the weather. The subjects were occasionally peppered with questions for Madison, and I tried to fight my immense satisfaction that I already knew the answers before she said them. Our weeks of constant phone calls had let me get to know her well.

Chin-hyuk was laughing at something really hard. I laughed too, unable to help it after I'd seen his face. Tai brought out some chips and banana milk, passing them around and offering one to Chin-hyuk. Chin-hyuk was still smiling as his hand reached for it and then his expression morphed into one of shock as he realized what it was.

"Agh, no!" he said. "What are you trying to do?"

Tai laughed and brought out the strawberry milk from behind his back, giving it to Chin-hyuk, who harrumphed "That's better."

"Why, is it poisoned or something?" Madison asked, eyeing it dubiously as Tai handed the banana one to her instead.

"I hate bananas," Chin-hyuk announced. "They're like... like... what's that thing that hurts Superman?"

"Kryptonite?" Madison said.

Chin-hyuk tilted his head, thinking. "Yes – yes! I think so. It's like Kryptonite to me."

"Chin-hyuk's English is the weakest," Tai said, licking his chopsticks. "But he watches English movies to try to get better."

"That's what I did!" Madison said. "Korean dramas."

"Uh-oh," said Tai. "Well, I hope you didn't imitate them. Chin-hyuk talked like Loki whenever he spoke English for weeks."

"Then we made fun of him, and he stopped after that," Dyeong joined in, an evil sparkle in his eye.

"I did *not,*" Chin-hyuk was protesting, but the others were talking over him.

I couldn't help smiling, watching them all. The conversation was still bubbling long after all the ramyun was gone, and then Tai stacked the empty bowls and brought out a pack of Go-Stop. Madison had never played it before, and they were more than happy to explain – but it was difficult when everyone tried to say the rules all at once. Dyeong and Tai kept interrupting each other.

Madison carefully moved to the floor so we could all sit in a circle and lay out our matches, seeming to take it all in stride. I marveled at her calmness.

"I like the cards," she said, admiring the flowers patterning the cards and the bright red borders as Dyeong shuffled. Her gaze strayed to me, and her breath hitched as she realized I was watching her.

My lips quirked up in a smile, and she smiled back, quickly, embarrassed, looking back down again.

"Okay, okay – listen up, everybody," Dyeong said loudly, drawing everyone's attention. "We're playing to four points. Whoever wins gets a package of Mongshell from each loser."

"But's that's four whole boxes!" Tai gasped, setting his empty banana milk bottle on the coffee table. "Why don't we all just chip in and get *one?*"

"I agree with Dyeong," I said. "Everyone buys a package of Mongshell and gives it to the winner."

"Within three days," Dyeong added seriously, holding up three fingers. "After that, they owe another box for each day they're late."

"What's Mongshell?" Madison asked, looking cautious.

"A sweet cake coated in chocolate and filled with cream," Chin-hyuk said. "They're amazing – the *best* kind of choco pie. Imagine fluffy clouds."

"Sounds good to me," she said, her eyes widening.

"If I win, you don't have to buy one for me," I told her. "However, the rest of you have to pay up."

"That's so not fair!" Tai yelled.

"Good thing I plan on winning, then," said Dyeong with a wicked smile.

As it turned out, I was the one who won the game, and I smugly informed the other members that they owed me Mongshell, promising to share some with Madison so she could try it. We played several more times, Madison getting the hang of it so that she too won once, and by the time we were winding down and I finally looked out the window, it was pitch-black.

"It's late," Dyeong said, sounding surprised as he looked at the time on his phone screen. "Past nine."

"Oh," Madison said, brushing her hair distractedly away from her face with her fingers. "I need to go home."

"You can stay here," Tai offered cheerfully. "If you want. There's an empty dorm down the hall."

She hesitated, seeming to consider it. "No, I really should get going."

"Are you sure you're going to be alright?" I asked her. I didn't want her to lie and say she was fine just because she didn't want to inconvenience us by staying here. "Can you really make it?"

She nodded. "It feels much better now. The distance from the door of the complex to my place isn't too bad. It'll be over quickly, and then I'll be able to get a good night's rest. I have a hard time sleeping in places that aren't my own bed."

"Whatever you think is best," I said. If she stayed here, *I* probably wouldn't be able to sleep either because I'd be hyperaware of her in the same building. The thought of waking up and eating breakfast with her filled me with both happiness and nerves, and I was both disappointed and relieved that she was refusing. I couldn't tell which one overpowered the other, though I was a little sad that our night of fun was coming to an end.

Dyeong offered to call a taxi and stepped out into the hall, where I could just hear his muffled voice under the sounds of Chin-hyuk and Tai carrying on a conversation with Madison.

Soon the taxi arrived – Tai saw it pull up through the window – and I offered to escort Madison downstairs. She shrugged her parka back on, but didn't zip it as we rode the elevator back down. Neither of us spoke much, but it was a comfortable silence. A content one.

Outside was cold and black, the empty, pale gray concrete frigid like a slab of ice. The city lights around us glittered like magic, and I could see my breath stream out in a large cloud in front of me as I helped her to the taxi, opening the door for her so she could slide in.

"Be careful," I said, my voice coming out quieter than I expected. "Take care of yourself."

She smiled up at me from her seat in the car, her eyes reflecting the lights of SMK Entertainment behind me. It was a happy smile, but still one to reassure me. "I will."

I gave a nod, shifting my position slightly on the sidewalk. I didn't want to say goodbye to her. But I had to.

She pulled her parka in all the way from where it'd been draped, and I closed the car door behind her. The reflective black glass window made it impossible to see her. I smiled at it anyway as the taxi started slowly pulling away, tires crunching under the gravel, its taillights casting me in a red glow.

It joined the main road and other cars, picking up speed until it had to slow down to turn the corner, pausing to make a left turn. I didn't move, standing there and watching it until it turned away and out of sight.

매디슨
MADISON
15

It was the next day, and I had stupidly decided to walk home from work like I usually did.

I was insane for thinking I felt fine enough to do this today, to think I could do this like I normally could. I'd thought a little exercise would help me – my ankle had hurt this morning, but by the middle of the day I could barely feel it. It was a *mild* sprain, after all, and didn't hurt if I moved carefully. Even the swelling had gone down. It had felt perfectly fine at the beginning of the walk, but now I wasn't sure if I could make it the whole way. I wasn't even halfway there.

I stumbled a little further before heaving a deep breath, righting myself. I had at least made it to the bridge in the middle of the park, and was halfway across. The railing was here for support, for now.

Why had I been so stupid to think that this would help my ankle? One day was far too early for exercising it. And now I wasn't even sure if I could swallow my pride and ask someone to pick me up. I should just make it home.

My phone pinged with a notification. I slipped it out immediately, thinking it was a text from Wooyeong.

A social media post filled the screen instead. It must've been one of those things I'd followed a while back, Ambition-related, long before I'd met them all in person. The header read *Wooyeong and Tai caught!*

The breath felt like it'd been punched from my lungs.

"Oh no," I said. "Please no."

My finger trembled as it pressed the icon, making the post fully open up.

It was a picture.

A picture of me and Wooyeong and Tai on the sidewalk, me piggybacking with Tai's arms under my legs as I leaned forward, my arms around his neck, Wooyeong gazing on with fervor. He looked intense and preoccupied, so that he hadn't even noticed someone taking a picture. It was a good shot. Clear, with all of us in focus. You could see Wooyeong's distinctive profile, that instantly recognizable nose and jaw. My face was half-hidden behind my hair, revealing only my lips, chin, and nose. I was lucky that no one could see my eyes. There was a possibility that I was a Korean citizen, just with dyed and textured hair.

A possibility. They didn't need to see my obviously white eyes to guess that I was a foreigner. My hair was enough. Even from the side, I did not look Asian.

Tai's face was the most hidden, but his ruffled dark hair, his broad back and his tallness next to Wooyeong made it clear who he was. Trying to argue it wasn't him would be ludicrous. He was unmistakable.

Wooyeong and Tai with a girl??!? the post was labeled. *I caught this in Jiuji market!*

Then a bunch of crying, angry-devil, and skull emojis. I felt a chill run through me that had nothing to do with the cold. My heart racing, I scrolled down slowly with my thumb.

The comments section was explosive. This was going viral, fast.

Ew! Tai can do better than that! I mean come on.

Our boys wouldn't date anyone! They love Aim. They're wayyy too busy.

Look at the way WY is looking at her. Is she his girlfriend? I will literally murder her. She's not good enough for him.

Duh it's obvious she's Wooyeong's girlfriend. Look at his face.

Why does she need to be carried around?

What a witch. Wooyeong's girlfriend is just tricking him.

Oh my gosh. Aim, we need to protect our boys.

Isn't she Tai's girlfriend since he's carrying her? Wait, is she double-timing?

Ambition wouldn't date anyone, nor spend time with some random ugly girl. This is Photoshopped.

I can't believe Ambition would betray us like that.

You know how kind our boys are. They would never do anything like that. Maybe Tai's carrying her because she's faking an injury. I hope she feels like killing herself because of the way she took advantage of their kindness and fooled them.

WY's girlfriend needs to back off. She doesn't deserve him.

I exited the post and stuffed my phone in my pocket, feeling my heart in my throat. The worst was happening. Had Ambition seen this? It had been posted hours ago.

I felt sick to my stomach. The nasty comments stuck to my mind like thorns. *Some random ugly girl... I hope she feels like killing herself...*

I swallowed, taking short, fast breaths. People on the internet were cruel. I shouldn't take this to heart. I could *not* let them break me. This was something all four of those guys I'd hung out with last night had to deal with all the time. If they could, I could. I needed to.

I pulled out my phone again quickly, unsure of what to do and not able to help myself, then looked up "Tai and Wooyeong with girl" in the internet search bar.

A tabloid site came up first. *Scandalizing picture of girl with Ambition members!* Then a K-pop news site. *Tai and Wooyeong caught giving a piggyback ride to girl in Seoul.* Then yet another news site. *Does Tai have a new girlfriend?* And another. *Breaking news – Ambition members dating!*

Then the flurry of social media links where it'd been posted, reposted, and talked about for hours straight.

I was too afraid to check the VLive fan page. I heaved a deep breath and then went to SMK Entertainment's Instagram page.

They had released an official statement just thirty minutes ago. My heart rocketed to my throat as I clicked to enlarge it.

The photo taken yesterday was when Tai and Wooyeong were out with an assistant general manager, who slipped and sprained her ankle on ice. As she couldn't walk, Tai carried her so that she could receive medical attention.

The comments were full of people gushing over Ambition's kind hearts and ridiculing others who believed that Tai and Wooyeong would ever commit the unforgivable sin of hanging out with a girl.

Would you complain if you were the girl? I thought, my emotions so jumbled I didn't know what I was feeling. Anger? Fear? Relief?

But then I saw one comment, with 750 likes.

Of course they're going to say that. We'll just have to see if they're ever spotted together again.

I had an ominous feeling about that one. I swiped up to get rid of the page and then opened my text. Still nothing from Wooyeong.

I stared at it like that would help, feeling slippery desperation worming its way into my heart. Desperation, ringed with panic. *Please, please, please talk to me!*

He hadn't contacted me since the photo was released.

I stared out at the snowy trees. A tear slid down my cheek, leaving a stinging trail. I sniffed, wiping my eyes with the back of my glove.

People passed by me but I stood still, hardly aware of them. I blinked back the water in my eyes, a lump rising in my throat.

I guess that's it.

It had to end, of course. I'd known that. It's not like we could be together. He was a K-pop idol.

Something had to ruin it sometime. This was it. He couldn't – *shouldn't* – be with me anymore. What if someone took another picture? He might not be able to explain that away.

I'd known we could never be together, and he would never even want to. Why did my heart still ache like it'd been broken?

I let out a choking sob, pressing my face into my hands. Then I slowly, painfully, shuffled off the bridge.

My ankle let out another flare of pain. I gasped, falling onto the cold metal rail for support. I was bent over, still letting out involuntary sobs.

If only they could see me now. Broken, pathetic, crying, hardly able to walk. They would never say I was Wooyeong's girlfriend.

People pushed past and around me but still I couldn't move. I pressed my arm harder on the metal rail, feeling the cold leak in through my wool sleeve. Tears fell onto the ice coating the metal, liquid on the snowflake pattern snaking up the surface.

It was over now. I should savor what I'd been given. Appreciate that we had even gotten the opportunity to be friends. That I had the opportunity to love him.

Maybe he'd still call occasionally, even if we would never meet again.

Maybe.

I pushed myself up off the rail, trying to balance on my good leg. I should just flag down a taxi, because walking all the way home from work would be agony. There were none around, however, except for one which wasn't vacant. I bit down on my lip, a tear falling off my cheek.

I pulled out my phone. Who should I call? I wouldn't be able to make it home.

The first contact that popped up was Wooyeong. I put my hand over my mouth, muffling my sob. I wanted *so badly* to call him. But I couldn't rely on him for help. We may never see each other again. Calling might just make it worse.

I couldn't ask him for help.

That felt lonelier than anything.

I scrolled down, seeing Jeongsook's name. I pressed the call button before I could hesitate, bringing the cell phone up to my ear.

I bit down harder on my lip to stop myself from crying as I waited for her to pick up, listening to the neutral sound of the ringer. Then I heard a click as the sound cut off and a familiar voice said, "Hello?"

"Jeongsook," I said, overwhelmed at the sound of her voice, relief making my fingers tremble. I swallowed. "It's me, Madison. I need a ride."

"Hmm? What? Why? Okay. Where are you?"

"I sprained my ankle yesterday. I came into work this morning because I was extra-careful, but it feels really bad now. I'm right by the Peace Coffee, in the mini park on the bridge."

"Ahhhh," said Jeongsook, and there was shuffling in the background. "I'm getting my car key. I'll be right there! I'm hanging up."

"'Kay," I said softly, my phone letting out a gentle little beep as it exited the call.

I kept it in my hand as I looked out at the main road, the teardrops on my face stinging in the freezing cold. Then I started across the bridge, holding the rail in a death grip. The concrete wasn't icy here, meaning I could just hop on my good leg for most of the way.

I tried not to draw attention to myself. No one stopped and asked if I needed help, though I almost wished they would when I got to the end of the bridge and there was no longer something to hold onto on the path from the rest of the park to the road.

I took a deep breath and put my good foot forward, then my bad one, as lightly as I could – and still gasped from the pain, my legs nearly buckling.

I'd sprained my ankle before when I was a kid, but it hadn't been like this. It was a good thing I'd had Wooyeong and Tai with me when I'd slipped on that ice, because it could've been worse.

I wished they were with me now. I wished Wooyeong were here.

The cold wind made my shiver. It was starting to sting my chapped lips and make my cheeks raw. I continued limping down the path to the road, losing my balance near the end.

I fell, my hands firmly on the ground. I pushed myself back up to a standing position, lips pressed together in desperation.

That was when a white car pulled to a screeching stop in front of me. The window rolled down, revealing Jeongsook's horrified face.

"Oh my gosh!" she said. "You look horrible!" She threw the car in park, hair swinging, and then got out, rushing to me.

"You sprained your ankle? Can you walk?"

"Kind of. Can I put my hand on your shoulder?"

"Of course, of course!" She grabbed underneath my arm, supporting me as I also put my weight on her shoulder when I had to step with my sprained ankle.

She helped me to her car and then shut the door for me, sliding into the front seat.

"Oh my gosh, Madison," she said, eyes wide and a crease between her straight eyebrows. "What were you doing out there all by yourself? You should've told me! Wait, have you been crying? Oh my gosh."

"It's okay," I said, trying to calm her frantic worry, though I was touched at her concern.

Jeongsook threw the car in reverse and did a three-pointer, peeling out of here. "What were you doing in the snow all by yourself with a sprained ankle? You could've frozen to death! Do you want me to take you to my place?"

"No, that's okay," I said, closing my tired eyes to the blast of hot air hitting my face from the vent. I felt like melting butter.

"Why were you crying? Are you okay?"

"I'm fine," I said.

Jeongsook made an indignant noise. "Don't tell me you're fine! You could've been really hurt! Oh my gosh, I'm so glad you called me! Don't ever do that again!"

I shifted my position in the backseat, elevating my leg and breathing a sigh of relief when the throbbing became less pronounced. "I'm sorry."

She glanced worriedly in her rearview mirror, then her eyes widened again. "Oh my gosh! Are you crying again?"

"I'm sorry," I said, sniffing and rubbing the tears from the corners of my eyes. "I'm just so happy that you came..."

"Don't cry!" she said, sounding even more anxious than before. "I can drive you to and from work the rest of the week too, as long as you need!"

We stopped at a traffic light. Jeongsook swiveled her head around to look at me. "Why were you crying before?"

I swallowed. What could I tell her? That I was undeniably and irreversibly in love with Lee Wooyeong? She would laugh, pity me, or worse, tell someone else. We couldn't be together and I couldn't tell Jeongsook.

So I said as much of the truth as I could say without endangering Wooyeong. "I love a guy but I don't think I'm going to see him again."

"Ohhh!" Jeongsook's eyes were sympathetic. "Oh no! Your heart is broken. I'm sure it'll work out, right?"

I shook my head slowly, my vision blurry from my welled-up eyes.

"I'm ready to listen if you want to tell me more," said Jeongsook. "Do you know what's really good for a broken heart? Throwing down five shots of soju. Should I take you out to a bar?"

I didn't answer, my dead gaze on the seat in front of me.

"Or not," Jeongsook sighed. The car was stopping. Another light, and then we were pulling up to my apartment. I felt disconcerted, with no idea how we'd gotten there so fast. I scooted over in the seat and opened the car door.

Jeongsook was already racing around to help me. "Don't get out!" she said hysterically. "Do you want to make it *worse?* Oh my gosh, Madison, it's already bad enough as it is!"

She took hold of my arm, putting it over her shoulder, mini high heels clicking on the pavement. "Come on. I'm going to take you to your apartment."

I winced as I bumped my foot against the side of the door as I slid out. Jeongsook looked extremely worried, not just at my ankle but at my barely-holding-it-together expression.

She walked me inside and then to the elevator, talking anxiously all the while. I pressed the floor number, and then when the elevator was done we went a little down the hall to my room.

"Thanks, Jeongsook," I muttered.

"It's nothing! Do you want me to help you inside?"

~{★ 105 ♥}~

"No, I'm probably fine."

"Where did you get that sprain, anyway? It's really bad! You need to rest it, Madison! Do you want me to order you something to eat?"

"No thanks." I wasn't hungry. I felt too crushed too eat. I would probably just cry myself to sleep.

"You look sick. Are you sure you're okay? You're pale and not in a good way."

"I'm fine," I repeated automatically.

"By the way, do you want to borrow one of my moisture packs? Your skin's really dry and irritated. Crying when it's freezing out is really bad for your complexion. Well, never mind – just take it," she said, flustered, digging around in her purse and pulling out a blue plastic pouch with a picture of a mask and an elephant on it. I took it numbly.

"Works miracles," she added.

"Thanks, Jeongsook. I'll see you later."

She started walking down the hall back toward the elevator. "Call me if you need to get picked up! Don't do anything crazy, alright? Just take care of yourself!"

I waited until she was gone and then shuffled inside, leaning against the wall, closing the door behind me with a soft click.

As soon as I was alone, tears started streaming from my eyes again. I limped to the couch, the closest available place to sit down, face screwed up in pain. Had it gotten *worse* over time? By the time I actually reached the sofa and fell on it, I was gasping from how much it hurt.

I reached for a pillow on the floor and picked it up, stuffing it behind my back. I took off my jacket and tossed it away, hearing a dull thump that was my forgotten phone in the pocket. I didn't care. With blurry vision I unlaced my shoes and gingerly slipped one off my injured foot, then rougher on the other, throwing them underneath the coffee table.

I pressed my face into the pillow miserably, my sweater-clad shoulders giving an involuntary shiver. It was too cold in here. But there was no way I could make it across the room to kick up the thermostat.

"I miss you," I whispered into the pillow, feeling wetness spread on the fabric as I started to cry.

It had been so perfect last night. How had everything changed so quickly?

I would probably never see him again. He couldn't afford that. Ambition had just barely gotten away with it one time. If they saw me again with Wooyeong – there would be no recovery. Would Ambition have to disband? Or would Wooyeong be forced to resign, with Dyeong, Chin-hyuk, and Tai carrying on without him?

There was no way that would ever happen. Because we wouldn't be seen together again. We wouldn't *be* together again.

Maybe there would be a few solitary texts from Wooyeong. Or even an ongoing conversation that lasted a while. But the fact remained that even that had a ticking clock.

We couldn't even be friends.

My heart felt like it was being ripped in two, crack by crack. Never had I wanted to see anyone this badly. Never had I cried over anyone like this before. Never had I experienced this much pain.

It was knowing that I might not ever get to see him again that hurt the most.

Even though this was probably my last chance to tell him anything over text, I didn't have the guts to confess how I felt. To tell him I loved him. That I wished he would be happy no matter what, even if he was happy with someone else.

Because I already knew I was a fool. No matter how deep our friendship became, no matter how much we liked each other, it could never lead to love on his part. He was Wooyeong. I was a fan. That was the way it would stay.

So I wasn't ever going to tell him the way I felt. For what? Just for the sake of telling him? To feel his awkwardness and pity? No.

...No.

I just wished that it wasn't like this. That we could be friends at least. I wished that we weren't from completely separate worlds. I wished that that photo of me and Tai and Wooyeong had never been released.

I wished our future was different.

I doubled over, though that did nothing to stop the pain in my heart. Why did it hurt so much?

The doorbell rang, its chime ringing out cheerfully through my small apartment.

I stared at the door. I half-sat up, breathing hard through my mouth. Who would be coming to see me? I fell back onto the couch, curled up, my ankle throbbing as tears ran off my face and onto the pillows.

A few moments passed. The doorbell rang again.

"Go away!" I shouted, my voice cracking and thick with sobs. "I can't answer right now!"

The door opened a tiny crack.

I watched in fear and shock as it slowly opened, revealing...

Wooyeong.

The surprise and concern and confusion he felt was written all over his handsome face as he stood there in the doorway, a stuffed grocery bag in one hand. My wide, wet eyes met his deep, intense brown ones.

"But..." I whispered. The sound was so faint that I barely formed the words on my lips.

His intense, caring gaze never moved from my face. He stepped inside and shut the door behind him, slowly, softly, almost like he was asking permission as he did it.

I just watched him in shock. My throat seized up at my relief at seeing him, the deep longing I felt that I knew would never happen, the gentleness on his face.

He moved closer to me, stopping in front of where I was on the sofa. We looked at each other for a long moment, and his dark eyes were so warm and worried that I had to look away, wiping my eyes on my sleeve, letting out another sob.

"Are you okay?" he asked, his brow creased, sinking on one knee so our eyes would be level. I looked at him, in the exact same position as he would be if he were proposing.

Something that could never, ever happen.

I started crying again.

His hand reached out and took mine, his fingers warm as he squeezed.

"What's wrong?" he whispered.

I was crying too hard to answer him. Tears were spilling down my face. When would they stop? I was angry with myself but so sad, so relieved to look into his beautiful face again. I gulped in a breath. "Why are you here?"

"Your ankle is hurt," he said. "You can't stand on it. You need someone to take care of you."

His voice was quiet, his fingers still gripping mine with a steadiness that felt grounding. Butterflies filled my stomach as I looked into his face, so close to mine. Closer than it had ever been.

My breath caught. My gaze flicked to his lips, which were parted, and then back up to his eyes – so dark they were almost black, framed by straight lashes.

He sucked in a sharp breath when our eyes met again. But he didn't let go of my hand, nor did he move.

I remembered his expression when Tai had been carrying me. Almost unreadable, carefully neutral, but... hard. The way he had pressed his teeth into the side of his lip, his eyes that looked even darker than usual.

I got shivers just thinking about it. Had he been... had that been... *jealousy?*

Wooyeong closed his eyes, exhaling. My stomach was filled with a strange, light, nervous feeling. My heart pounded almost painfully in my chest and I could feel everywhere where the lines of his palm, his thumb, met mine, his touch electrifying my skin.

All he had to do was lean forward mere inches...

Then he opened his eyes and his hand slowly slid from mine. He stood up, the strangest expression on his face, one that I could not read.

"I've come to cook for you," he said, something in his voice different from usual. He swallowed, glancing down, then back at me. He lifted the shopping bag at his side to show me. "I went to the market earlier today. But I had too many things scheduled to come then, so I had to wait until they were over."

I stared at him, speechless.

He reached into the pocket of his black leather jacket and pulled out a silver case, opening it to reveal a pair of black glasses, which he slid on his face.

We looked at each other for a long minute. He was just standing there in my living room, so out of place that I might've conjured him from a dream. His slightly scuffed white sneakers; his gracefully falling hair that was a subtle shade somewhere between the palest brown, blush pink, and silver; his spiked earrings, without the chains and extras today; and now his glasses, framing his steady brown eyes in a way that I had never seen before.

I wanted so *badly* to fall into his arms, to press my face against his sweater and feel his strong, warm hug. I wanted it so badly it ached.

"I didn't know you wore glasses," I sniffled, adjusting my position so I was at least sitting up straight, trying to hide the longing I felt.

"No one does."

"They look nice on you," I said, which was not a lie. My heart was fluttering as a fresh wave of emotions toppled onto my chest, threatening to come out in a new rush of tears.

"Dyeong and Chin-hyuk already wear glasses," Wooyeong said, his head turned sideways. "The agency decided that one more member would be too much. I don't wear them when I'm out just in case someone snaps a picture."

I nodded, not knowing what to say. My gaze flicked down to the bag he was holding, but I could not tell what was in it.

He clapped his hands, making me start a little with the loud noise. "So," he said. "I guess I should start."

I watched him walk over to the kitchen, dazed, hardly processing what was going on.

The kitchen was so close – and with its open layout, I could see him at all times, except when he bent down to look for pots in the cupboards. He was doing so now, and I could hear him making little "hmms".

"What is it?" I asked, but quietly enough so that he didn't hear me. My voice sounded slurred because of how long I'd been crying.

Wooyeong looked in my pantry and refrigerator, gathering black pepper and some garlic, then set his own shopping bag on the counter and started pulling out items. A light brown tub, a package of red meat, potatoes, tofu, zucchini, a variety of mushrooms, an onion, a container of chili powder, Korean white radish, a blue home container, and a small bottle of rice wine came out.

He looked back at me. "Do you have flour?"

"It's in the far-right cupboard," I said numbly, aware of the thickness in my voice.

Wooyeong moved around items in the cupboard, pushing things aside and finally finding the hardly-used package of flour. "Ah!" He set it next to the other items, then took out a cutting board and knife and slid some vegetables out of their bag, rinsing them under the tap and setting them on the board.

It sank in then that he was really going to cook.

"You don't have to do this," I called, feeling my face burn warm. "Really. I'm okay…"

He shot me a look that seemed to call that out as ridiculous. Why was he so handsome in glasses?

Wooyeong sliced vegetables and cubed tofu, setting it all aside as he put a pot on the stove and turned the heat up, fiddling with it at first as he checked that it was on. I watched helplessly from the couch.

Butterflies had filled my stomach. Not only because he was here, but that he had bought all those things so that he could come cook dinner for me – to take care of me. He'd come to my apartment when he'd never been here before, walking around as if this was normal and we did this all the time.

Wooyeong was sizzling the meat in the pot now, stirring it and breaking it up with a wooden spoon, and I smelled rich beef. His back was to me because of the way the stove was situated.

I held out my hands and framed him. Then I took a long mental picture.

If we couldn't ever be together, I wanted to be able to, someday, look at that stove and imagine him there. The knitted material of his sweater against his broad back and shoulders as he worked, his leather jacket that he'd dropped onto a chair, the back of his head with his ruffled, colored hair. The way the yellow kitchen lights above him cast a warm glow on his figure and his busy hands.

My hands dropped back into my lap. I wiped my nose with a tissue, throwing it into the wastebasket underneath the table, feeling happy and wistful and heartbroken all at once. Finally the tears seemed to have stopped coming.

Whatever he was cooking was starting to smell really good. I eased myself off the sofa, trying not to move my ankle, gasping in pain when I bumped it against the cushion and made it bend slightly. My face screwed up, then I took a slow, deep exhale as the pain faded.

I carefully, quietly, moved across the living room, hopping on one foot and stopping to brace myself against a chair, leaning over it as my hands clutched at the backrest for support.

Wooyeong turned around like he'd heard me. His mouth opened in surprise. "You – you shouldn't be standing up!"

"I'm okay," I said, smiling, but he was already striding toward me. "I want to watch you cook. It's good for me to move around."

Wooyeong had stopped in front of me with his arms slightly held out like he wanted to support me but couldn't. He made a small noise of frustration and then offered his hand, palm up, fingers splayed gracefully.

I looked at it and then at him, and his beautiful eyes, which were intense with his emotions.

I gingerly placed my hand in his, feeling his warmth burn my skin, seeing my small fingers over his larger ones.

Wooyeong was already turning, helping me make my way to the kitchen. His strong grip let me lean my weight as I tried to get my balance. I felt clumsy compared to his steadiness – he looked like he might as well be escorting someone to a ballroom, while I was awkward and hopping like a kid playing hopscotch. With my ankle, I *was* clumsy, and there was nothing I could do about that.

When we got to the stove, which was seconds but felt more like minutes, he made sure that I had one hand on the cool counter before he eased the strength of his hand, finally letting go. He quickly picked up the spoon again and stirred the pot, which made violent hissing and sizzling noises with steam rising up.

I leaned forward to peek inside, scooting a little closer. There were strips of beef and chunks of potato and onion. As I watched, he broke the seal on the brown tub, taking a spoon and scooping out a generous amount of a chunky, light brown paste. Next was a shake of chili powder and a splash of rice wine, which hissed even louder.

Wooyeong stirred it all to blend the sauces together, his expression ultra-focused and serious.

"What are you making?" I asked.

"Stew. You'll see what kind. Do you have any liquid measuring cups?"

I bent down to open the cupboard next to me.

"I'll get it, I'll get it!" he said hurriedly, moving past me and sinking down to a squatting position as he moved things around. There was a small *chink* noise and he pulled out the glass measuring cup, closing the cupboard door behind him and going to the fridge for water.

When he poured the water into the pot, it turned a rich brown color because of all the flavorings.

Wooyeong fiddled the knobs on the stove as he adjusted the heat, trying to bring it up to boiling. I watched him – the set of his jaw, the shine on the frame of his black glasses, his intense eyes. His gaze flicked to me as he noticed me looking at him. I turned away, feeling my pulse racing.

"I hope I wasn't too late," he said. "I came here straight from SMK."

I was speechless again. "You... did?"

"Yes."

Would the butterflies in my stomach ever go away? I swallowed. There was something nice about imagining him stepping out of SMK and catching a taxi right to my apartment.

"Do the others know you're here?" I asked, not sure why I wanted to know that.

"Mm. Tai does."

The soup was starting to simmer and bubble. Wooyeong picked up the wooden spoon and gave it a stir. There was that strange, unreadable expression on his face again.

I picked up the bottle of rice wine and leftover, un-chopped vegetables and started to put them back in his bag.

"What are you doing?" he asked. "Those are for you."

"Me? Why?"

"What am I going to do with that food? I'll just buy more. But you have a hurt ankle. It might help you to have something more around. Your refrigerator isn't very stocked yet."

My face burned. He'd noticed – but he'd also bought all that before he'd even stepped into my apartment. It didn't matter what my fridge looked like, since he'd pre-planned it. I had no idea what to think of that.

"Thanks," I muttered.

He didn't respond, but picked up the cutting board with the sliced vegetables and slid them into the boiling soup with one hand.

We were quiet the rest of the time. It was comforting to have him so close to me. I felt the ache to lean forward and wrap my arms around him. With his proximity, and the warmth of the stove, I felt like I could never leave.

A tear slid down my cheek.

I turned away a little, hoping to discreetly wipe it away, but he noticed the movement. He froze mid-cut into a green onion, dark eyes widening. "What's wrong?"

I shook my head, unable to speak. My shoulders started to shake.

He let out a breath, reaching out a hand and resting it lightly on my shoulder.

I couldn't stop crying. "Is this – is this the last time I'll get to see you?"

Wooyeong was quiet for a moment.

"Is that why you're crying?" he asked finally.

I nodded.

"Then don't cry. It's okay. I came here, didn't I? Couldn't I do it again? I might just have to be more careful, is all."

The weight of his hand was still on my shoulder. I inhaled a shaky breath, my eyes closed, trying to calm myself. I wanted with everything I had to believe him. I *should* believe him. He had never lied to me.

My breaths became steadier, and I opened my eyes again, looking into his face. "Okay," I said.

Wooyeong helped me over to the table, pulling out a chair. I sat down, elevating my ankle by propping it up on the chair next to me.

Then he brought the wooden cutting board to the table, set it in the center, and put the soup pot on top of it. I leaned over it, inhaling the umami-rich, slightly spicy scent. It was wonderful – a bubbling stock with cooked vegetables, beef and cubed tofu, sprinkled lovingly with green onions.

"This looks like it should be in a picture," I said, wrapping my arms around myself. The air was colder away from the stove. "It's beautiful, Wooyeong."

"Where are the bowls?" he called, opening up random drawers until he found one with spoons.

"Top left. And there's a ladle in the drawer next to you."

He came back to the table with a smile on his face. He ladled some soup into one of the bowls he had brought, taking care to get some of everything.

"Here you go," he said, setting it in front of me.

I picked up my spoon and dipped it in, getting some of the broth and a piece of beef and radish. Wooyeong watched me expectantly as I blew on it, then put it in my mouth.

It was hot and rich and savory, with a smoothness and a mild spice. It had just the right amount of salt and was almost nutty. The beef was flavorful and tender, and I didn't know how radishes were supposed to be cooked, but it was delicious.

It spread warmth down my throat as I swallowed. It felt the way chicken soup did when you were sick – comforting, nourishing, and feeding more than just your stomach.

I let out a sigh of bliss, feeling the warmth tingle up my arms. "Korean winters aren't so bad with this."

"You like it?"

"Of course! It's wonderful."

He smiled as he ladled some into his own bowl. "I thought you might. It's doenjang jjigae – soybean paste stew. Nothing is better when you're hurt or sick."

I slurped up some more, sighing in contentment. We ate in silence for a few minutes, with me deep in thought. If he hadn't come, I would've been alone.

I was so grateful for his presence here. Just him being across from me was vastly comforting.

"You're a good cook," I said. "Do you think you might've worked in a restaurant... if you hadn't become a K-pop star?"

Wooyeong stilled. For a second I thought I'd said the wrong thing – I'd never mentioned his status so directly before. But then he sighed and leaned back in his chair.

"I don't know," he said, voice low. "Maybe, since I've always loved food. But it's hard to imagine. My life has undergone extreme change since we debuted."

"Before..." My voice faltered. "Before you debuted, did you ever date anyone?"

Wooyeong looked at me for a long moment. I could feel a blush creeping up my cheeks.

"No," he said, looking away and picking up the ladle.

"Why not?" My voice was breathy.

Wooyeong stirred the soup slowly.

"No one liked me before I became an idol," he said finally. "They didn't care. I was a nobody."

His voice was edgy, laced with bitterness while it was still calm.

"I bet most girls in my class didn't even remember my name. And then I became a trainee. Hardly anyone knew that I had." He paused. "I debuted eventually. The fan mail started washing in. SMK has a whole mail bin for Ambition due to how many pounds of it we get. I had so many love letters I couldn't even open them all. I read some at first – 'Wooyeong, you're so handsome'. 'Wooyeong, I love you, I want to kiss you.' 'Wooyeong, marry me.'" He let out a short, breathy laugh. "I stopped reading those after I started getting ones from the girls in my class. Funny how they didn't care before."

He set down the ladle abruptly, propping his elbow up on the table, his eyes glazed over.

"I don't know," he said quietly, almost to himself. "I was a nobody all my life. Isn't that proof that everyone just likes me because I'm a K-pop idol?"

I was silent for a few moments. This... this is what he thought? I wanted to blurt out all the things I liked about him, all the things that would stay the same whether he quit Ambition or not, but my own fear stopped me. Fear of him seeing what I really thought of him. Fear of rejection. Because, truly, why would he like *me* when he could have anyone he wanted? And besides, I was already a fan when I met him. He probably thought that I was one of those people who only liked him because of his fame....

"I... think there's a lot of things about you people like," I said, not meeting his eyes. "The staff and management don't care who's famous and who's not, right? They're not impressed by it. They like you, don't they? And Tai and Dyeong and Chin-hyuk."

"Mm." He played with his spoon, turning it over and over in his fingers.

I like you, I wanted to say. But I couldn't.

He sighed. "I shouldn't have said anything. I'm sorry."

"Because I was a fan when I met you?" I asked quietly.

Wooyeong looked slightly startled, slightly frozen, like I'd caught him in something. But then he looked away. "No."

"You don't have to lie. That's okay. I know it's true." I nodded, trying not to show my hurt. "It only makes sense." *You can't trust me.*

"No," he said firmer, his hand seizing mine. I looked down at it in shock, then up at his face. "Madison, it's not... not like that. We're friends. *Real* friends." His breath seemed to catch.

His gaze slowly followed mine to our hands and he quickly released it, seeming to realize what he'd done.

"Don't think like that," he muttered. "I don't want another thing to be ruined by my career."

I felt instant regret slam me. "You're right. I'm sorry. I was being..."

"Honest," he finished for me quietly. There was a pause.

I swallowed. "If... if we're real friends... you should be able to tell me stuff like that."

Wooyeong nodded, slowly.

"So don't apologize," I continued, not meeting his eyes. "It's fine."

He let out a little sniffing noise that I realized was a small half-laugh. I looked at him, surprised. "Even when I'm trying to support *you,* you're supporting *me.*"

I smiled. "Not nearly as much as you've helped me."

Wooyeong sighed, pushing up his glasses. "I'm glad you're feeling better."

I stirred my warm soup. "This helps."

우영
WOOYEONG
16

It was late afternoon in the studio. We were having a recording session for our next comeback. I'd sung my parts into the mic over and over, but the supervisor was still looking for the perfect sound. I was used to it. It was like this for all of us – this was what music was.

We were currently taking a short break. I took a swig from my water bottle, trying to soothe my vocal cords, while Chin-hyuk held his in his hands beside me. His lavender hair was pushed off his forehead by a bandana. Manager Pak had thought the look suited him rather well, and was busy calling the stylist to recommend it for the next music video, if it fit nicely with the mood and overall aesthetic.

Dyeong and Tai were in the bathroom, and we were going to resume recording as soon as they came back, especially since we had some unison parts that sounded better if we did it at the same time rather than record our voices separately and layer them.

I scrolled listlessly through my phone, not really seeing anything that was going past. I couldn't get yesterday out of my head. The tears on her cheeks as she looked into my face, her wide, beautiful eyes.

I had almost kissed her then. I had almost... but I hadn't. I wasn't sure if I regretted that or if I was glad for it.

We were friends. I'd said so, *she'd* said so. Even though I loved her.

Just friends. Just friends. Don't ruin it.

But I couldn't get her expression out of my thoughts. She had been crying because she was afraid she wouldn't be able to see me again. And then, the way she'd looked at me...

I passed a hand over my face.

Even if I got what I wanted – Madison feeling the same way about me that I did about her – how could I know how it started? If she hadn't been an Ambition fan, hadn't already seen my face everywhere, would she have found me attractive in the first place? Would she have liked my personality? Or was it just because I was an idol that this all started?

That was how anyone had ever liked me. Just because I was a K-pop idol. How could I believe that this would be different? Was it just wishful thinking on my part simply because I wanted it to be true *so badly?*

I hadn't lied to her yesterday when I said we were real friends. We were. I never wanted to lose her, no matter what happened. She was a great friend to me. The only thing that had complicated things... was me falling for her.

Unhappiness was crushing my chest like a weight. Regret came, stronger than ever before, as I wished, once again, that I could be normal. If I wasn't an idol I wouldn't have to think about any of this. I could love anyone I wanted and they would love me, and I wouldn't have to second-guess their motives or the reason they liked me in the first place.

My hand clenched into a fist on my leg. I couldn't help myself. I couldn't stop the way I cared about her so much. More than I'd ever cared about anyone.

Yesterday I'd gone shopping in the morning and waited all day until work was over so I could go and cook for her. *All day.* That was what happened when I followed my feelings, what I wanted to do, my instinct.

But then the old fears took over. Just because I ignored them, did that mean they weren't true?

I sighed.

"You seem like you're going through some trouble," Chin-hyuk noted quietly.

I raised my head, my hand with my phone falling back in my lap. He was tracing the letters on his water bottle, not looking at me.

"You've been sighing all day," he said. "You have this expression on your face – sometimes heartbroken, sometimes wistful, and sometimes you smile for no reason."

"Mm." I leaned back against the leather seat, taking a deep breath.

"Is it Madison?"

My teeth bit down on the side of my lip. I glanced at him. He was studying me now, his light brown eyes searching mine.

My heart swelled with gratitude toward him. No matter what happened, Chin-hyuk would always be there for us. I knew I could trust him with whatever I wanted to say. His inquiries came out of concern – always wanting to help us, to make us feel better, to check that we were doing okay.

"Yes," I said. "I... we... had very clear boundaries from the beginning. Far-away. Just friends. We're still like that. But..."

It took courage to say what I was going to say next.

"I love her."

He nodded, slowly, then sucked in a breath. "I thought so."

"I don't know if she feels the same way about me," I continued quietly, "but if she does, I'm not sure what I would feel about that either."

"You're afraid she only started liking you because you were an idol?"

"Yes."

He smiled. "So she liked you before. She likes you a lot more now, right?"

"Maybe."

Chin-hyuk glanced at the door. "Just don't let Dyeong get a word of this. You know he'll be angry. And to be honest, I can understand why."

"But you're not," I said.

He smiled. "I know that our heads often get overruled by our hearts. Even the most logical of us can't help how we feel. But you're being careful. Idols... we still have to be people. If you be only Ambition Wooyeong instead of Wooyeong, you will destroy yourself."

I nodded pensively. Just then Dyeong came through the door, laughing and saying something to Tai behind him.

"Ready to resume?" said the recording manager. "Let's try the chorus."

Chin-hyuk and I stood up.

The four of us took our respective places around the mics, slipping on the headphones. The beat started playing with the instrumental backtrack, addictive and fresh together. Dyeong was already nodding, his eyes squeezed shut. My eyes were open, but my head tilted to the side as we all sang the chorus – *"So baby, tell me, should I hold my breath..."*

Our voices blended together, delicious like candy with the backtrack – Tai's harmony, vibrating higher than lower, Chin-hyuk's main melody in his distinctive voice, me and Dyeong joining in with a mix of main and harmony. The overall sound mixed together in the smoothest way.

The manager gave us the thumbs-up through the recording glass. Tai slipped off his headphones and smiled from ear to ear. "Aim will love this!"

"*I* love this," added Dyeong with a laugh.

"Just imagine it with my high notes and Dyeong's rap layered over it for the bridge," said Chin-hyuk, his grin mirroring everyone else's. "That's going to be *fire.*"

We got back into position to try again. I shut my eyes this time. I wanted to do my best for Aim – to make them happy. They would listen to this song over and over and over, and I wanted to make sure that each time was just as thrilling as the first.

People said that this music has saved their lives – when they're depressed or even thinking about harming themselves, Ambition was there. The songs gave them hope that there was still happiness and love in the world, and they would find it. I believed it. I knew what songs could do.

So I wanted to give this my best shot. Like I always did. For them. If it wasn't for Aim, we would be nothing. I was grateful to them for allowing me to achieve my life's dream, even if sometimes it had downsides. Everything did – nothing was perfect.

I sang extra-hard as I thought of the faces of all the people I'd seen at the last concert. As I thought of fans listening at home, like Madison did for six years without ever seeing us in person. I sang for them.

Chin-hyuk, Tai, Dyeong and I did it again as the backtrack started up again. When we'd finished, the sound coach came in.

"Wow," he said. "Wooyeong, can you do that again? That inflection on the last 'tell me'."

"Yeah, okay," I said, wiping some sweat off my neck. "I can do that. I'll try my best."

"So *serious,*" Dyeong said, punching me in the arm. I grinned at him. I loved Dyeong to death. He was my brother.

Even if I had to keep secrets from him.

I ignored the sinking sensation in my stomach, like a stone.

Forgive me, I thought, feeling pain as I watched him smile and say something to Chin-hyuk.

"And, Chin-hyuk, maybe try to be a little more buoyant. Your voice is the most distinctive, like the brand of Ambition. We really need to hear that."

"Yes sir!" said Chin-hyuk, taking a deep breath and adjusting his headphones. "Distinctive *energy.* Let's try this again."

The glass door to the recording room closed again. We watched everyone take their places at the recording board, and then the beat started.

We tried it again.

"Everyone else is spot-on," the manager said. "But even though you did the inflection on the end, you sounded sad, Wooyeong. We're not doing that. It should give a mood of caring and happy, with attractive possessiveness thrown in. The good-boy bad-boy mix."

I nodded, my eyes cast down. We'd been through this a million times before. "I apologize. I'll try harder."

We tried it yet another time. I focused hard on singing for the fans, for my brothers, just like I'd always done, taking care to do the inflection on 'tell me' that the manager wanted.

"I think that's it!" he said, clapping his hands once we'd finished. "You guys are doing great. If you can repeat that five more times, we'll be great."

"Okay," we said in unison. The manager gave us another thumbs-up. He'd been our supervisor for six months now, and was used to us saying things at the same time, but he did smile slightly whenever it happened.

"You guys hang around each other too much," Manager Pak liked to tease us. *"You're going to go crazy one day. You better watch it."*

We started again. Chin-hyuk was passionate about singing the entire chorus instead of just singing it once and playing the same recording over and over, so that it sounded authentic instead of canned. We all agreed on that.

In the breaks in between singing, I couldn't help pulling out my phone to check if there were any texts from Madison. There were none.

I wondered what she was doing right now. She was probably still at work – or did she have the day off?

Did she know I was thinking about her? Did she wonder what I was doing, too?

After fighting with myself for a few minutes, I opened our text chat. I stared at it, then decided.

How's your ankle? I typed, then blew out a breath and clicked Send before I could change my mind, ignoring the nervousness in my stomach.

Two minutes passed, then five. She didn't answer. I didn't know how to handle my disappointment.

We resumed recording again. She was probably just busy.

매디슨
MADISON
17

Jeongsook would not stop talking as she drove me home from work in the evening.

She talked about the weather, the latest scandals with actresses, corporate news, and everything in between. I listened, staring out the window at the gray sky as she drove.

"And Valentine's Day is two days from now!" she said enthusiastically. "I'm going to get my boyfriend something special."

I turned to her in surprise as the light turned red and she braked, all the traffic around us slowing. "What? Valentine's Day? Already?"

Jeongsook nodded, her perfect hair bouncing up and down. "Yep, of course! You should've noticed all the advertising. Everything's practically colored pink and red now in the stores, and the online ads are terrible."

"Well, I haven't been out much," I said numbly. "But it doesn't feel like it's close to Valentine's Day already."

Jeongsook swiveled her head to look at me. "You know this is the day we give gifts to the men, right? It's the perfect way to solve your heartbreak problem. You look like you're doing better, by the way. How are you so *composed?* I'm impressed."

"I think I probably don't have a reason to be heartbroken anymore," I said. "That's why. Oh, and I used your moisture pack last night. I think it helped a lot."

"I thought your skin looked better," Jeongsook said in satisfaction. "So, care to tell me all about it?"

"Jeongsook, the light's green."

She gave a little yelp and punched the gas. "Oh my gosh. Sorry about that."

My phone in my bag went *ping!*

I looked at Jeongsook, then decided that I couldn't pull it out and check it without her asking questions. If it was a text from Wooyeong – which made me burn with curiosity – there wouldn't be a way for me to explain that away easily. So I kept it in my bag.

"Valentine's Day," I repeated softly to myself. Why did it sound like an impending execution date and exciting all at once?

"Jeongsook, in Korea isn't Valentine's Day where the girls give stuff to the guys?" I asked her suddenly.

She nodded. "Uh, that's what I just said. We give gifts to the men. Like chocolate. And White Day, a month from now, is where men give things to *us*."

So I wouldn't be getting anything from Wooyeong in two days. It was all up to me whether I wanted to give him something or not – but no, that was impossible. I shouldn't. Why the heck would he like me back when he could have someone far prettier, far smarter and far more talented than I was?

"Is it different in America?"

"Yeah, Valentine's Day is the only romantic day. That's it. Just one. And it's up to the girls *and* the guys."

Jeongsook laughed. "Oh my gosh. I can just imagine the chaos. Both people wanting the other to just give them a gift to confess! How would that even *work?* If they're shy they'll just wait for the other person every Valentine's Day and no one does anything!"

"Pretty much," I said.

"I mean, can you *imagine?* What if one person gives a gift and the other doesn't? How awkward would that be? That makes *no* sense. Taking turns on Valentine's Day and White Day is way better."

I tried not to be offended at this slight on my home culture, but I could admit she had a point. "So..." I said. "What happens if a guy likes a girl and she doesn't give him chocolate on Valentine's Day?"

"Then he downs five bottles of soju –"

"Jeongsook! I'm serious."

"So was I! Anyway, he'll be disappointed for sure. Haven't *you* ever missed a romantic confession you were hoping for on your American Valentine's Day?"

"I guess," I sighed.

Jeongsook switched lanes, biting her lip in concentration and moving her head to see. Then she glanced at me. "Oh my gosh, you *are* in romantic trouble, aren't you?"

I figured it was clear by the pained expression on my face. Jeongsook tut-tutted. "Good luck out there," she said.

우영
WOOYEONG
18

Many things were within walking distance of the SMK Entertainment building, but my friend Du Yohan was not one of them. It was my turn to catch the train to go to a coffee shop closer to where he lived in Seoul.

He was already there, leaning against the outside of the building with a shock of teal-blue hair – obviously professionally done with just the right amount of ruffle. But he looked so leisurely and casual, with his arms crossed over his chest to keep in the warmth, that I couldn't help a burst of happiness in my chest. No one but Yohan would look so casual in a daring bright orange puffer jacket. Everything about him positively screamed *idol* today; but people were only glancing at him, seeming to have no idea that he was actually the persona known as ONEDAN. I almost laughed as I walked up to him among the many other customers.

"Yohan," I greeted him in relief, feeling a smile on my lips.

"Wooyeong. It's great to see you." He cuffed me lightly on the arm. "Should we go inside?"

We found a tiny table shoved up in the corner of the room. The shop was bustling with people, but it made me feel safer instead of exposed. More people sometimes meant more anonymity. Who would notice me in this crowd?

By unspoken consent, I took the chair with my back to the room and he took the chair facing it. We couldn't be a sharper contrast – Yohan with his striking teal-blue hair and eyebrows, sitting comfortably in the shop with his eyes freely roaming, and then me, with my baseball cap pulled low over my face, my black hoodie and my leaning-forward posture.

He had just debuted as a soloist after the disbandment of his old group. K1L just hadn't caught any traction. They'd had a small, dedicated fan base, but it wasn't enough. Their disbandment had hit Yohan hard, but here he was, debuting again as a soloist.

The last time I'd talked to him had been two weeks ago on the phone, right after the promo shoots of his latest music video.

Yohan stirred his coffee slowly with a straw, lost in thought. "The new song – I composed and produced it myself, and I can vouch for it. It's really, really good. But it's not getting enough views."

"I listened to it," I said. "It's catchy. Dynamite, even. It should go viral."

He gave me a wry smile. "The world doesn't function on 'should'."

We both knew how hard the industry was. Every day there were perfectly deserving groups, ones who worked as hard or harder than everyone else, fading out. Yohan's group K1L had been one of them. They were talented dancers and vocalists, good-looking, had great stage presence and a decent budget. And yet....

It reminded me of how incredibly lucky Ambition was to have made it this far.

How much we had to lose.

How much /had to lose, for not only myself but also my soul brothers, by being seen together with Madison again.

Everything we had could just float away, destroyed, just like with K1L...

Disbandment had hit Yohan hard. He'd been bitter, at first. But unlike me, he hadn't let experience jade him. He cherished his fans now more than ever, laughed often, and enjoyed being alive. Even allowed himself to dream again.

"Being a soloist is a shock," Yohan said, sipping his drink. "In a lot of ways it's more free. I don't have a dorm at the agency but I have my own apartment. The music, the lyrics, the aesthetic – it's focused around me only, so I have a lot more control. When the stylist from K1L told us we were going to wear emerald velvet suits, we did so. Now, they're asking me – 'what do you want the mood for this to be? The aesthetic? Do you like this costume?'"

"I guess you're better than anyone else about deciding who you want to be."

Yohan smiled. "I still have a team of people in charge of all of it. But I like them. We get along well."

"Even your backup dancers?"

"All my friends."

I whistled. "Well, it's almost impossible not to like you. You're cheery, for one thing."

He laughed. "Thanks."

I stirred my coffee, staring down at it. "I see you're not afraid of someone recognizing you."

Yohan ruffled his teal-blue hair. "It doesn't matter that I *look* like an idol, because no one can figure out *which* one I am. You know how small K1L was. Well, my career as ONEDAN is even smaller. When I run into a fan, I'm genuinely happy to see them. It's like 'Wow! Someone has actually listened to my songs!'"

I felt a pang of jealously. I knew what he was talking about, but I hadn't experienced it for a long time. Ambition was too popular now. Talking with fans, hugging them, and taking pictures were some of my fondest memories. Just seeing the smiles that blazed across their faces because they saw you was like precious gold.

But then we got more and more famous, and we learned to be afraid of people recognizing us instead of thrilled. To sit in the corners of rooms like I was doing now. To hide our faces behind masks, hats, and sunglasses.

Ambition had thousands of great fans. But there were also others who would completely disrespect us, our privacy, or act like lunatics. It was those people, in greater and greater numbers, that we were avoiding. Just last week I heard that a 'fan' shoved a member of Tr3sure and nearly injured him.

"Enjoy it while you can," I said. "If you're going to become more popular, expect that to go away. You haven't experienced the sadness yet of knowing you can't even greet a crowd because of the fear that's holding you back. It's a real heartache."

"Despite my dreams, there's something to be said for staying small," Yohan agreed. "There's a golden spot where you can do what you love and keep loving it. We've seen too many stars go big and then feel unhappy or even commit suicide. That's not going to be me."

I nodded pensively. "It helps that you have Nari to support you."

Nari was Yohan's girlfriend. They'd met in high school and were still in love, though they kept their relationship secret because of Yohan's job – Yohan confided to me that when they went to church on Sundays, they even made sure to sit in different rows. Their relationship had survived through his idol training, his debut and disbandment in K1L, and now his career as ONEDAN. They were closer than close.

"That's true. Nari is the light of my life, and I know I can trust her. She's seen the real, messy, gritty, pathetic version of me." He laughed. "If I'd met her after I debuted, it might have been harder. But I guess you know all too well..."

"I can't trust anyone," I said, bringing my coffee cup to my lips and then setting it down again as I realized I didn't want it. "I guess that makes it easier, to stay single... Dyeong would be happy about that. He's watched too many dating scandals wreck groups, and thinks none of us should fall in love until we're about thirty."

Yohan laughed. "Good luck. He can't control *that*."

"Exactly," I said darkly, sipping my coffee.

Yohan's teal-blue eyebrows shot up. "Pardon me, sir? Is there something you want to tell me?"

I made a noncommittal gesture, taking another swig of coffee to buy me some time, alarmed that I'd just betrayed myself.

"Don't tell me you're falling in love!" Yohan said, a big grin on his face.

"We're friends," I said, my tongue burned. "But every time I think about us being more, the old fears return. That anyone who dates me will only like me because I'm famous, or will only want to suck off it to make themselves feel important, or will only like the *idol* version of me and not the everyday me..."

"Well, who is she? Does she really know who you are?"

I didn't break eye contact. "She's a fan," I said flatly.

For a second Yohan looked shocked. "Yikes," he said, letting out a long breath and leaning back. "That *does* complicate things, doesn't it? But it's not impossible. If she likes you, and you like her, and you're friends to start out with –"

I was suddenly reminded that if it wasn't for Yohan, I wouldn't even be thinking about Madison. The restaurant where we'd met by chance – it was the one that Yohan had been urging me to try for a while, gushing about how fresh and tasty the food was. I wasn't sure if now was the time to mention it.

"She's a good friend," I said. "She's thoughtful, kind, loyal –"

"Then you already know who she is, don't you?"

"It won't stop the old fears. Would she have wanted to be even friends if I hadn't been one of her favorite idols?"

Yohan leaned his head on his hand. "You'll never get the answer to that."

"I know," I said in a low voice. "I still don't even know who her bias was."

We sat there in silence for a few minutes, watching the hustle and bustle of the busy coffee shop.

"And – it's clear she likes you, then?" Yohan said.

I shook my head slowly.

~{★ 129 ♥}~

He clapped his hands, startling me. "Unrequited affection? Gosh, Wooyeong, if she doesn't want you in the first place then why are you worried about the whole famous thing?"

I groaned. "I'm a mess. Let's not talk about this. Let's talk about what we were on before. That dynamite new song of yours. You never told me how you came up with it."

"Well, I composed it and wrote it myself," said Yohan cheerily. "That's another thing some other artists are missing – freedom to express art as they want. I know you guys write a lot of your own songs..."

"Tai does it, mostly," I said, cracking a smile. "I'm terrible. Dyeong's pretty good though."

"He's an all-rounder," Yohan agreed. "So I'm writing everything, coming up with all the music. My manager was thinking about having me sing a song written by a known hitmaker but I'm just not feeling it. I told him I'll make my own hits."

"That new dynamite song already sounds like one," I said. I secretly filed away a mental reminder to play it during a VLive as part of our song playlists.

We talked about our careers for the next long hour, about our personal lives, about anything and everything just like we'd always done as best friends. But we didn't talk more about Madison.

After a long time Yohan said he had an appointment he needed to catch. We parted ways, cheerfully, Yohan asking me to drop by his apartment sometime so we could hang out and watch TV and eat together. I agreed. His happy face was fixed in my mind as I rode the train home.

My phone buzzed in the back pocket of my jeans. I slipped it out, looked at the screen, and smiled. It'd been a full two days since I'd seen Madison, but she'd responded to my text yesterday late at night. There wasn't much back-and-forth conversation. It was oddly formal, polite. But at least she'd responded. That was all I could ask for.

매디슨
MADISON
19

Tomorrow was February 14, Valentine's Day – Korean Valentine's Day, where the girls gave gifts to the guys.

That was why I felt like it was now or never. I could practically feel the axe at my neck. I couldn't tell if all the other women here in the store with boxes of chocolate in their hands felt the same, or if they were actually excited.

I had a plastic bag filled with apples on my arm; the original reason I'd gone shopping, or maybe that was just a weak excuse so I'd have the opportunity to look at Valentine's Day gifts.

If I was going to buy Wooyeong something, it would have to be today, if it was going to arrive on time at SMK Entertainment tomorrow. There was no way I was going to ever deliver anything in *person*. Just the thought made me want to run away.

I blew out a breath as I stared down the display of chocolate. The packages were covered in pink, white and red, matching the balloons floating overheard. There were ones with ruffles, hearts, and bouncy cheerful script. *Show him you care!* said an adorable illustrated butterfly with the help of a speech bubble.

I stuffed my hands in the pockets of my parka, nervous. Should I...?

Cheerful music played over the speakers, interrupted by the occasional ad where the announcers sounded like they were ecstatic about whatever they were selling. A girl moved past me with a huge smile on her face, clutching a big heart-shaped box of cherry chocolates to her sweater.

I shuffled to the side to get out of her way, almost bumping into a gray-haired woman behind me who was perusing the more serious-looking chocolates decorated with less bubblegum pink and more dark brown.

I bit my lip, stretching my hand out in front of me and picking up a red rectangular box gingerly. It felt light, and the plastic wrap was slippery. I turned it over in my fingers. On the back, it showed a picture of all the heart-shaped chocolates inside with a smaller pink heart in white chocolate on top.

I swallowed, taking a deep breath. I imagined him holding it in his hands. I couldn't imagine his face or expression.

Would it be happiness or pity?

I shoved it back on the shelf like it'd given me an electric shock. I shivered, rubbing my hands up and down my arms. No way. There's no way I was doing it. Just imagining the look of confusion and sympathy and heck, maybe even annoyance on his face was giving me hives.

"I swear," I muttered to myself.

But my irritation was giving way to sadness. What was I thinking? Was I delusional? He would never like me. Those comments online were right. I didn't deserve him. He could do much better than me. Maybe at the very least he could find someone who was actually pretty.

Literally thousands of girls had crushes on Wooyeong. I wasn't any different. I was just one of his many fans, and not one of the most interesting ones either. Of course we were just friends, and would stay that way. I should be appreciative for even that – it was too good to be true already.

This place was starting to be clogged with people. It was hard to move. I had a group of three girls in front of me, giggling with each other, and a bunch of people behind and to the side of me. One person in particular caught my eye. Her black hair was cut short in a cute bob and she was a few years younger than me. She was touching a box of chocolates with a wistful expression on her face.

An older woman, probably her mother, touched her lightly on the shoulder. "He'll love it, Sohyun," she said. "You've been just friends for so long, I'll be so happy to see you two finally together!"

The girl, Sohyun, smiled wider, blushing.

I watched them, fascinated and frozen, until they moved on. Their heads were no longer visible in the crowd anymore.

I looked down at the chocolate display in front of me.

Would it be so bad to just give it to him anyway?

I picked up a box of chocolates again, staring at it. Maybe I should just buy it. No harm done if I gave it to him, right? I wasn't brave enough to confess to his face. There was always the smallest chance that he would like me back. Really small, but not impossible.

Wooyeong had come to cook for me when I'd hurt my ankle. He cared about me... he had taken care of me. Just thinking about it still gave me butterflies.

I cursed myself. Yeah, he'd come because he was a good guy, not because he *liked* me. What an *idiot* I was. This was impossible. So I'd give him the chocolates, and then what?

Did I really want to suffer from the disappointment of both him and me, the awkwardness between us, his pity, even the end of our friendship? Of course not. I couldn't decide if I was being rational or a coward. I took a deep breath to calm the anxiety tight in my chest, stretching out my hand to put the box back.

"Excuse me," said a deep male voice behind me.

I gasped and dropped the box. It clattered to the floor as I whirled around, coming face-to-face with...

A random guy trying to get past me.

I was just in the way. I moved aside, my heart still racing, bending down to pick the box up on the checkered linoleum floor. When I straightened up, he was walking away with his back to me. He was too tall to be Wooyeong, with completely different features. Even his clothes were different, and his voice sounded nothing like any of the Ambition members.

Gosh. For a second there I'd really thought it was him behind me. I pressed a hand to my pounding heart, clutching the box to my parka. I was definitely paranoid.

If I gave it to Wooyeong... would he be surprised, with no idea that I'd been crushing on him? Sympathetic? Okay with it? Or maybe even... open to the idea of us as a couple?

I held out the box, looked at it, and then made my decision.

우영
WOOYEONG
20

The sidewalk was icy and the sky was dark, but I could see my breath illuminated in the bright light coming from the buildings. I kept my hands in my pockets, moving quietly back to SMK. It would be dawn soon and I didn't want to be spotted by anyone.

A few cars flew past on the road, throwing me in the glare from their headlights and lighting up my face. But I didn't flinch like I normally did.

I couldn't sleep last night for some reason. I'd woken up at four and hadn't been able to go back to bed. So I'd gotten dressed, quietly so I wouldn't wake the others, and headed out. That shift between late night and early morning was the perfect time to go out – when there were considerably less people, and those that were present were mostly too tired, too busy or too drunk to notice me.

I'd just gone for a walk through the city. Though it was freezing cold, I'd enjoyed having my hood thrown back and my scarf dangling off my shoulders as I strode, my face completely exposed.

It felt... free.

Even though my eyes stung and my ears ached from the frigid air, every gust of wind was both painful and exhilarating.

This was the only time where I could be myself, without hiding. It was thrilling to be normal again. To just escape. To not duck every time a car went by just in case they recognized my face in the illumination from the headlights, or turn my head away when someone passed by like I was a wanted criminal.

I strode briskly down the sidewalk, for once feeling like I had nothing to hide, my head completely revealed.

Even though the sky was pitch-black, the ground was still lit up in a pastel white-blue light from the windows of the city buildings around me. It was beautiful. Every once in a while I would see the slick shine of ice patches on the pale sidewalk and I stepped around them, unhappily reminded of sprained ankles.

SMK loomed up ahead, a clean white against the black sky. Most of the windows were dark, especially on the higher-up levels that were the dorms. My eyes scanned the top windows on the right, looking for ours. Still dark, of course. There was no way Tai, Dyeong or Chin-hyuk were up this early. It was what – five in the morning, six? I'd been out walking through the city for a while, but it was in the middle of February. The sun wouldn't start to rise for another hour at least.

The glass automatic doors of SMK opened for me as soon as I walked up to them, blasting me with hot air that made my cold face tingle. I nodded to the security guard as I went to the elevator, and he nodded back. One of his many tasks was making sure that when I went out at night, I came back.

I punched in our floor number, gingerly touching the tips of my ears and wincing. Freedom came at a cost, I suppose. It'd been worth it just to feel the wind through my messy hair.

The elevator dinged cheerfully as the doors opened on my floor. The hallways were black, except for a small dim light that was always on through the glass doors of the dance studios. I walked quietly, trying not to wake anyone up, using my phone light to guide me.

Eventually Number 10 came. I turned off my phone light and slipped it in my coat pocket, knowing it would wake up Chin-hyuk instantly. I also slipped off my shoes and held them in one hand as I slowly turned the door handle with a faint click.

I slipped inside and very slowly, very carefully, closed it behind me. I breathed through my mouth silently. I'd done this whole routine before – I could easily make it to our dorm room and back into bed in the pitch-black, as long as I was mindful. It was rare that one of them woke up. My socked feet were quiet on the floor as I took one step forward, then a few more, then another –

I just managed to silence the colossal yell that came to my throat as I toppled over. Something – some*things* – went everywhere with a loud noise as my body slammed into them, making peculiar crunching noises.

I swore, louder than I had intended. I heard voices in the bedroom and inwardly groaned as the light under the door clicked on. Whatever I'd tripped and then fell on had made a huge noise. It was impossible not to sleep through *that.*

Sharp corners were digging into my back and legs. "What the *heck?*" I hissed, sitting up. I was crushing whatever it was underneath me. I crawled away, the objects – they felt like boxes – sliding underneath me and probably scattering wider across the floor.

There was a thump and louder voices and then the bedroom door swung open, revealing Chin-hyuk with his cell phone in his hand as he turned on the flashlight mode.

"What the *heck?*" he said, sounding groggy as it clicked on, shining bright light in my eyes. I held up my hand to block it.

"Exactly," I muttered, feeling like a burglar who'd just been discovered. I looked down at what I was sitting on, gleaming in Chin-hyuk's phone flashlight, and then let out a loud groan. "Oh no. It's Valentine's Day, isn't it?"

Tai was right behind him. He took one look at me and then started laughing.

I stood up, throwing my arms out for balance as I walked off the pile, the boxes slipping and moving underneath me. I nearly fell again but caught myself.

Dyeong had found the light switch and clicked it on, flooding the room with yellow light. Tai and Chin-hyuk blinked several times.

"You tried to sneak back in, didn't you?" Tai exclaimed. I pretended to hit him and he ducked, but didn't stop his raucous laughter.

I picked up my shoes from where they'd fallen when I'd tripped, then looked back at the doorway. Just a few feet from it, in the start of our living room, was a *mountain* of chocolate. Valentine's Day chocolate, in pink, red, white, and brown boxes, each wrapped in cellophane.

"Did you try to dive like it was a leaf pile?" Chin-hyuk asked, grinning.

"Where did *that* come from?"

"Staff delivered it late last night," Dyeong said. "You were asleep. They tried to put it out of the path of the doorway. And it was, since you snuck out okay. Why would you walk there on the way back in?"

"There's a wall so I always know where I... never mind. Who's that for?"

"All of us. They'll probably have enough chocolate to fill our entire living room when they drop off the next batch today."

"Mm." I nodded, looking at the mountain of chocolate boxes, some of them squished because of me. Last year we'd read the notes, helped ourselves, and then distributed the rest to the staff. It was a side benefit of their jobs.

My pulse quickened. The fact that it was Valentine's Day seemed all the more real now. The day when girls gave chocolate to the guys they liked.

Was something from Madison in there?

"You guys should go back to sleep," I said, really hoping they would. "Sorry about that."

Dyeong didn't need telling twice. He went back to the bedroom, closing the door. But Tai and Chin-hyuk didn't have the ability to go to sleep instantly.

"It's morning, even if it's black outside," Chin-hyuk yawned. "I should start the day." He walked into the kitchen, clicking on the light and flipping switches on the coffee maker.

Tai wasn't so energetic. He collapsed on the sofa, curled up, and started watching videos on his tablet.

I looked between the two of them. Chin-hyuk was busy, and Tai might as well be a puffy-faced, pajama-clad zombie for all he moved. So I sat on the floor, cross-legged with my scarf still dangling around my neck, and picked up the first box of chocolate.

To Tai, my adorable baby, I love you -Hyojoo

I set it aside and moved on to the next ones. *To Ambition from Park Sangmi. Dyeong, I am in love with you, please marry me. For Chin-hyuk, my handsome oppa. Wooyeong, you are hotter than the sun, from Jung Hanna.*

It was split pretty evenly between me, Chin-hyuk, Tai, and in general "To Ambition", but Dyeong had the most. As soon as I saw his name I tossed it behind me. He could look through them later. I didn't care about anyone else's – nor had I ever cared so much about mine before.

My heartbeat started pounding whenever I saw my name, but sank when it didn't have the words I wanted to see.

I put those aside in a stack. I appreciated the fan's love, knowing I might even be the first big crush of some younger girls. I wish I could acknowledge all of them, give someone a really great memory of a personal letter from their idol, but I knew I couldn't possibly write to everyone. And then other people would feel left out and wonder what was wrong with them. I'd gone through all of this before for the past Valentine's Days.

But this time, my pulse was racing and I felt... nervous. Anticipation rose and fell like a crashing wave every time I picked up another box. I hoped so badly to see the name Madison Hart.

Why would she give me chocolate? She probably didn't like me. We were just friends, and that's how she thought of me. That's how it had always been, since the beginning. Good friends.

I couldn't stop the nervous feeling in my stomach though. Especially since the pile was considerably smaller since I started, and still nothing from Madison. But we'd get more later in the day, as SMK was flooded with gifts confessing love. These boxes were just the earlier arrivals.

"What are you doing?"

I jumped. I twisted around to see Tai looking at me as he sipped coffee, standing behind me. I'd been so distracted I hadn't realized that he'd gotten off the sofa and helped himself to some of Chin-hyuk's coffee, but he looked sharp and wide-awake now.

"Just – looking through the chocolate," I said as casual as I could.

"You never looked through all of them before," Tai said suspiciously.

I swallowed, struggling to find something to say. It must've shown on my face, because one of Tai's eyebrows lifted slightly.

"I always look through some," I said, stalling, trying to look normal. "You guys do too."

"Yeah, but we've never sorted through each and every one."

I shrugged.

"Hmm," said Tai, watching me skeptically. Then he took another sip of coffee, fixing me with an overly intense stare as he turned away.

I exhaled in relief as soon as he was far enough away, avoiding Chin-hyuk's gaze from the kitchen, because of course he knew exactly what was going on. Luckily Tai didn't think to interrogate Chin-hyuk, because he was a terrible liar. I finished up the pile of chocolate boxes, but there wasn't one from Madison.

I exhaled again, sitting back and pinching the bridge of my nose with my eyes squeezed shut. *Relax, Wooyeong. It's fine. It doesn't matter how badly you wish something would happen if it doesn't. She just thinks of you as a friend.*

I pressed my mouth into a line gloomily. I looked down at the traitorous mountain of chocolate. Then I impulsively grabbed one and tore open the cellophane, opening the box and popping one in my mouth.

It was sweet and creamy, a milk chocolate truffle. I chewed it miserably, then grabbed another one.

Hey, she might've sent you something. It could be in the next batch the staff will deliver here.

I ate another chocolate, then tossed the box sideways, standing up. I guess I'd have to wait until the next boxes came.

I groaned. It'd been almost two hours since I had started my next batch of chocolate-sorting. I'd swept the old one to the bedroom before the staff had dumped the second, and much bigger, pile in the living room. Manager Pak had personally driven one of the wheelbarrows, amused and laughing by the insane amount of chocolate we'd received this year. Dyeong had been smiling ear-to-ear as well. We may be famous, but we didn't get a mountain of chocolate just every day. Valentine's Day was special.

Dyeong, now awake and fully dressed with his hair sticking up in the back, lounged on the sofa with a heart-shaped package. "To Dyeong," he'd read aloud with a smirk, "for being the hottest, the coolest, the smartest, the funniest, and the cutest man alive."

"You made that up," Tai had accused, but then Dyeong had shown him the back of the package, which actually did say that.

"The chocolate tastes excellent," he added now a few minutes later as he took a bite of his third one. "They really didn't cheap out. You should try one, Wooyeong. Here, catch."

I looked up, startled, just in time to clutch a flying chocolate to my chest. I gazed down at it. It was dark brown and in the shape of a square, with a pretty crosshatch pattern. I bit into it, my mouth flooded with the taste of rich coffee.

"Wow," I said, amazed. "That *is* good."

Tai was looking down at the back of one, sitting cross-legged on the rug in the middle of the pile like someone had attempted to bury him alive. You couldn't see the floor until almost the bedroom, since we'd accidentally spread the boxes in a thin layer as we looked through them. Chin-hyuk, meanwhile, was drinking a green protein smoothie next to Dyeong, with the self-restraint to not eat sweets before he finished his breakfast. Even he couldn't help himself a little, however.

"Do you have raspberry flavor?" he asked, leaning over Dyeong's shoulder.

"Yes I do," said Dyeong. "Help yourself."

Chin-hyuk grabbed it for safekeeping as he chugged down the rest of his smoothie.

"To Tai, the king of my heart, whose eyes are the color of the best chocolate," I read aloud on the back of a circular box, handing it to him. "That one's got caramel clusters."

Tai gasped, tearing it open. "I was hoping for one of these!"

Chin-hyuk picked up a square box that had accidentally gotten half-pushed under the sofa. "Dear Chin-hyuk," he read seriously. "You will always be more handsome and talented than Dyeong. Everyone knows that shorter guys are the new hot."

Dyeong choked on his chocolate, grabbing the box from Chin-hyuk. "You liar," he said, coughing. "This is for Wooyeong."

I could feel my adrenaline rise. "Give it to me," I said as casually as I could, holding out my hand.

Dyeong tossed it to me. "Nice note on it too."

My heartbeat was going very fast as I flipped it over, seeing the note. *You're a great friend. Keep it up, WY! Love –*

Yeseo.

I nodded, trying to conceal my crushing disappointment. For a second, I'd really thought...

"Didn't you meet at that first Mnet we did?" Tai asked. "She's the one who's in Shooting Star, right?"

"K4Y," Dyeong corrected. "They're doing pretty good. Yeseo was really nice to us too."

I nodded, not really listening, zoning out.

"Euch!" Chin-hyuk said suddenly, covering his mouth with his hand, face screwed up in disgust. He looked like he wanted to gag. I looked at him in alarm, then realized.

"Banana-flavored?" Dyeong asked.

Chin-hyuk nodded, getting up off the sofa and going to spit it in the trash. Tai laughed at the expression on his face.

He may tease Chin-hyuk about being sickened by all banana-flavored things, even the universally popular banana milk, but just wait until Dyeong 'tainted' the group ramyun with some cooked spinach. Tai could act like a seven-year-old when vegetables were involved.

I was looking through the packages must faster than the others, my mood considerably more dampened than theirs, though I tried to hide it. There were all types of girls' names I knew on these – except for the one that I wanted so badly to see.

The way that Tai and Chin-hyuk and Dyeong were randomly moving boxes around was making me stressed, though there was no way I was telling them what I was trying to do. What if I missed her box in all the others because it got pushed to my already-looked-at-pile? Well, they wouldn't be able to tell it was a pile; I was trying to make it look casual. I thought Chin-hyuk was already on to me, even though he wasn't saying anything. He would never pester me about what I was feeling, trying to pry all my secrets – it was more his style to let me choose whether to confide in him or not, and to leave me alone to just naturally work through whatever was going on. He already knew I was in love with Madison, and that was enough for him.

I did appreciate his silence as I sorted through, growing increasingly more despondent.

Give it up. She doesn't feel that way about you. She hasn't gotten you anything.

I suspected this, so why did I obsessively keep looking? I might miss hers anyway in all this abundance. I should just ask her tomorrow – or today. No, tomorrow. Casually. Just mentioning how much chocolate we got so it was easy to miss some, and by the way, did you send me anything? If I slipped that into conversation, she might not guess what was in my head. It wouldn't be awkward. None would be the wiser, right? She'd say yes or no, and that would be that.

I just had to ask her. It was that simple, as long as I was smooth about it.

I leaned my head on the coffee table, my stomach a jumble of emotions that I couldn't pick apart or recognize. Mixed with the chocolate I'd had for breakfast, it wasn't a good combination.

"Can I get you some apple and toast?" Chin-hyuk asked. "You look like you don't feel so well."

I lifted my head from the coffee table. "I'll get it."

Two hours, and it still wasn't here. I ambled to the kitchen, throwing a slice of whole-wheat bread in the oven to get crispy and taking out an apple. A hardly filling breakfast, but it balanced the calories from all the chocolate I'd eaten in my dejected stupor. Manager Pak would be happy.

How come I was so desperate? I wasn't used to feeling this way. This was new.

I pulled out my phone. No texts from Madison either. I sighed, pocketing it again. I wondered what she was thinking this morning. Maybe she just hadn't realized that it was Valentine's Day today. Maybe her work was keeping her very busy and she'd want to see me later. Maybe she'd give me chocolate in person!

She also just could've not realized the significance of giving chocolate to boys on Valentine's Day. Did they have that in the US? I sure would feel stupid if I brought it up tomorrow and it turned out she had absolutely no idea that it's how you show you like him. I mean, the guys would do the same on White Day in a month. She might not know about that either.

I sighed, sliding down the cabinets until I was sitting on the ground. This was torture.

매디슨
MADISON
21

The wind was frigid as I walked home from work. I shivered, glad for the flat dress shoes I'd bought after my sprained ankle. It let off a small thrill of pain if I stepped too forcefully on a hard surface, but otherwise it was fine, especially compared to how bad it'd been a couple days ago. I could still do my routine of walking home. I was thankful for that.

It might've been much worse if Tai and Wooyeong hadn't taken me to SMK to elevate it and get some ice. Usually I smiled when I remembered that day. But not now.

I let out a breath, seeing it dissipate in a cloud in front of me. Then a tear rolled down my face, stinging my eyes.

I did *not* want to cry today. I was sick of crying. Apparently my emotions hadn't gotten the message.

I angrily wiped my eyes on my chilly parka sleeve, hardly paying attention to where I was walking, my body on autopilot as I headed back home, staring at the ground.

Cold wind blew my hair back away from my face. I shivered again, trying to tuck my chin into my scarf.

This was the worst Valentine's Day I'd ever had.

Before, in the US, it's not like I ever got a real valentine from anyone. No secret or not-so-secret admirers. But that had been fine. This... this was *hard*.

I hadn't bought any chocolates yesterday. There was no way Wooyeong would ever like me. He was *Wooyeong*. I was delusional for thinking otherwise. Why send him chocolates? So I could just humiliate myself?

It's not like we could be in public together ever again anyway. A second picture of us would seal the deal.

I wondered what he was doing right now. I wondered if he had expected me to confess that I liked him, or maybe even if... a small part of him... might want me to.

"You're a fool," I whispered angrily to myself. Even though I *knew* there was no way anyone might like me, let alone Wooyeong, I still couldn't stop that tiny, irrational hope.

It didn't matter whether I had given it to him or not, anyway. Didn't matter that I couldn't bring myself to give him chocolates, that I was too cowardly. This was still the worst Valentine's Day ever. Nothing would've changed.

I reached my apartment. By the time I took the elevator up to my floor, my fingers were still so numb that I fumbled the keys when unlocking the door.

I stepped inside and closed it behind me, twisting the lock. I need ramyun, or something – no, that would remind me of when we'd eaten together in his dorm and played Go-Stop and drank banana milk. Too much.

I pulled open the fridge, seeing all the food he'd left here for me to cook with. Even a small container of leftover stew that I hadn't eaten already, the last of the doenjang jigaee he'd made while I watched.

I think the truthful reason I hadn't eaten it already was that I had been saving it. But you couldn't save food, no matter how precious the memory was to you. It went bad eventually. I should eat it soon while it was still fresh. But right now I didn't want to be reminded of him...

I let out a loud, sudden, frustrated noise, pounding my fist into the fridge door. It hurt. I gasped, shaking out my clenched fingers.

I wouldn't eat anything, then. Maybe I'd order takeout and have it delivered. I pulled out my phone, shrugging off my parka and throwing it against the wall, yanking off both my gloves and taking off my shoes. Then I collapsed onto the sofa, looked up the nearest fried chicken place and dialed them up.

Crunchy, delicious fried chicken. It was treat I hadn't had in so long. I popped open a Coke while I waited, taking a swig of the sugary liquid and relishing the way it burned my throat.

Stupid health. Who needed it?

I'd already chugged the whole can before the fried chicken arrived. I paid for it and then went back inside, popping open another and hearing the satisfying hiss.

The fried chicken was heavenly – the white meat was moist and tender, the shell craggy, abundant, and insanely crunchy. I savored the salt and that unmistakable fried taste, and the light layer of grease that coated my fingertips.

What was Wooyeong eating now? I hoped something substantial, and that he wasn't depriving himself...

Don't think about him, I told myself furiously. *What is wrong with you?*

What was wrong with me was that I loved him. And he would probably never, ever love me back.

"I hope you had a good Valentine's Day," I said sullenly, speaking even though he couldn't hear me. "I'm not."

I took another swig of Coke. The sugar was sour in my mouth.

My phone rang, sudden and sharp and loud next to me. I jumped, nearly cursed, and then flipped it over so I could see the screen.

L.W. said the caller ID.

I inhaled a sharp breath, my hands firmly in my lap, my fingers entwined, as I watched it ring twice. Three times.

I wanted to pick it up, but whether I should was another matter. My pulse was racing, I was a mess of emotions including majorly cranky, and I'd just drank nearly two cans of soda in a very short period of time.

My ringtone went on one last round, looking dangerously close to going to voicemail.

I couldn't help myself. I clicked *Accept,* bringing the phone to my ear with my lightly greased fingers.

"Hello?"

"Madison," he said. The sound of his voice made me ache. I swallowed the tangled knot of emotions that were threatening to reveal themselves. "Hi."

Was that all he was calling to tell me? I waited.

"Hello? Are you still there?"

"Of course I'm still here," I said, my tone coming out less sharp than I expected. "What do you want?"

Wooyeong was quiet for a moment. I guess he hadn't expected me to be mad at him – well, mad at myself, mad at everything – or maybe he didn't know and was trying to figure out what was going on.

"I thought you were going to call me," he said. "I got a little worried when you were quiet all day."

I looked down, smoothing out the napkin on the table with my fingers. "I don't call you every day."

"A text. Something."

I didn't answer.

"Are you doing okay?" he pressed on.

I held the phone out at arm's-length away from me so he wouldn't hear the incredulous little gasp that escaped my lips. After all this he still wanted to know if I was okay. I couldn't believe it.

"Madison?" he asked softly.

I nodded, trying to swallow the lump in my throat, then realized he couldn't see me. *Don't speak to me like that!* I wanted to snarl at him. How dare he use that quiet voice that made me blush, made me feel vulnerable like my heart had been cracked open, even when he wasn't there. "Yeah, I'm fine. Did you have a good Valentine's Day?"

I didn't know why I said it. It was stupid. I regretted it the instant it came out of my mouth.

The silence that followed was pained.

"It was fine," he said lamely.

"Mm." My finger flicked up and down on the corner of the grease-stained fried chicken box. "I'll call you later, okay? I'm eating right now."

"Okay," he repeated, something unreadable in his tone.

I tapped the *End* button, setting the phone back down. I slumped in my chair, pressing my face into the table.

Why did it have to be you? Why couldn't I have fallen in love with anyone else? But it had to be you. You who will only ever think of me as a friend. You who is untouchable. You who is an idol, who I can never be with.

He was too gorgeous. Too kind. Too talented. Too *everything* for me. He was one of the most desired guys in the K-pop industry, with thousands of girls crushing hard on him. Who was I in the face of all that? What made me different? I could never have him. Wooyeong was too good for me.

"We'll just stay friends," I muttered into the table. "Like we have been."

I ate the rest of my fried chicken, but it didn't make me feel any better. I felt drunk with grief.

Why had I let myself crush on him for six years? Why hadn't I shut my heart away like I did with everyone else?

"You're an idiot," I muttered to myself again. "This is just like any other day. Nothing's changed. It's just Valentine's Day that's making you feel things."

I sighed. I should probably call him back. It wasn't his fault that he was too good for me. He was probably worried about me right now, anyway, or thinking he'd done something wrong. I had to make him feel better so he didn't think he'd offended me, at least.

I swept the fried chicken containers and napkins in the trash along with my two Coke cans, washed my hands, and shrugged on my parka, grabbing my phone and making my way downstairs. I hated cold, but a little of it might shock me back into my senses.

The freezing air outside the apartment doorstep was, indeed, shocking. It felt like an icicle had slapped me in the face. I shivered, pressing the call-back button.

He answered on the third ring. "Hello?"

"Hi, Wooyeong," I said, my tone forced and cheerful. It was so good I nearly fooled myself. "Sorry about that. I was eating fried chicken."

"It's fine," he said. I couldn't read his voice.

"Hey, um, how about we meet up somewhere a week from now? I'm a little busy, but a week should be good." That would give me long enough to get over this.

"Oh," he said.

There was a short silence, and I rubbed my forehead with the back of my hand, unable to think of anything to fill it with.

"SMK, probably," Wooyeong said, when I didn't say anything. "It's safer that way, especially after they said that you're one of the assistant general managers."

"Okay," I agreed. "See you then."

"See you then," he repeated dully.

I hung up, then stared at the phone, my heart feeling like someone was driving a knife through it. A week never seemed so long.

매디슨
MADISON
22

The shiny SMK Entertainment building loomed over me. The last time I'd been here was when I'd sprained my ankle, but I'd been distracted at the time. I hadn't remembered it being so cold and formidable-looking, its slick surfaces shiny and spotless. The windows were all tinted black, probably so that passerby couldn't see the secret things going on inside. I wondered which one of those windows belonged to Wooyeong's dorm.

I looked up at it, swallowed, and then steeled my nerve.

I felt sicker and sicker as I approached the sliding-glass doors. But as soon as they swished open, there was no turning back.

The desk clerk, a man with round glasses, looked at me in surprise. "Oh, hello," he said as I went up to the desk. "What can I help you with?"

"I'm h–here to see Wooyeong," I managed, but hating the unexpected stutter in my voice. I was hyperaware of my surroundings, of the clean carpet beneath my feet running to the silver elevator across the room, the security guard watching us.

The clerk surveyed me suspiciously – my probably pale bloodless face, my nervous mannerisms, my foreignness.

"I'm sorry," he said carefully. "What do you need to see him for?"

"I'm – I'm a friend," I said, feeling an edge of desperation now. He thought I was a stalking fan. Of course it was going to sound like I was lying. Hadn't Wooyeong told the staff to expect someone like me? He was the one who'd told me to come over today whenever it was a good time.

His squinting eyes looked very small under his glasses. "Hmm. I'm sorry, Wooyeong didn't alert me about this. You're going to have to leave. If you're friends, you can call him."

It was obvious by the tone in his voice that he didn't think I had his number. He was challenging me. The security guard next to the elevator had shifted in his position, started to move toward me.

"That's okay," I said hurriedly. "Right. I'll call him." I quickly walked out of the building, pulling out my phone, trying to fight the fear and dizziness threatening to overwhelm me.

I heaved a deep breath of the cold air, trying to blink away the tears I could feel coming on. I looked back at the door – at least the security guard hadn't followed me out here. I rubbed my arms and pressed *Call* on Wooyeong's contact.

I listened to the dull tones of it ringing. I felt like a very small, very fragile criminal. I'd *never* been on the bad side of a security guard before. I wasn't a stalker or out of control or trying to harm someone. I hadn't done anything wrong.

The last ring sounded. Wooyeong wasn't picking up.

"Where are you?" I whispered as it went to voicemail, trying harder not to cry.

"Right here," said low voice behind me.

I spun around, my fear melting away as I saw Wooyeong standing there, holding his phone, which must've been vibrating on silent mode. His hair was slightly messy, lifting in the breeze, and he was in black jeans and a leather jacket over a gray knit sweater.

"I'm sorry," he said. "Let's go inside."

I didn't say anything, walking past him indoors.

"You shouldn't do that," I said, trying to control my voice so he wouldn't see how upset I was. I could hear him following close behind me to the elevator. "What if someone sees?"

There was a pause. "Yes. You're right."

I half-wanted him to argue with me, to tell me I was wrong, that it didn't matter who saw us together. But that would never be the case.

The clerk was staring at us with huge eyes, looking shocked as the doors closed, but I couldn't even muster up the energy to be satisfied.

We were silent on the elevator. So much for me trying to seem like I wasn't angry with him.

Wooyeong moved ahead of me as soon as we stepped out into the hall, leading the way. I watched his broad shoulders in front of me, trying to control my feelings. I shouldn't be upset. Why was I so upset?

~{★ 149 ♥}~

"I'm sorry the clerk didn't know you," Wooyeong said. "I didn't tell him you were coming. It was supposed to be Eun Ae today, and she would recognize you."

"It's fine," I said, my tone coming out dead and automatic.

Wooyeong turned around suddenly and stopped, making me step back so I wouldn't bump into him, backing into the hallway wall to the side. "It's not fine. The security guard scared you."

"It's fine," I repeated. Why should I care if Wooyeong had told anyone that I was coming or not? It's not like I was anyone important in his life.

His dark eyes never left mine, though I was determined not to look at him. He reached for my hands, his warmth sudden and surprising. "Your hands are trembling."

I didn't have anything to say. Wooyeong didn't move, still holding my hands.

"I'm not," I mumbled, hoping he couldn't see my cheeks flushing.

My hands slowly slid out of his grip as he let go. I took a shuddering breath, trying to ignore my racing heartbeat.

He seemed to sense my reaction, stepping closer to me. He reached out his arm, placing his hand on the wall behind me, above my shoulder, so he was square in front of me.

I was motionless, confused, his proximity making warmth and adrenaline rush through me. My stomach was full of fluttering, even though we weren't actually touching.

"You don't have to lie to me," he whispered. His chest was inches from me; I would hardly have to lift my hands to touch his sweater.

His lips were barely moving. I was frozen, my heart racing. He didn't like me back. He didn't love me. If he didn't.... then why... was he so close...

My breaths were coming fast and shallow. His dark gaze strayed to my lips and stayed there. He swallowed, and I could see the movement at his masculine throat.

"I've... told myself what to feel," he said, his voice quiet and husky. "But it never works..."

His free hand, slow and trembling, reached up and lightly touched the hair on my forehead, gently brushing it back. I watched with wide eyes, my cheeks prickling.

"And the one person... who I want to like me... I can't have..." His hand swept lightly across my hair, sliding to the back of my head for one brief moment before dropping again. His mouth was parted, and I could hear every breath passing by his lips. He moved ever so slightly closer to me, his head tilting to the side as his face moved toward mine, his eyes closing.

"WOOYEONG!" someone roared, sudden and angry.

His lips were a centimeter from touching mine, his nose already brushing my cheek. For one beat, he was frozen, his breath light on my mouth. He leaned away from me, his hand falling from the wall. My heart plummeted into my stomach. Dyeong was standing in the doorway, right across from me. I could see him over Wooyeong's shoulder, fists clenched. Wooyeong swallowed, blinked several times, and then slowly turned around.

"Hello, Dyeong," he said, his voice low.

I was still pressed up against the wall, petrified, my cheeks still flushed and hot and my heartbeat racing. Now it was pounding so much it was painful.

"We need to talk," Dyeong said, his tone seething and dangerous. His previous roar still rang in my ears. *"Now."*

I gulped in a breath, my skin burning like fire where Wooyeong had brushed me right before we'd almost kissed. I pushed away from the wall and ran, my mind a confused jumble, punching floor number 1 on the elevator. I didn't hear anything before it closed over the rushing noise in my ears.

I didn't remember the seconds that passed as I descended, didn't process them, just barely aware of the blur around me as I sprinted, out the doors of SMK, running away.

우영
WOOYEONG
23

Madison darted down the hallway. I turned away from Dyeong to go after her, making it only a few steps, reaching out – and then Dyeong hissed *"Stop."*

I jerked to a halt almost like he was holding me by some invisible force. Madison vanished from view. She shouldn't be alone. Did she even have a ride home? But I already knew I was too late and too slow.

I stared down the empty hallway, the air completely silent except for the deep *chung* of the elevator doors closing. The sound echoed loud and lonely in the stillness.

My chest rose and fell with my breath. I was turning around to face Dyeong again when he did it himself, yanking my arm and spinning me around, his grip rough. Dyeong was breathing just as hard as I was. His eyes were bright and wild, his fists balled as he towered over me. For a second I thought he was going to punch me in the face. He looked like he wanted to.

"Dyeong," I said, struggling to keep my voice calm, "Dyeong, I didn't mean to –"

"You lied to me."

"Dyeong, I didn't mean – it was an – an accident –"

"And accident that you lied to me? Or that you were going to kiss her?" He made a disgusted snort, stepping away from me, his shoulders still tight like he wanted to hit me. "Must've been holding in your feelings for a long time if kissing her was *an accident.*"

"I wasn't going to tell you what you didn't want to hear –"

Dyeong laughed, harsh and fake. "So it's my fault? Good one." He was breathing hard through his nose, trying to control himself, but his sudden, raw roar still made me flinch. "HOW COULD YOU?"

I didn't have the words to answer him. I almost wished he would punch me like he wanted to, so we'd be even. I'd been lying to my best friend, my soul brother. I wanted to be angry with him. I wanted to fight back. But instead my insides just felt like they'd been ripped in two.

"I see where your priorities are," Dyeong snarled. "Can't even defend yourself. More than six years together, *everything* we've worked for – you want to throw it all away."

"That's not true!" I yelled. "It doesn't have to be one or the other!"

"And yet I asked you over and *over* whether you liked her, and then the next minute you're kissing her as soon as you get the chance. You're a selfish liar and a *backstabber.*"

"Dyeong, I'm sorry – I didn't mean to, it just happened, I'm sorry –"

"Don't talk to me," he snarled, and turned around and stalked the way he'd come, back to the dorm.

"Dyeong! No – *Dyeong!*"

He was out of sight. My heart was beating against my chest so hard it felt like a hammer. I sunk to the floor, feeling almost lightheaded. It was all going so wrong. I had broken the trust of one of the people I loved most. Dyeong, my soul brother. One of the only people in the whole world who knew me as I really was. Who had witnessed all my failures and insecurities as well as my triumphs and strengths. Who'd accepted me. Supported me. Loved me as I was and not for who I was in Ambition.

I pressed a hand to my face. It was still burning hot from my almost-kiss with Madison. This was what happened when I let my guard down... which kept happening more and more around her. I had to admit I wasn't in control of my feelings at all.

He was right. This was dangerous. And I'd lied to him, intentionally. Yet there was one thing I knew for sure, and that was that I would *never* let go of Madison.

The pain in my chest came from the impossible choice he wanted me to make: Her, or the group. Her, or our friendship.

Had I truly ever thought it would be possible to have both? But I couldn't choose one or the other. I *couldn't.*

I loved her.

It had seemed like, in that moment, she had been feeling the same. I'd been telling myself the whole time that she wasn't attracted to me, didn't love me because of the way she went along with Tai's flirting, and the way she was only ever polite to me... but now I wasn't sure. When I'd touched her hands...

And when I'd almost kissed her. Her flushed face, beautiful lips, the way her eyes had started closing too when I'd leaned in. It had felt so right. She wanted it to happen.

Dyeong had come just when she might've confessed, just when /was going to confess...

Everything was going wrong. He hated me now. I'd shattered his trust in so many broken pieces I wasn't sure if it could ever be whole again – if things between us would ever be the same.

Most ironic was how close we'd been in mindset, in the beginning. By one simple twist of fate we might've switched places, and it might've been Dyeong that day who'd gone out and met someone he couldn't stop thinking about.

Then I would've been the angry one. The levelheaded rational one, furious with him for being weak enough to do the most dangerous thing a K-pop idol could ever do – fall in love.

I pressed my face into my hands, rubbing my forehead, trying to clear my head.

Dyeong would probably be reporting me right now. In that switched-places scenario, it might've been what I would've done. I didn't blame him.

The sharp buzz of my silenced phone in my pocket gave my senses enough of a shock so that my head at least felt clearer. I stood up and drew it out, answering it as I started to walk down the hall to the elevator. "Hello?"

"Wooyeong, I'd like to speak with you. Come to the modeling room."

"Already on my way," I said, trying to control my voice, trying to be calm.

Manager Pak hung up without even saying goodbye. I swept my hands on the soft knit materiel of my sweater, trying to forget the way Madison's hair felt against my fingers as the elevator descended.

The dating ban had been lifted since what felt like ages ago. So then why was I being called downstairs?

When the doors opened, Chin-hyuk and Tai were right there in the hallway, standing on the polished floor outside almost like they'd been waiting to get in. Tai's eyes were wide and surprised, but Chin-hyuk looked more neutral. He, of course, had been expecting something like this at some point.

"Wooyeong, what's going on?" Tai said quickly as I stepped out.

"What are you guys doing here?" I said, ignoring the question. It was strange that they should be right outside the elevator as if waiting for me.

"On our way to room 117," Chin-hyuk said. "Manager Pak called all of us. Apparently Manager Gu's there too."

I sucked in a slow breath, having an ominous feeling about why our publicity manager should be coming. "Ah."

I walked down the hall, Chin-hyuk and Tai in step beside me. Dyeong was nowhere to be found.

I'm sorry, Dyeong. I'm so sorry.

I should've done things differently. I should've been honest with him from the start. We were best friends, but I hadn't been acting like it.

We reached the door to room 117. I reached for the cold steel handle... and then hesitated, my fingers wrapped firmly around it. I exhaled and closed my eyes, not wanting to open it, not wanting any of this to be real.

But it didn't matter what I wanted, as I knew I would be told soon enough.

I opened the door and strode in.

"Hello, Wooyeong," said Manager Pak. He was standing in the middle of the empty room looking a bit nervous, next to the folding metal table where Manager Gu was seated, examining me critically. "Please sit down. And Chin-hyuk and Tai too, of course."

I said nothing, pulling up a chair with a scrape directly across from Manager Gu, not afraid to look at him. Chin-hyuk and Tai sat next to me, both on my left.

No one spoke for a long time. One minute passed, two, three. I was just starting to count the seconds in my head when the door swung open and Dyeong walked in, pointedly not looking at me, taking the seat at the end and crossing his arms.

"So," said Manager Gu, after a long silence. No one said anything, so he continued. "We've just been having a little chat about your new... acquaintance."

I nodded, measuring my breathing, trying to stay calm. I had lied to myself, lied to the other members and especially to Dyeong. I was sick of lying.

I still felt flushed. I couldn't stop thinking about Madison, replaying what had happened, worrying about her. Even though I needed all my concentration right now.

Manager Pak had a strong expression of curiosity as he stared at me – Lee Wooyeong, the most cynical, jaded K-pop star of his industry, the one always in control of himself. I could understand how he saw me. The last person likely to ever fall in love. I was a conundrum for everybody.

"We hear this... acquaintance..." Manager Gu struggled for words, fighting the smile of disbelief and condescending amusement that kept appearing on his features, "is your girlfriend?"

"Not yet," I said, with difficulty.

He leaned forward. "Wooyeong, you should've told us," he said sorrowfully. "You know we would've wanted to know what's going on in your life."

"The reason he didn't," Dyeong said quietly as he examined his fingernails, "is because she's a fan."

Manager Gu's expression went slack. *"What?"*

"Manager Gu, I can explain –"

"You should know the dangers of fans!" he said, venom lacing his voice. "Obsessive, toxic, willing to bring down this group as quickly as they supported it."

"She's not like that. Not her. I know that now."

"That's what they *all* said, Wooyeong. You're endangering this corporation. As soon as you do something to anger her, or try to break up with her, she'll expose everything over social media and go on a crusade until *all* of you are destroyed. She doesn't love *you*, she loves feeling special because she gets to date a famous idol!"

"She's not like that," I repeated, my teeth gritted. I looked into his jaded, hate-filled face and felt revulsion.

Revulsion because just a few months previous, I would've had the same expression.

I could almost hear my own voice now in my ears, see my curling lip as Dyeong told me about Hak Beomsoo dating a fan. *She only likes him because he's a K-pop star.* That was what I'd said, word for word, feeling like I was the one on top of the mountain, that *I* was the one who was wise, the one who knew better....

I was different now.

"How long do you have to be in this group to get this? You know how desperate people are for fame. They get the smallest glow from your radiance, and it makes them feel good. Special. Important. They're addicted to it, and it's never enough."

"The dating ban is lifted," I said firmly. "Under our contract – which holds until two years from now – I am allowed to date whoever I want. Why is this a problem?"

Manager Gu's eyes widened and he leaned forward, careful not to crease his suit. "We thought you would date other industry stars! Girls with as much interest in secrecy as you have! The most gorgeous, most desirable girls in Korea! Not some random *fan!*"

For a second I was speechless with outrage and disbelief. He thought that anyone would want to date the female stars just for their looks? And he thought that everyone else was inferior, and so I was *settling* by choosing Madison?

"So... she's a fan," Manager Pak said, breaking the stunned silence. He nodded. Then nodded again, almost like he was trying to convince himself. "Right. And what's her name?"

"Madison," me, Dyeong, Chin-hyuk and Tai all said in unison. Dyeong met my eyes for one brief second, but I couldn't read his expression.

Manager Gu looked at all of us uneasily. Unlike Manager Pak, he wasn't used to us speaking at the same time.

"I'm not *settling* by choosing Madison," I said, trying to hide my seething anger. "I love her the way I will never love anyone else. It's her, or no one."

I realized as I said it how true it was.

It was Madison, or no one. For the rest of my life.

Manager Gu sensed the hostility in my expression and backed down, switching back to a calm, pleading tone that he would use to convince an illogical child.

"Wooyeong," he said, leaning forward earnestly and tapping his pen on the table. "This girl may be a nice person, but you are not a normal man." He shook his head in an exaggerated manner. "Even if she likes you only *partly* because you're an idol, the relationship could end in disaster!"

"It doesn't have to be so extreme," Chin-hyuk said, speaking for the first time. "Many other idols date."

"Many other idols get caught and have their career destroyed," Dyeong retorted. "Don't tell me you're ready for that kind of hate that's going to be thrown our way. I'm sure you've read even some of the comments on the photo released of Tai carrying Madison." He turned to me, eyebrow raised. "Do you want to put her through that again? Except imagine it a hundred times *worse.*"

I flushed with anger remembering some of the cruelty said about her. "No," I admitted stiffly.

"Wooyeong, as Ambition's publicity manager I can tell you that dating a fan is the worst thing you can possibly do," Manager Gu jumped in. His eyes narrowed. "You don't know what's at stake."

"I will consider your advice," I said coolly, formally.

Dyeong stood up, pushing his chair back with a loud scrape. "I can't believe you," he spat, and left the room. The door slammed behind him.

I swallowed, anger and despair tight in my chest. I wanted to call him back, beg him. But there was nothing I could say.

Manager Gu stood up too, giving a dismissive wave of his hand before he left without looking at me. Manager Pak uncertainly followed him.

Tai's eyes were round and unsure. "You're taking a chance for all of us," he said. "You realize that, right?" He gave me a worried glance before grabbing Chin-hyuk's arm, not waiting for an answer. Chin-hyuk's face was covered with regret, but he went with Tai. The door shut behind them, leaving me all alone.

The silence was suffocating. I sat there for a long time, frozen, unmoving, then heaved a gulping breath, wiping tears from my face angrily with the back of my hand. They took me off guard. I pressed my lips together, squeezing my eyes shut, as my shoulders started shaking.

I was so lost. But in all this, I still had her. I still had her. No matter how hard this was, no matter how my heart felt like it was splintering.

She is worth fighting for.

I put my hand against my mouth as tears ran down my cheeks.

It was hours later when I stood up from the chair, cold and stiff, my legs cramping. I slowly shuffled to the door, pausing as my hand fell upon the icy metal of the doorknob.

I drew it away, turning it over palm-up, brushing one index finger lightly down my fingertips, remembering the feeling of Madison's hair as I'd gently swept it away from her precious face. I swallowed painfully, a sad smile on my lips.

I wondered if she was okay. What she was feeling right now, about what happened, not only me almost kissing her but also about Dyeong.

She liked me. She felt the same way about me as I did about her. I was more sure of that now after today.

But I needed to check if she was alright. I needed to talk to her.

The door jerked open from the other side. I stepped back in surprise, seeing Manager Pak. His expression was resolute, like he'd been planning this and wasn't going to chicken out, but I could see the nervousness in his boyish eyes.

He stepped into the room. "You've been here a long time," he said. "I think maybe it's time we had a little talk."

I opened my mouth, but just then my phone buzzed in my pocket, ringing on silent mode. Manager Pak looked down at it, and I pulled it out.

Madison Hart.

For a moment I was stuck in limbo, awkwardly staring at the phone and the waiting Manager Pak in front of me, unable to satisfy both. But then I was moving past him, opening the door. "Sorry, Manager Pak," I said, breathless, ignoring his shocked stare. "I have to go." And then I was running down the hall, pressing *Answer.*

매디슨
MADISON
24

I'd run from SMK, confused and overwhelmed, Dyeong's angry roar still ringing in my ears. It terrified me, sent my stomach twisting up in a knot.

I'd made it several blocks before I stopped, hardly remembering how I'd gotten there, my memories a blur except for the image of Wooyeong's closed eyes and his nose brushing my cheek. I'd stopped, panting and gasping for air, my weak ankle giving a small thrill of pain.

I was breathing hard as I leaned against a building wall, dazed. He'd almost kissed me. He was going to – wasn't he? He was. I let my eyelids flutter closed with a sigh. I wished he had. I wished Dyeong hadn't come.

He had sounded so furious. I knew kissing in public was still mainly taboo in Korea, mostly among older people, but Wooyeong and I had been alone until he'd stumbled upon us.

Dyeong had been madder than that. Much madder. Remembering his voice still made me shiver.

I wondered desperately what was going on. But what was I supposed to do – call him? I didn't even know what to say. He had almost kissed me. Where did that leave us, relationship-wise? Were we still technically friends? Did he love me the way I loved him?

I've told myself what to feel.... But it never works....

My stomach felt nervously queasy all over again as I thought of what he'd said. Kissing me didn't seem like a spontaneous mistake.

He'd meant it.

I took several quick, shallow breaths. I should've been happy. Ecstatic, in bliss. But somehow, I couldn't muster up the feeling after hearing Dyeong's voice...

I hoped Wooyeong wasn't in trouble now. My head was whirling, a mess of my own emotions – disbelief, euphoria, confusion, and a million other things – and my concern for Wooyeong.

I walked home, slowly, still dazed. I got to my apartment, unlocked the door and took off my parka. I sat at the kitchen table, and laid my phone faceup there.

I had no idea where we were supposed to continue on from what happened. He would probably at least text me, if only to tell me he was doing fine, that everything was alright. I felt nervous as I waited.

But the minutes passed, and then hours. I lifted my head from the table, realizing I'd fallen asleep, and frantically checked my notifications.

Nothing.

I felt deep in my gut that something was wrong.

I had to call him.

I inhaled shakily, biting my lip. Somehow the thought of pressing that button made me more nervous than I'd ever been. But I had to do it. For Wooyeong.

I picked up my phone, pressed *Call,* and waited.

It rang three times. I suddenly felt sick, closing my eyes to the wave of nausea that washed over me.

"Madison."

His voice on the other end was like a gasp of thirst. Relief crashed over me. "Wooyeong," I said, my desperation obvious. "I'm not interrupting anything, am I? What's going on?"

"I'm – I'm fine," he said, though he sounded slightly hoarse. "Nothing's going on."

I closed my eyes, dread and fear sinking deep in my gut. No... I knew him too well know. He could try to hide from me, but he couldn't. He was lying.

"Tell me the truth," I whispered.

There was a long pause.

I swallowed. "Dyeong?"

"He's not speaking to me at the moment. I think he hates me now. It's fine, though. He'll get over it. Where are you? Are you okay? You didn't even have a ride home..."

"I'm okay, Wooyeong. I'm okay."

He'll get over it. Even I could tell he didn't believe it. Dyeong *hated* him? Dyeong, who was like a brother to Wooyeong? Because of me... because of *us.* The dread and fear I felt just got stronger.

"Good." He inhaled. "I was so worried."

"Why didn't you call me?"

"I'm sorry, for a while I couldn't... the... the managers came and called us all, so I had to talk to them... Dyeong reported me and the publicity manager wanted to have a talk. He didn't think dating would ruin my career like Dyeong does, though, so they're kind of on different parallels." Wooyeong laughed, but it was worried, slightly bitter.

Dyeong thought dating would ruin Wooyeong's career. The manager had so much of a problem with it that he wanted to talk to Wooyeong, with everyone else there....

How could I have been so *selfish*? I'd seen the destruction that a single photo could bring for Wooyeong, and I'd still stayed around him, when I knew better. How could I have been so *stupid?*

I remembered that comment from weeks ago.

Of course they're going to say that. We'll just have to see if they're ever spotted together again.

I was frozen, with chills running down my body.

"Hello? Are you still there?" He sounded anxious.

I opened my mouth to respond but found that no words would come.

All this time, from the very first day I'd met Wooyeong, I knew it couldn't last.

I loved him. More than I'd ever loved anybody. More than I ever would. But we were on different paths. He was a K-pop star. I was a fan. The difference between us, the huge, invisible chasm, couldn't be wider.

He wanted me back. But it was costing him so much, he couldn't even tell me the truth of how bad it was.

It was destroying his relationships with the other members. And if we were seen together ever again, it could destroy his career too. His dream.

"Hello? Hello? *Madison!*" Wooyeong was panicking now.

My voice came out squeezed. "I think you should stop seeing me."

"What?"

My whole body felt numb and disconnected. "I'm not letting you throw away everything for me. You need Dyeong. He's right. If we're ever seen together again, it will ruin you – and maybe them too."

"What?" He was breathless, stunned, like I'd just hit him in the chest with a hammer. "Madison – Madison, no –"

Hearing his voice was shattering me in a million pieces. I took several hard inhales, fighting the grief that was overwhelming me. My fingers tightened on the phone as I spoke the words I'd always known to be true, when I was crushing on him from thousands of miles away, when we were friends, when I loved him.

"I'm not good enough for you anyway."

"No – Madison, you're amazing! I've never met anyone like you!" he said desperately. Wooyeong let out a little gasp and when he spoke next, his voice was thick and cracking. "No one else will ever come close to how I feel about you. You are good enough for me. Better than me. Please don't leave."

I squeezed my eyes shut, unimaginable pain tearing through me at his words.

There were so many things I hadn't told him yet, would never tell him. I couldn't. This was my only chance.

I drew in a calming breath. "Do you know when you asked me what the best moment of my life was?" I asked. My voice was even and steady. "I said it was arriving in Seoul. I was lying. It was meeting you."

I could hear him inhale on the other end. "Do you remember that day when I lost my wallet?"

I nodded slowly, even though he couldn't see me.

"I found it. But I lied and told you I hadn't, just to see you longer... even back then, when we barely knew each other, I knew you were special." He was crying, the first and last time I would ever hear it. I loved him. I loved him so much it hurt.

I loved him more than I loved my own happiness.

"I'm sorry," I said. "I can't be in your future."

"Don't leave me," he begged. "I'll... I'll quit Ambition! *Please!*"

"I'm not letting you do this to yourself. I'm not letting you destroy your relationships and your dream. Goodbye, Wooyeong."

Wooyeong sounded like he was running. *"No!"* he yelled, the raw, grief-stricken desperation in his voice ripping right through me. "Just tell me where you are, I can come meet you! *Please!* I – I –"

~{★ 163 ♥}~

"Goodbye, Wooyeong," I whispered. "Please don't come to my apartment."

I hung up.

I let out a low sound of pain as I slipped out of the chair, suddenly aware of how badly my hands had been shaking, releasing a sob. I pressed my forehead to the cold floor, letting go of the phone, not even able to support myself, a knife feeling like it was being driven into my heart. I was crying so hard it hurt, the shrill sound of the phone ringing filling the air as he called me back. Then again and again, not relenting, the ringtone never stopping.

I hit *Block.*

우영
WOOYEONG
25

She wouldn't answer.

I was shocked, numb, heartbroken, calling her over and over. She would pick up. She had to pick up.

This number is no longer available.

Madison had... blocked me?

No. This wasn't happening. I needed to tell her I loved her. I was going to.

I had to find her.

I had already run out the doors of SMK down the street, my stupid, useless phone still clutched in my hand. *The metro.* I had to get to the metro. I still had time.

I smeared the tears off my face as I ran, remembering I was completely exposed and not caring. Nothing else mattered but Madison. The world was a blur as I made it underground to the subway station.

I sprinted down the subway platform. I was almost there. I could come find her, stand at the door of her apartment and refuse to leave until she'd heard me out. I had to. I panted and doubled over, despair and grief feeling like they were slowly ripping my chest in half, desperate to plead with her in person, to see her one more time, to tell her I loved her. Even though it would only tear my heart to shreds worse. I *had* to.

I reached the train... and hesitated at the open door. There were only a few people filing in, since it was an odd hour without the after-work rush. No one payed attention to me as I stood there to the side.

Madison had cut off contact with me. It sounded like she'd meant forever. She didn't want to be convinced.

I didn't care. I had to see her again – that couldn't have been the last time, the only time, when I hadn't even said goodbye and she'd run away. It couldn't end this way – just hours ago we'd almost had our first kiss.

I hadn't even said *goodbye*. My lungs felt like they were constricting as the weight of it, the panic, sunk in.

I was not going to lose Madison. My friend – one of my best friends. The love of my life. I would do whatever it took, standing vigil outside her apartment or work, *begging* her to come back. To change her mind.

I was going to step on the train. I would've. I wanted to, so badly.

But remembering her soft, broken voice stopped me.

Goodbye, Wooyeong. Please don't come to my apartment.

I stayed bent over, slowly, numbly sinking to the ground as the train started moving, gliding past and vibrating the concrete beneath my feet. Its noise filled the vacuum in my ears.

If there had been any tiny sliver of doubt left in my mind of whether she truly loved me, it was gone. She'd just proved it, and her actions screamed it louder than anything else could. But it was too late. /was too late.

She didn't want to see me. She'd blocked my number and told me not to track her down. It was over.

I choked out a dry sob, wrapping my arms around myself, burning hot through my sweater.

That's when someone screamed.

"It's Lee Wooyeong!"

Like a wildfire, it was catching, spreading faster than I could process it.

"Wooyeong! Look over here!"

"Wooyeong, I love you!"

I didn't turn to see the source, panicked, hiding my face, staggering to my feet and running away from the sound of rushing footsteps and cameras clicks and more screaming behind me.

"Wooyeong!" someone shrieked.

The screaming was sharp like shards of glass stabbing my mind, overwhelming me, and I turned, half-blind through the flashes of camera lights.

Someone grabbed my arm but I wrenched away, running, running, dodging obstacles in the sea of people and bags. I leapt up the flight of stairs two steps at a time, then stumbled at the top. My phone flew out of my hand and hit the smooth floor with a *crack,* sliding and spinning across the concrete. People moved out of the way of its path to avoid slipping on it, and I got the barest flash of their confused faces before I scooped up my phone again and kept running, the cracks in the glossy black glass digging into my fingers.

I dodged through people, the world a chaos of noise and movement until I burst out into the light, into the fresh air from the metro entrance. The sky was gray and bright and the air was icy on my skin, harshly stinging the tears I realized were running down my face. The sidewalk was nearly empty, and even the roads just a few feet to my left had only a few cars whizzing by.

Still, I didn't stop running. I didn't know who was behind me or how determined they were, but it was unlikely they could keep up with a fear-fueled idol who made stamina and endurance part of their career.

I kept my head down, running down the broad sidewalk to SMK, nearly crashing into a pedestrian with a briefcase and a suit who yelled "Hey!"

I didn't stop until I'd made it through the automatic doors, slowing down and collapsing against the wall in safety.

My eyes were closed and my breath came ragged and harsh, stinging my throat. I was numbly aware of the security guard moving past me to check if there were any threats outside, standing sentry at the door.

Fear and adrenaline were still pumping through me. I swallowed with difficulty, my mouth dry.

"Wooyeong?" asked Eun Ae softly from behind the clerk desk. "Are you okay?"

I felt a tear slide down my face from my closed eyes. I wiped it away with the back of my hand, still breathing hard, not having the energy to answer.

"Wooyeong, answer me, please. Do you need a medic?" Alarm was sharp in her tone.

I shook my head, eyes still closed, breathless.

It was over. Madison was gone.

It had been three weeks since that day.

I had gotten used to the pain. The lonely hole in my heart.

The silent moments where I realized she was gone.

~{★ 167 ❤ }~

The ringing where I heard in my head the words I had been too cowardly to say right when it had mattered most.

I love you.

Chin-hyuk found me that moment where I'd just escaped from the metro, slumped against the wall of SMK's lobby. He'd knelt by me, wiped the sweat from my clammy forehead and damp hair, not saying anything. Just like a dad would to his young kid. I was too exhausted to move.

"It's over?" he asked.

"It's over," I said. Somehow speaking any more, explaining, felt like it would split me apart in agony. I didn't tell him anything else, and he didn't ask, probably because he was trying to be sensitive.

We'd gone up to Number 10.

"I was caught at the metro," I told him on the elevator, my voice scratchy and painful. "People recognized me. They took pictures."

"You were alone?" Chin-hyuk asked, and I could hear the strain through his tone.

I nodded.

"Good," he breathed, closing his eyes with a sigh of relief. "Don't worry about it. I'll scan all the platforms and see if I need to notify our public relations or social media team. I'll take care of it."

"Thank you," I rasped.

Chin-hyuk turned my broken phone over in his hands; he'd picked it up from the floor beside me before helping me to the elevator. The screen was cracked in three large splits across the face, though it still lit up when he absentmindedly pressed the home button.

He hadn't needed to say it for me to hear what he was thinking. I had never, ever broken my phone before.

The past three weeks had been hard for everyone, I suspected. Dyeong and I still weren't talking. He was still angry with me.

Madison had said he was right. She said I needed him.

I had been so angry at him the first few days. He was part of the reason why she ended it. Maybe even a big part. But I knew that by directing my wrath toward him, all I was doing was hurling the storm inside me at a target. It was just a distraction, and one Dyeong didn't deserve. He didn't want me to date. Of course he didn't. That wasn't a surprise or a betrayal. *I'd* lied to him. *I'd* betrayed him.

My anger at Dyeong had already faded away. In its place, all I felt was weariness, and frustration.

Tai was less bubbly and puppy-like than his usual self, and the carefree smiles I could always count on had vanished. Chin-hyuk seemed like he was always working, but he was also more tired. They both spent energy trying to smooth over the massive chasm that had cracked between me and Dyeong. It wasn't working very well.

Number 10 used to have a peacefulness about it if nothing else. It was home. It was our safe place, the place we could be a family.

But not anymore. The air was filled with tension and a heaviness.

I still hadn't told them the truth of what had happened. They all had no idea that Madison had cut it off with me. It seemed like, by the way Tai and Chin-hyuk tried to cheer me up, they thought *I* had cut it off with *her*. After all, what reason would she have to leave?

I didn't think any of us could've predicted the possibility that she cared so much about me that she would make the hard choice, so I wouldn't have to.

Dyeong hadn't relented very much. I'd thought that he would, since Tai and Chin-hyuk were guessing that I'd cut it off with Madison. That should've made him happy. But I thought he knew that if I had truly cut it off with her, I would tell everyone. The fact that I hadn't told anyone *anything* besides confirming to Chin-hyuk "It's over" made it seem like I had something more to hide.

Maybe I did. I could've told them what she'd done, but I knew the question Dyeong would ask me – "What if she comes back? What will you do then?" – and I knew he wouldn't like my answer.

We struggled through our dance practices each day. I did poorly, so poorly that even the filming staff were raising eyebrows. Tai, Chin-hyuk and Dyeong all said nothing, though I could see the frustration and concern on their faces.

I was so depressed that I barely felt the shame and guilt added on. The others watched me sliding into despair with alarm.

"Life will get better," Chin-hyuk told me, standing over me as Tai and Dyeong left the dance practice room. I was sitting down against the wall, struggling to regain my composure and the crushing sadness weighing on my heart. "Eventually."

I turned my face away before I could see his expression, swallowing the lump in my throat.

"Life without her hasn't gotten better," I said hoarsely. "It's gotten worse."

She'd given me up to protect me. Even in our last moments together she was trying to protect me.

There was nothing left. I was shattered beyond repair. Over the past three weeks, everything had grown number. I felt like I was half-dead. At those moments where I had the chance to forget for just one second why I was so anguished, everything came rushing back. It was a pain that I couldn't stop, that couldn't be solved or helped. I wanted to forget.

I longed for her so badly. Every car that parked near SMK below our window I wished had her in it. Every pedestrian I saw from far away I wished was her walking. Every scuffle outside our door, as it opened, I wished was her.

The hope didn't last. Different people got out of the cars, the people walking headed in directions away from SMK, and the faces that greeted me when the door opened were always Chin-hyuk, Tai, and Dyeong.

Madison was gone, and she wasn't coming back.

Nothing made me happy anymore. It felt like nothing ever would.

The others were trying to fix it. Trying to get back the Wooyeong they'd lost. Even Tai tried to talk to me about it, late at night when we were lying in bed.

"Your heart will heal sometime," he told me clumsily, on the bunk below me.

I passed my hand over my eyes, though the room was pitch-dark except for a thin slice of light from the window coming from all the city buildings surrounding us. It didn't feel like my heart would heal.

"There will be other girls," Tai continued, and I could just imagine the awkward grimace on his face. He didn't usually have heart-to-heart emotional chats, and I knew it was a testament to how much he cared about me that he was trying. "You can always date after Ambition's slowed down."

My arm was draped over my eyes. "Okay." There would be no other girls. It was Madison or no one.

I could tell by Chin-hyuk's and Dyeong's breathing that they were awake and listening, though they were both silent.

"I'm sorry," Chin-hyuk said softly, breaking the stillness.

I had forced a hard swallow, an escaped tear slipping down my face and onto my pillow. I didn't trust my voice enough to reply.

That night was days ago. How many, I couldn't remember.

But now, today, on March 14, it had been almost a month since I last saw Madison.

I walked slowly along the concrete back to SMK, the bitter, callous air stinging my face and hands. Usually I didn't mind the harshness. Now the iciness hurt more than just my skin.

The sun had already set. It was five in the evening. Soon, all the office workers would flood out of their buildings, go back home to their own lives, Madison among them.

I'd called her again, this morning. Hoping she'd unblocked me after three weeks. Hoping she missed me enough...

Her number was still unavailable.

Today was the first time I'd been outside SMK in three weeks too. I'd disguised myself with a hat, sunglasses, scarf, and gloves, as well as a big trench coat, oversized for me, that I'd "borrowed" from Tai's closet.

I didn't know if what I'd just done – the purpose of that outing – was worth it, but it didn't matter. I needed to do it. Even though it just brought everything back to painful, heart-shattering clarity.

I reached the door to SMK, walking to the elevator and punching in my floor automatically. I didn't greet the desk clerk or the security guard.

I walked slowly down the hall to Number 10, taking off the sunglasses I used to hide myself, not able to muster the effort to remove my scarf and hat.

Tai looked up from his position on the couch when I walked in, but didn't say anything, looking back down at his tablet. His usual smile was gone, as it had been for three weeks. I headed to the bedroom, intending to shut the door and lose myself in some music for hours.

"Where've you been?"

I stopped at the sound of Dyeong's harsh voice behind me. We had barely talked since that day, and when we had it was tentative. Sometimes I caught him looking at me with worry and sadness in his eyes, but it's always gone as soon as he realized I was watching him.

I turned around, seeing him standing in the kitchen, motionless in his black turtleneck, messy midnight-blue hair with the black roots showing tousled on his forehead. I didn't like his tone, the way he was frozen and immobile behind the counter. It was not friendly.

~{★ 171 ♥}~

"You were gone for a long time," he said, his voice sharp. "And you left your phone on the table this morning. It had the walking directions to Gi – the place where she works."

I was standing there not moving, anger rising in me like lava.

"Seeing Madison?"

It was meant as an accusation. I felt like snarling, like throwing something at him. How dare he use Madison's name out of his selfish mouth, when he'd ruined it for both of us, still feeling high and mighty enough to be angry at me. What more did he want? What more was there to give him?

I ground my jaw. "That's impossible, considering three weeks ago she broke up with me. So my relationship with *you* and Ambition wouldn't be ruined. She gave up what she wanted so you could have what *you* wanted. Are you happy now, Dyeong?" And I yanked off my scarf, slamming the door behind me in his shocked face.

매디슨
MADISON
26

It was ten o'clock at night and the windows outside were pitch black. There was no one in the Gi office except me, and the lights were off too, except for a lamp that was always on through a glass door to another office.

I pushed back in my chair and stretched, tired, turning off my light so I was sitting in dimness. I packed up my work bag and shrugged on my winter parka, not able to bring myself to care enough to zip it up.

I was used to the quiet stillness and desertion here. Every night since that day – three weeks ago, since it was now in the middle of March – I had done this. Stayed and worked hours late at the office, long after everyone had left, alone.

I was not giving myself time to feel, delaying the trip back to the cold silence of my apartment that awaited me, until I was so exhausted that there would be no other choice.

I picked up my work bag and walked heavily, slowly, across the thin carpet into the hallway toward the door. The faint yellow glow of the lamp from the other office, though no one was ever there, was enough to guide me through the dimness to the front door. The darkness pressed in, but I was used to it now.

I opened the door, stepping out into the frigid air. It was pitch-black outside except for the streetlight over my head between the buildings, illuminating the entrance to Gi in clean hospital-white light. Thick, fluffy snowflakes fell from the sky, dodging and dancing in the light from the streetlamp and then vanishing into the darkness again. A layer of snow had already covered all available surfaces, piling in corners on the front step of Gi.

I dully turned around to make sure the door was locked, reaching for it as I always did since I was the last one out, when the toe of my boot kicked something solid in the pile of snow on the front step.

I looked down at it, paused, still dead on the inside. After a few seconds I nudged some snow aside with my foot, revealing a surface of something pink.

I stopped and slowly picked it up, shaking off the freshly fallen snow. It was a light, smallish rectangular box.

A box of chocolates, with a note attached to the ribbon.

I smoothed my hand across the top to get rid of the residual coat of powder. The paper was damp and the ink, although once written carefully and perfect, was smudged and bleeding from the wetness of the snow, almost ruined. It said M and W, one letter above the other, nothing else.

An M and a W...

Madison and Wooyeong. He had noticed how our initials were mirrored in English...

For a split second I was confused, my mind too weary to understand. But I blearily remembered, for the first time in weeks. Today was March 14, White Day.

My eyes welled up, tears threatening to spill over. I staggered off the front step into the empty road, holding the forlorn box of chocolates, gazing into the night.

The street was completely deserted. The box was cold, had probably been placed with care there hours ago.

Wooyeong was long gone.

I hugged the box to my chest, alone in the light of the streetlamp, as sobs wracked my shoulders.

우영
WOOYEONG
27

I grabbed my sweater and pulled it on as the last member of the film crew clicked off the lights in the dance practice room. "Are you coming, Wooyeong?"

"Yeah, I'm coming."

But after they left I sat down on a chair in the corner, in the dimness.

We had just finished filming all the dance practices for the release of our next album. I had struggled, been out of sync, not even energy in my movements. None of us had enjoyed ourselves as we had before. It had taken twice as many takes as it should've just to get to a dance practice they could call decent.

I took a deep breath. It was late. We'd been obsessively working all day, prepping for interviews, filming, and working on the songs' compositions to adjust them so they were perfect with the help of our sound manager. Chin-hyuk had done a solo VLive this morning before I'd even woken up.

I was exhausted. And not prepared for the door to open again and for a quiet voice to say "Wooyeong?"

I'd known that voice for six years, had laughed at its teasing, heard it teary as we accepted our first award. It was more familiar to me than my own, yet I was not prepared to deal with it right now.

I rubbed the crease between my eyebrows, trying to lessen the dull pounding there. "Yes, Dyeong."

He clicked on the light, closing the door behind him.

"Could you not?" I said, shielding my eyes. "I have a headache."

"Sorry," he muttered, clicking it off again and coming to sit next to me, pulling up another chair.

We sat there for a while – side by side, in silence.

The door opened again, and I saw a tall figure silhouetted against the light in the hall – Tai. He paused, then walked in, Chin-hyuk behind him. I noticed they didn't bother turning on the light.

"Is it okay if we join you?" Chin-hyuk asked quietly.

"Fine," I murmured absentmindedly.

They pulled up two more chairs, sitting next to me and Dyeong in a circle. I was reminded of the old days where we used to put our hands together before every concert.

"Were you coming in here to tell him something?" Chin-hyuk asked Dyeong.

He shook his head, and I could barely see the movement in the darkness. There was a pause before he spoke. "It can wait."

"Okay," said Chin-hyuk. He looked at me for a long moment. "I'm glad we're all here, together. I want to talk about Madison."

The weight pressing on my lungs got heavier. I felt so weary. "There's nothing left to say," I whispered.

"Life was nicer when she was around," Tai said, resting his face in his hands. "That time when we carried her here, to this room? And then ate together and played cards and talked? That was the most fun I'd had in... well, a really long time."

"Me too," Chin-hyuk and Dyeong said together. I looked at Dyeong, surprised. I wanted to tell Tai to stop talking, to stop making me hurt more with remembering, but my lips refused to move.

"You were happier too," Tai said, gesturing to me. "All of us were happier. Now you barely eat, hardly sleep – don't even deny it, I can hear your breathing – and you can't even dance. You used to be so good at that."

"I'm sorry," I said hoarsely, rubbing my eyes. "I'll try harder. I don't know what happened when she left. It just..." Everything was harder. He was right about eating and sleeping, too. For the first time in my life, food didn't interest me any longer. And at night, lying in bed, the ache in my heart was often too painful to fall asleep. I was too sad.

"Wooyeong," Chin-hyuk said gently. "We know you're not doing it on purpose."

"No, don't keep making excuses for me. I'll try harder, I promise." I rubbed my forehead again, my headache getting worse.

"That's not the point," said Dyeong, and even he sounded sympathetic.

Chin-hyuk sighed. "Tai and I have been talking. Wooyeong, it's empty around here without Madison. We thought you'd get over it and move on, but you haven't. I'm not sure you even *can*." He leaned forward and gripped my hand. "You need to get her back."

I was shocked. He *wanted* me to pursue her again? My heart gave a jump, only to fall again.

My throat was dry as I spoke. "She doesn't want me back. She told me not to visit her. She thinks that us being together will ruin me."

"Right. She broke up with *you*. You said that earlier." Tai still sounded stunned. "Why?"

"She saw how angry Dyeong was. She heard me speak over the phone, heard a little of what had happened with the publicity manager. She didn't think... after what had happened with that photo of her being leaked... it was just too much. She didn't want to ruin my relationships with you, and my career. *Our* careers."

Dyeong pressed a hand to his face. I couldn't tell what he was thinking.

"Well, we're telling you to get her back," said Chin-hyuk. He looked at Dyeong. "With your permission. He needs everyone's permission, Dyeong. This is about all of us."

"I need to talk to Wooyeong," Dyeong said. "Alone."

"Okay," Chin-hyuk agreed calmly. "We've said our piece. Goodbye, guys. Is it okay if I want all of you to be at dinner in half an hour? We need to all sit down together again and have a meal like a real family."

"Yeah," I murmured. "I can do that."

Dyeong nodded. Tai and Chin-hyuk stood up from their chairs and left the room, the door swinging slowly, softly shut behind them.

We both didn't say anything. I waited, unsure of what he wanted to tell me. Dread curled in my stomach.

After a few minutes the silence seemed to be too much for him.

"I'm sorry, Wooyeong."

I thought I'd misheard. "What?"

"I'm sorry," Dyeong said, his voice throaty. "I made you so unhappy. That's the last thing I want to do."

I shook my head, even though he may not have been able to see me all that well in the dimness shining through the glass door of the dance practice room from the hall.

~{★ 177 ♥}~

"You didn't. Madison cut it off with me. Facing life without her made me..." I trailed off. I was starting to feel emotional, and I didn't like tearing open the stiches on my heart again.

"No, that's not true. She only did that because she didn't want to destroy your career and your dream, and... well, because of me. I was so angry."

I wondered if Madison had moved on already. I wondered if she thought *I'd* moved on already. I hadn't, and I wasn't going to. My heart was forever and only hers.

"It was my fault."

"It's fine, Dyeong. I don't hold it against you." And it was true.

He seemed to struggle for words, running his hand through his black hair. "I still can't believe she did that," he said softly.

"Manager Gu won't believe it," I said, giving a harsh laugh. "The fan, willingly giving up her idol."

Dyeong shuffled around, pulling a letter out of his back pocket. "He already did believe it," he said nervously. "He approves now – he's changed his mind after I told him what happened. Madison sacrificed her relationship with you because she wanted to save the rest of your life." He wasn't looking at me, holding out the letter. It fell gently into my lap. "I think he knew it must be the truth if I was the one telling him. This is for you."

I swiveled to face him, eyes wide. "*What?* He *approves?* You told him? Why did you...?"

"I want you to be happy. And I still don't feel completely comfortable with it. It's not easy. It's not safe." Dyeong wrapped his arms around his knees, and I was suddenly reminded of the boy he was six years ago – more vulnerable, more unsure. "But you love her, and she loves you. I can't keep you from that. You're a wreck without her. You can't even dance."

I was speechless, the letter in my lap, so he continued.

"Training wasn't easy or safe, was it? And neither was our debut. There were moments where I felt like my soul had been crushed, or I'd wasted years of my life when I would just turn out to be a failure. All of us felt that. And when we all met, we still felt that, though we were in it together now."

"It was worth it," I said huskily, and I meant every word, down to the core of my bones. "This is our dream."

"And it's not the only dream that matters."

I struggled for words, feeling chills run through me at his statement. "And... if she hasn't moved on already... what if my relationship with Madison does come out, like you feared? You were right. We could lose a big portion of our fans, and more."

He looked at me for a long moment, and I saw determination in his wet eyes. "Some risks are worth taking."

매디슨
MADISON
28

I knew I should get up from the sofa. But I couldn't seem to move. I was staring without really seeing at the coffee table, at the box of chocolates I had been afraid to open. At the note. M and W.

It was the last part of him I had left.

I missed him so badly. I hadn't known what pain was, before coming to Korea. Now I did. Every day I had to wake up knowing it was over, that I would never see him again. I couldn't even look at my phone without resenting what I fangirl I was, every screenshot I'd ever taken, every social media account, username, wallpaper and app I had downloaded with my obsession with Ambition. It all looked so different after I had known him personally. Every reminder was thrown in my face like a slap.

Every day I doubted my decision. But it was better this way. One thing kept me going, every time the pain felt like it was too much to even get out of bed, every time I found myself walking past the restaurant where we'd first met, every time I cried myself to sleep.

I'm protecting Wooyeong.

That was all that mattered. He was safe from me now. There would be no angry members, no fear of being discovered, no mobs of hate-filled fans. Everything would go back to the way it was, and he would be safe and well.

I needed to be out of his life to save the rest of it. *I'm protecting Wooyeong.*

I'd thought about leaving Korea, the first week, when the pain was the most intense. I wanted to flee so badly, get as far away from here as I could. But I realized that it wasn't actually Korea I would be trying to escape, it would be my feelings. Pieces of Wooyeong were embedded in my heart like shrapnel. I *loved* him.

That would be true no matter where in the world we would be, whether we were together or apart.

I was thankful for the chance I got to love him. To know him. And no matter how much time would pass, wherever I would be, I would never, ever forget him.

I hugged a pillow to my chest, curling up tighter on the sofa. I wished I could go to work again, to distract myself from the gaping hole in my heart, but it was Saturday. There was nothing to do at Gi. It was closed. I had hauled myself out of bed this morning, collapsed it back into a sofa and then tidied the house – even gotten dressed – something I hadn't done on previous days off. I had been too depressed. Now I was sitting here at ten in the morning, and I couldn't even muster the energy to turn on the television to fill the void in the chilly air – the suffocating silence.

It was so quiet I could hear my heartbeat. I closed my eyes, the crushing sadness I'd been running from washing over me like a wave.

I had never been so alone.

I needed to leave here. Get out of the house and somewhere where I could lose myself in a crowd and be nothing more than a number.

If I didn't open my eyes all the way I could almost imagine him in front of me. At the kitchen counter, in his sweater with his back to me, cooking something on the stove as I watched him, just like he'd done when my ankle had been hurt. I'd taken a mental picture then, trying my best to memorize every detail, thinking I wouldn't get to see him again.

Now it had come true, and I was left with just the memory of him, the place where he should be standing cold and empty and silent.

I should get off the sofa. I should grab my shoes and parka and go out somewhere. Anywhere, it didn't matter where, just as a distraction. I should...

I didn't move.

My phone rang from across the room, where it was on the kitchen counter. The chime was sharp and annoying, its loudness making me start a little.

I got off the sofa and grabbed the phone just before it was about to end, grateful for a diversion away from everything else I was feeling. It was a number I didn't recognize, but I answered it anyway. Anything to distract myself from the longing. "Hello?"

"Hello."

It was a man's voice. A voice I would recognize anywhere.

"Dyeong?" I stammered. Had Wooyeong given everyone my number? Why was he calling me? Dread surged through my stomach as my last memory of Dyeong, furious and shouting, came rushing back.

But he wasn't angry now. He gave a breathy little chuckle, surprised. "You recognized my voice."

"Of course I did, I..." I stopped myself. "Why are you calling me?"

Dyeong ignored me. "Are you at home?"

I shifted my phone to my other hand, walking around the house in circles just to clear my head, cautious and edgy now. "Why? What does it matter?"

"Just tell me, Madison. Are you at home or not?"

Why was he calling me? If Wooyeong wanted to find a way to call me even though he was blocked, he could've just swiped one of their phones. Was Dyeong going to tell me to stay as far away from them as possible, or interrogate me about whether I was still in contact with Wooyeong, or something? I hadn't even gone near SMK.

Unless.... Had something happened to Wooyeong? The thought made my blood turn to ice. "Yes, I'm home," I said sharply, my tone hiding the fear in my voice. I sucked in a breath and held it.

"I'm calling to say...." There was a pause, and he started again. "I'm calling because Wooyeong said to tell you: He's sorry he's always late."

I muffled a sudden sob with my hand.

"I also wanted to tell you one more thing."

I waited, the tears in my eyes threatening to spill over. I gulped, trying to control them.

"Look out your window."

My gaze dragged to the window, and I took a few steps toward it, until I could see the street outside. And the person there in the road, with a black coat, looking upwards.

"Wooyeong," I gasped. I looked down at the phone, but Dyeong had hung up. I gasped again and dropped it, running to the door and slipping on my shoes, dashing down the stairs so fast I nearly slammed into the wall. I flew out the door into the icy air, rounding the corner and seeing Wooyeong standing there, looking at me.

Seeing him was like an electric bolt to my heart. I slowed and then stopped, suddenly, ten feet away from him. Every part of me wanted to throw myself into his arms, but I didn't move. Had Dyeong given his blessing? Even if he had, there was still the management. There was still the rest of his life. The life I couldn't be a part of – *shouldn't* be a part of.

Wooyeong's lips were parted as he took a breath, his eyes vulnerable and glossy with tears that hadn't fallen. He looked at me, not moving either. Standing there, he looked so uncertain, so alone.

I was frozen, hugging my arms tightly to myself. The cold air was cutting right into me and I realized I'd forgotten a jacket. I just stared at him through my stinging eyes. My longing for him, the ache, was overwhelmingly powerful. I wanted to sob, to bury my face in his chest. But I didn't. I couldn't.

I didn't look at him, taking slow breaths of the icy air as I tried not to cry. "Why did you leave me chocolates?" I asked finally, my voice coming out thick.

His voice was steady and undoubting, yet also full of tears that wouldn't fall. "Because I love you."

I looked at him then, my eyes wide. He took a step toward me, butterflies falling low into my stomach as his black shoe hit the concrete between us, one step closer.

"I was afraid to say it before." Wooyeong swallowed, hard. "In case you didn't feel the same way. But now I know that... even if you walk away and never talk to me again... at least I'll have told you."

I didn't want to walk away. I closed my eyes and nodded as a fresh wave of pain and emotion washed over me, pressing my lips together, a tear escaping down my cheek. It was a few moments until I could muster up the composure to trust myself to speak.

"But you can't be safe if you're with me," I whispered. "If someone finds out... even though Dyeong's changed his mind... the management... your career..."

"It doesn't matter," he said softly. "None of it matters if I don't have you, Madison." He took another step toward me. Then another.

The butterflies in my stomach got stronger as he got closer, his voice dropping quieter and quieter. "It's you, or no one for the rest of my life."

"I... just don't want to hurt you...." I was crying.

Wooyeong stopped right in front of me. He reached up slowly, and then his fingers slid against my jaw. Electricity shot through every place where his skin contacted mine. He tilted my face upwards, gently cupping it in his hands, which were burning warm.

I was suddenly still, my stomach doing flips. My eyes were locked on his soft, dark ones as his thumbs slowly glided along my jawline, making my skin prickle.

"You won't hurt me," he whispered. "I know. And even if you still want to walk away.... I won't regret what I'm about to do."

Wooyeong's face was slowly, slowly tilting toward mine as he closed the distance between us.

I could feel my cheeks burning feverishly as I slowly reached up a shaking hand, touching the side of his face with trembling fingers.

He paused at my touch, centimeters away with his breath brushing my skin, and the last thing I saw was his lips curling up in a slight smile, so close that I could see every swirl of brown and almost-black in his intense eyes.

Then his mouth pressed against mine. I surrendered to his gentle warmth, his lips incredibly soft like velvet as they moved against my own. He kissed me more intensely, yet ever so slow, savoring it as one hand went to the back of my head.

It seemed like forever before he pulled away, his ragged breath light on my mouth. I could feel his racing heartbeat through his sweater, my hands on his chest. He was breathing hard, his dark eyes smoldering as they looked into my own.

My legs were weak. Wooyeong seemed to sense it, gripping my waist strongly as he kissed me again, harder. I was floating in bliss, every ounce of longing pouring into this moment as I kissed him back.

I felt disorientated when he pulled away, reaching up and brushing a tear from my face with his thumb.

"Why are you crying?" he asked, his voice soft and gentle. "I'm here. I'll be here for as long as you want me."

When all I could answer was a sob, he wrapped his arms around me, enveloping me in a tight hug. I felt him rest his chin on the top of my head, his arms snugly pressing me against his heat.

I cried into his chest, my shoulders shaking as he held me, stroking the back of my hair. "It's okay," he murmured. "It's all going to be okay."

I had complete trust in him. I hugged him tighter, knowing somehow that no matter what happened, it was true. It was going to be okay. *We* were going to be okay.

"I love you," I whispered.

Wooyeong kissed the top of my head. "I love you too."

우영
WOOYEONG
THREE MONTHS LATER

"I'm back with the bungeoppang!" Dyeong said, holding up the paper bag he was carrying full of fish-shaped sweet bread filled with sugary red bean paste.

Manager Pak strode into the room. "Save one for me."

We were all inside a room of SMK Entertainment – me, Madison, Chin-hyuk, Tai, and most recently Dyeong – having a little party to celebrate the end of our most recent concert tour. It was filled with a long table, chairs and plates and silverware, and streamers that Madison had taped everywhere as a surprise. We'd dragged in a portable barbeque and Chin-hyuk was making bulgogi, ultra-focused, while Tai used a side burner to make kimchi fried rice. I was glad to be back home, and with Madison.

I reached for her hand underneath the table, and she looked at me and smiled.

"Hey loverboy!" Tai yelled from over his shoulder. "Come help me with this!"

"It's kimchi fried rice, Tai," I said as Manager Pak pulled up a chair, eager to taste some sweets. "Everyone knows how to make kimchi fried rice. A seven-year-old could do it."

"Fine! Just get me some more kimchi from the dorm. This isn't flavorful enough."

Madison and I got up as Dyeong plopped the bag of bungeoppang on the table. "Sure is nice not knowing how to cook sometimes," he said. "No responsibility at all except running errands at bakeries."

Chin-hyuk let out a frustrated yell as some of the beef stuck to the barbeque grill, scraping quickly with the tongs as some smoke rose up in the air. Dyeong sauntered over and stretched languidly next to him.

"You watch it!" Chin-hyuk said, flustered, pointing at him with the tongs. "This is harder than it looks!"

Madison was laughing softly as the door closed behind us. I held her hand as we walked down the hall, my heart full to the bursting as I looked at her beautiful, familiar face. I wanted to see that face for the rest of my life.

"This is fun," she said.

"It is," I agreed, a smile tugging at my lips. It was nice to have Madison here hanging around, as she'd been doing a lot over the past few months. The others enjoyed having her around in SMK. Manager Pak liked her, and even Manager Gu had given a respectful nod of acknowledgement when we'd passed him in the foyer once.

Madison tucked some stray hair back into her braid. "I never would've believed this six years ago if you told me where I would end up."

"What did you think of me back then?" I asked, intensely curious.

Madison glanced over and smiled to see me anxious and on the edge of my seat. She was slow to answer, enjoying the tension on my face.

"Come on, tell me," I laughed, stepping in front of her so she had to stop.

"You were my bias," she said, and turned and gazed down the hall, a faraway look in her eyes. "Since the very first time I saw you."

"Was it my charming good looks?" I said, leaning against the wall next to her flirtatiously.

"And your personality," she said. "You are very hot, but I liked you as a person. That's why it lasted six years."

And she loved me completely, selflessly, with an unbreakable bond, today. I felt out of breath. "I was hoping I was your bias," I said. "I know it shouldn't matter but I really, really hoped it was me."

"You were my *ultimate* bias," she said. "Still are."

"And you're mine," I whispered, kissing her.

Wooyeong listens to a lot of songs and has a *long* list of favorites. It would go on for more than a page, but here's just a few:

Your Difference by **Lucente**
Lit by **ONEUS**
Killing Me by **iKON**
Say My Name by **ATEEZ**
Dr. Bebe by **PENTAGON**
Love Me Harder by **WOODZ**
Make This by **1TEAM**
On by **BTS**
Déjà vu by **Dreamcatcher**
Love Shot by **EXO**

LOOK FOR YOUR NEXT K-POP ROMANCE READ:

BEHIND THE IDOL

COMING SOON

www.ingramcontent.com/pod-product-compliance
Lightning Source LLC
Chambersburg PA
CBHW050138110726
47898CB00008B/2577